Sanibel Sunsets

A Shellseeker Beach Novel
Book Six

HOPE HOLLOWAY

Hope Holloway

Shellseeker Beach Book 6

Sanibel Sunsets

Cover designed by Sarah Brown (http://www.sarahdesigns.co/)

Introduction to Shellseeker Beach

Come to Shellseeker Beach and fall in love with a cast of unforgettable characters who face life's challenges with humor, heart, and hope. For lovers of riveting and inspirational sagas about sisters, secrets, romance, mothers, and daughters...and the moments that make life worth living.

For release dates, excerpts, news, and more, sign up to receive Hope Holloway's newsletter! Or visit www.hopeholloway.com and follow Hope on Facebook and BookBub!

Chapter One

Eliza

"Are you nervous, Mom?" Olivia asked, taking her gaze off the Fort Myers afternoon traffic to glance at Eliza with uncertainty.

"No, why? Are we late?" Eliza checked the clock in the car dash, calculating how much time until Dane's plane landed.

"Not late, but you have sighed noisily fifteen times, fidgeted like a toddler, and just about gnawed a hole in your lower lip." She threw a smile to temper the tease. "When Dane arrives, the Whitney fam will be living in the same town for the first time in years. Are you not over the moon about this mother-and-child reunion?"

"Dane isn't a child. He's twenty-eight as of his birthday last month and..." Eliza shook her head, realizing that her daughter really wasn't that far off the mark. "If I seem nervous, it's because he's not going to love the bombshell we're about to drop on him. In fact, he's going to be furious we didn't tell him ahead of time."

"I know, I know. I should have told him that Deeley and Bash moved back in with me, thus eliminating the opportunity for us to be bro-sis roommates like I'd offered. But I'm also one hundred percent confident that my little brother would have cancelled his plans to come to Sanibel Island. He'd have gone back to the idea of getting some raggy apartment out there in Northern California like a starving musician, which he'd have to do since he quit his job."

Eliza sighed—for the fourth or fifth time, it was true—and closed her eyes. "I still can't believe he walked away from that job. Remember the day he got hired as a lead engineer at Ambrosia Intelligence?"

"Not really," Olivia admitted. "But that was, what, five years ago? I was so busy climbing my own corporate ladder back then. I don't remember his career highlights. I know it was a big deal for him."

"Straight out of Caltech and into the engineering department of one of the top AI companies in the world? A *huge* deal." Eliza leaned her head against the window, taking a little stroll down memory lane. "Dad was so proud of him, he couldn't stop smiling. And the money! That company threw money at Dane."

"Well, I hope he caught it and saved a wad, because he's not going to be rolling in cash as a musician," Olivia said.

"He's saved enough to live easily for a year, he told me. Of course..." Eliza made a face. "He did kind of assume he'd split the rent with you."

Olivia winced in response. "And we're back to the bombshell. 'Well, good news, Dane! You can live at Mom and Teddy's house for free!'"

They exchanged a look, both of them holding back

laughter. "Just wait until he sees that room decorated in wall-to-wall Disney," Eliza said.

"Hey, it's a free room on the beach, so he should just sing *Let it Go* and channel his inner princess. Anyway, Deeley and I are planning to look for something bigger. Then he can take over my lease and maybe get a roommate."

"That could take a while, but you're right. Dane has a place to stay, even if that spare room has been overtaken by a five-year-old."

Olivia nodded. "The thing about the house for us is that Deeley and I would love to wait just a little longer. Then we could save up enough money to buy something. So I'm not dying to leave my rental, but I don't want to wreck things for Dane. He's in a tender place."

"He sure is," Eliza agreed. "And if it weren't the middle of the tourist season, I'd squeeze him into one of the Shellseeker Cottages. He'd love Sunray Venus, which, as a former resident yourself, you know is perfect."

"Divine," Olivia agreed.

"So divine that it generates way too much revenue in February and March," Eliza said, checking off a mental list of the reservations they currently had. "In fact, we're almost completely booked through May."

"But you still have that week open for *The Last Resort* feature, right?"

"Of course! Mia Watson is writing the piece herself and I have her in Slipper Snail when she gets here next week." She shifted in her seat, cringing when she realized she *was* as fussy as a toddler. "Oh, February turned into a crazy month, didn't it? Camille will no doubt want to get married the minute the doctors give her clearance, Dane is coming, a major review is being done of the resort, and..."

"And it's our first Dad-iversary on the twenty-fifth." Olivia gave her a sad smile. "Another reason I don't want to make life difficult for Dane."

"I can't believe we're coming to the end of one whole year without him."

"And look what's happened in that year," Olivia said, always so encouraging. "You're practically a co-owner in a beachside resort with Teddy, your new best pal in the world. You have friends, family, your son is coming to stay, and..." She lifted her brows playfully.

"I have a man in my life," Eliza said in a singsong voice that she imagined Olivia was about to use.

"I was going to say, your daughter is happy and in love, but, okay, this is about you."

Eliza laughed, her heart lifting just because that's what Olivia did for her. "You *are* happy and in love," she agreed. "And that is truly one less thing I have to worry about."

"Really? Because I'm petrified."

"Of what?" Eliza blinked at her. "Deeley's back, he's not going anywhere, you two are...perfect. And Bash is so settled and happy, Liv. His behavior is one thousand percent improved."

"It could only go up from where it was," Olivia said with a wry smile. "Actually I think a month with his Aunt

Christine was good for him. In his little not-quite-three-year-old mind, he wants to be good so his world doesn't turn upside down one more time." She gave a soft whimper. "That poor child has been through so much, losing both parents before he's even old enough to understand anything. All we want for him is smooth sailing and stability."

"Is that why you are petrified?" Eliza asked. "Or is it work? The new hire, Ileana? She's working out well, isn't she?"

"So well," Olivia said on a happy sigh. "I couldn't have managed the store alone while Camille is recovering from heart surgery. Without another salesperson on the floor, I'd have been at Sanibel Sisters twelve hours a day. But Ileana is amazing, with twenty years at Blooming-dales in Miami on her resume, and it shows. Did I tell you about the new summer line out by Elan? Gorgeous. The customers are going to inhale those sundresses."

"Then…" Eliza leaned a little closer over the console, not willing to let her daughter go down a work rabbit hole, her favorite way to avoid any topic that made her uncomfortable. "What has you petrified?"

Olivia let out a little groan. "What's the expression—the other shoe's going to fall? The next hurdle? The unexpected problem behind Door Number Three?"

"What are you talking about, Liv?"

"I'm talking about Deeley and me," she said. "Every time we get close to…to that place of peace, love, and perfection, something happens. Sanibel Treasures got set on fire, a shark darn near attacked him, then Bash's mother died, and Deeley was named guardian of a toddler. Just as we settled into that new normal, he took off to stay with his sister."

"Because he thought that was the right thing for you."

"Couldn't have been more wrong," Olivia said.

"He knows that now." Eliza patted Olivia's arm with a mother's touch that came so naturally to her. "Nothing to worry about, Livvie Bug."

But she didn't look at all convinced. "I have the feeling that my happy ever after is...just out of reach. Every time I get close, we get slammed. What's next?"

"Um...your brother moving here?" Eliza suggested.

"Dane being here is not a problem for me unless he pitches a fit and insists on living with me instead of you. But I think the spare room in the beach house decorated by a five-year-old girl will be more appealing than sharing a room with a real live toddler who has frequent sleep issues."

Eliza didn't think either option would thrill her son, but that was just the way things were.

"You just relax and focus on your new life with Deeley and Bash, which is ideal right now," she said. "Don't make up problems where there aren't any."

"You're right, as always, Elizabeth Mary, and you should listen to your own advice." She shot Eliza a quick look as she took the turn for Southwest Florida International Airport. "Dane coming here will be awesome. He might have a little adjustment period getting to know the friends who've become family and...and..."

"And Miles," Eliza finished for her, knowing exactly what Olivia was thinking. "You know he's going to try and find everything wrong with the very idea of me dating someone."

"I'll set him straight," Olivia promised. "Are you really worried about Dane's opinion of Miles?"

"It isn't going to be easy for him. I might not see Miles as much when—"

"Mom!" Olivia snapped the turn signal before whipping into the short-term parking lot. "You are a grown woman, a fifty-four-year-old widow with a whole life ahead of you, and well within your rights to go out with a wonderful man like Miles Anderson. If Dane can't see that, then he can…go back to California."

"But I don't want him to," Eliza said. "I want Dane to love it here, like you did, and my sister, Claire, and everyone who has become so important to us. I want him to stay for a long time and love his life and make his music and join our world. But you know Dane."

"Cold, devoid of emotion, and Spock-like in logic?" Olivia rolled her eyes. "How *does* he produce such beautiful music on the piano?"

"Because his rationality and mathematic approach to the world is a cover for a deeply emotional man who lets his feelings out in music. My concern with this change is, well, it's Dane. He's never met a learning curve he liked."

Olivia frowned. "What do you mean?"

"Dane despises any time of adjustment or learning," she said, thinking back on pivotal new experiences in her son's life, and how he vibrated with frustration when he didn't get something immediately.

"Like when he got his first Xbox and couldn't figure it out in ten seconds flat?" Olivia snorted. "Total meltdown. Yeah, you're right. Dane likes to know, not learn. Good thing he has a crazy high IQ so his learning curve is shorter than most mere mortals."

"But here, he'll have to learn a whole new life, new family, new surroundings, and new career—depending on what he's going to do. He has to navigate relationships that are already well-formed, and he isn't going to enjoy that."

"He'll have to work it out in his music," Olivia said. "Because it was his choice to be an unemployed wanna-be songwriter."

Eliza grunted and crossed her arms. "What was that boy thinking?"

She expected Olivia to agree with her, but instead her daughter parked the car and turned, her gaze serious. "Mom, we have to make each other a promise."

"What's that?"

"We can't make side comments or snide judgments once Dane gets off that plane. I made a mental commitment to emotionally support him the day he called and told me he'd quit his job. Do I think it was impulsive, rash, and financially, uh, questionable? So very much. But he's here and he hasn't felt the magic of Shellseeker Beach yet. He hasn't had the benefit of our found family to help him heal from losing Dad a year ago. He..." Her voice faded out. "Mom? Why are you crying?"

"Am I?" Eliza swiped under her lashes, only a little surprised to feel they were damp. "I guess I am kind of a wreck today. But the tears? Those are your fault." At Olivia's stunned look, Eliza pulled her closer. "How did you get so wonderful and wise and amazing and kind-hearted?"

She smiled through misty eyes of her own. "I had a great teacher named Elizabeth Mary Vanderveen Whitney."

"And now the teacher is learning from you." She kissed Olivia's cheek. "Thank you for the reminder on how to be a great mom. I promise to show Dane all the love and support and patience he needs."

"Without ditching Miles," Olivia added.

"Of course. Thanks, Liv."

"You bet. And you can have the honor of telling Dane that he's sleeping in a room that rivals *It's a Small World* at Disneyland."

"He hated that ride," Eliza said on a laugh.

"But this one has a *Frozen* nightlight and a jewelry box that plays *Let It Go* next to his bed."

"Well, he's a musician." Eliza shrugged and unlatched her seatbelt. "He should love that."

HE LOOKED DIFFERENT. Eliza peered at her son as he strolled through the airport toward the small group waiting for the plane's arrival, pulling a rolling bag and a backpack slung over one shoulder.

Was that Dane Whitney? The uber-perfectionist computer engineer who lived in light-blue button-downs and khaki pants, now in a T-shirt with Kawai Pianos emblazoned across the chest? And jeans with holes in the knees?

Where were his tortoise-shell glasses and the buzz cut, both of which he thought helped age up his baby face? His dark blond hair was downright shaggy, and he was either flying blind or had gotten contact lenses. And...what was on his cheeks? Stubble?

"He's gone Hollywood," Olivia muttered.

They'd seen him a few months ago, when Olivia and Eliza flew to California for a week to sell the family house in Pacific Palisades. Then, he'd seemed troubled. Not that Dane would show the world his emotional cards, but his blues were understandable that week. They'd said goodbye to a lifetime of memories, and all of them were still very much mourning Ben's death.

"Or at least lost his razor," Eliza replied, smiling around the words as she waved at him.

His return smile was a little tentative, and he touched those whiskers self-consciously, like he expected the two of them to comment or tease.

Good heavens. Had it always been so difficult to navigate her son's moods? Ben had done the heavy lifting in that area, while she and Olivia never met so much as a speedbump in their relationship. But Dane? He held his cards so close to the vest, he was truly an enigma, and that, she realized, was at the very heart of why she'd been on edge in the car.

"Hey, guys," he said as he approached, reaching out his free arm to Eliza. "Mom."

She hugged him with both arms, wrapping him in an embrace that felt utterly natural no matter what he was wearing or when he'd last shaved. She knew this hug, knew the feeling of her lanky, six-foot son who spent more time in front of a computer than at the gym. Except...

"Oh, my." She patted his shoulder, her eyes popping at the muscle. "You've been working out?"

"A little," he muttered, turning to his sister. "Hey, Liv."

"Hi, Dave," she teased, using the much-hated name so many people mistakenly called him, and poking his chest. Then she hugged him like Eliza had. "Welcome to Florida."

Inching back, he gave just enough of an eyeroll for Eliza to know how he felt about being here. "Humidity at nine-hundred percent in the home of newlyweds and nearly-deads?"

Olivia poked again, this time a lot harder. "Give it five whole minutes before you go all elitist on us, will ya? I think you're in for a surprise."

"Yeah, sorry. I swore I wasn't going to do that."

"But I called you Dave, so we're even." Olivia slipped her arm around his waist and tugged him closer. "Baggage claim next?"

"Nope. This is it."

"Really?" Eliza looked at the carryon, her heart dropping. "I thought you were staying for a while. Did you change your mind?"

"I'm staying until I'm ready to go back. I just didn't have that much to pack, to be honest. Shorts, beach stuff, some workout clothes. I'll get anything else I need here."

"Where did you put everything?" Olivia asked. "You moved out of your Palo Alto rental house, right? How'd that work out?"

"A breeze," he said. "You know the guy who's been my housemate for, like, three years? Jake? He got engaged, so his fiancée is moving in. We worked out a deal so that he could keep my furniture, TV, and a whole bunch of books and...stuff I don't need anymore. I packed a laptop." He shrugged the bag on his shoulder. "This, and the piano, is all I need."

"Ah, the piano." Eliza nodded. Of course, he meant the Whitney family grand piano that Dane had happily agreed to keep when they packed up the house a few months ago. "What did you decide to do about it?"

"It's on the way, or will be the day after tomorrow when National Piano Transport picks it up and drives it across the country."

Eliza froze. "Here?"

"Problem?" He looked from one to the other, narrowing his gaze at Olivia. "You said put it in storage or ship it here. When we talked on the phone about this, you said you had room and I could—"

"I didn't think you'd ship it *today*," Olivia said.

"The day after tomorrow. What changed, Liv? You promised!"

"Can you just chill for a second? The living situation changed, that's all." She shot a pleading look to Eliza.

"Whoa, whoa, whoa, wait a second," Dane said, not chilling at all. "I can't do...anything without that piano. I can't live without it."

"You just got it four months ago!" Olivia insisted. "How did you live with it before that?"

"I didn't. I existed. What changed in the living situation?" He directed the question to Eliza, as if he knew his mother was the one who had to deliver bad news.

"Deeley's come back," Eliza said.

"That's good." He frowned, still confused. "Isn't it? You like this guy, right, Liv?"

"I love him," she said simply. "And they've moved back in with me—"

"Seriously?"

"But we're going to look for another place soon, and then you can just take over my lease."

"And until then?"

"You're going to stay with me," Eliza said as brightly as she could.

"Oh, in one of those villas?" He considered that. "Could work. First floor, right? Can I get a piano in?"

"Um, no. The cottages are all booked for the season, but you'll be with me in Teddy's beach house, in the spare room."

He searched her face, processing this. "Isn't that house built up on stilts?"

She nodded, bracing for his response.

"I can't get the piano upstairs," he said. "So that won't

work. And, don't take this wrong, Mom, I totally appreciate the offer. But I have to write music. I don't really want to live with you and...that old lady who makes the tea and likes crystals."

Eliza bristled at the description of Teddy, who wasn't old and had so many more attributes to her lovely character she couldn't begin to describe them.

"Cool it," Olivia stepped in to say. "Everything is temporary. The change is in my life, and I wasn't expecting it. Just give it a few, will ya? You literally still have plane stink on you and you're complaining about where you're staying. We'll get everything worked out."

"Can't the piano stay in storage for a little while, Dane?" Eliza asked.

"No." He hoisted the backpack higher on his shoulder and started walking again. "I don't need a lot of things in this world, but I do need that. I can't breathe, live, or compose without it. So, we'll have to, what'd you say, Liv? Get everything 'worked out' real soon, or I'll just head back."

As he walked ahead of them, Olivia and Eliza shared a look that communicated their confusion, concern, and no small amount of dismay.

"So nice to see him again," Olivia murmured, then they both hustled to catch up with him.

A piano? Eliza had no idea what to do with that piano...or the son with a big brick wall around him. One was more of a challenge than the other.

Chapter Two

Dane

Destiny awaits!

Dane took one look at the words woven into a children's carpet at the foot of a double bed draped in pink and purple and laughed out loud.

How could he do anything else? The whole trip was a folly of an idea, completely lacking in rationality and reason. Yes, he'd originally thought that it all worked so well with his new outlook on life, which was, "Less logic, more music."

But standing here in Cinderella's castle with at least fifty plastic snowflakes hanging from the ceiling by fishing line? He craved logic and there was none.

"What first grader am I kicking out of this place?" he asked, barely able to take in the sherbet-colored walls and riot of pastel-spined books on a shelf.

"One who doesn't actually live here," his mother said from the doorway. "Harper Bettencourt is Katie's daughter. Katie's the housekeeper at Shellseeker Cottages, so Harper stays here a lot, and she likes *Frozen*, as you can see."

He had less than a vague idea what *Frozen* was, and

didn't want to change that. But the snowflakes finally made sense.

"But she doesn't have to use the room," his mother continued. "And since I'm in the guest suite now, and Teddy's room is upstairs, this is really the best place for you. Look, you can see the water right out that window."

He glanced, but he'd seen enough of the shell-covered sand and turquoise Gulf of Mexico on the mini-tour they'd insisted on giving him. That's when he met his official hostess, Teddy Blessing, who owned the place and had become some kind of surrogate mother to his own mother.

Teddy had hugged him and pronounced him "deep violet," whatever that meant. Then she had handed him a cold iced tea...which wasn't a *Long Island* Iced Tea, sadly. Because he could use something that strong about now.

"You shouldn't be here too long." Mom leaned against the doorjamb with a mix of pity, amusement, and maternal concern in her expression. "Deeley and Liv and Bash are crowded now in her little house, and they'll be looking. Then you can take over her lease and get that piano out here."

He gave her a tight smile. "It's fine, Mom. I'm not going to stay long. I'm going to text the moving company tomorrow before they load up, and cancel the piano transport. It can stay at my old house until I go back."

"Dane!" She took a step into the room. "You don't have a job or a house to go back to. I want you to stay. I want you to give Shellseeker Beach a chance."

"I appreciate that, Mom, but truth? It might have been a little too crazy and impulsive of a decision after all. Not my usual MO."

"Crazy and impulsive can be good," she said. "Look at me. I came here with less than what you have in that backpack, planning to stay one or two nights. That was, what? Eight months ago. My whole life has changed."

He shot her a look, trying hard not to give away exactly what those words did to him. "I know," he said quietly. "Didn't take long."

She exhaled harshly. "You mean after Dad died? Honey, we all grieve at our own speed."

He held up a hand, looking around for a surface to drop his backpack. But it sure didn't belong anywhere in this room. He dumped it on the floor. "It's fine, Mom. We don't have to talk about it. You're here, and Liv's here, and everybody's happy."

"And if you gave this place a chance, you might be, too."

He tipped his head and gave her a "get real" look. Happy? He'd be happy when he sold his first song or actually composed something people listened to, or got someone in the music industry to pay attention to him, or...or...

Or didn't wake up wanting to talk to his dad.

"Well, not happy in this room," she said, misunderstanding the look. "But I promise you, it won't be long. And tonight will be fun. You'll like everyone."

He felt his brows shoot up. "Everyone...tonight?"

"It's a Teddy thing," she explained, except that

explained nothing. "She loves to host small parties down on the beach by the tea hut. We want you to meet the... well, it's not technically a *family*, but some is. My sister, Claire, is certainly family, and you're going to meet her, remember?"

He nodded, recalling all the details about Mom's long-lost sister who was the daughter of one of his grandfather's many wives—some he even had at the same time.

There was a dark song in that story somewhere.

"And Claire's mother, Camille," she continued with a list that sounded like a lot of *socializing* to someone who abhorred it. "Do you remember me talking about Camille?"

"The one who got a new aortic valve? Livvie's partner at the store?" he guessed, hoping he remembered some of the specifics from all that his mother and sister had thrown at him since they'd moved here.

"Exactly! And Claire's son is Noah, and his father is DJ, and you'll love them. DJ quit the corporate world right out there in Northern California just like you did. Left his job as a big-time architect to become a world-class pizza-maker."

He nodded his approval. "Okay, that's kinda cool."

"And you'll meet Deeley, of course, who I have no doubt will be your brother-in-law in the not-too-distant future. And the little boy, Bash, and...and..."

When she hesitated, he waited for her to say the name he'd heard far too many times.

Miles Anderson, the great and powerful private investigator who thought nothing of swooping in on his innocent widowed mother and...Dane didn't want to think beyond that. All he knew from Livvie was that they were *dating* and Mom was happy.

Which really got under his skin because...Dad.

"Roz and George," she said, unaware of his low-grade discomfort just thinking about this Miles dude. "And their daughter, Asia, who has a brand new ba—"

"Mom, stop."

"What?" She frowned and looked genuinely surprised by his reaction. "There are a lot of people and—"

"I'm not going to memorize names and backstories of this ragtag operation of your new friends. The fact that Livvie's guy is back and I don't have a place to live—"

"No. *You* stop." She crossed her arms and for one flash of a second looked like the woman he remembered standing in the family room threatening to pull the plug on his Xbox if he didn't stop playing *Call of Duty*. "First of all, he's not 'Livvie's guy.' His name is Connor Deeley, he is likely going to marry your sister, and he's a fine man who you would be wise and honored to call a friend."

"Yeah, I—"

"Second, you have a perfectly adequate room in a gorgeous house, with full access to a well-stocked kitchen *and* a stunning beach on one of the most desirable islands on the planet."

"I told you I appre—"

"And third, and most important, there is nothing *ragtag* about the people you're about to meet. They are..." Her voice caught as she searched for a word. "They are

priceless," she finished. "And you are being a disrespect-
ful, ungrateful brat."

He grimaced at the word, letting it do the damage she
intended. For a moment, they just stared at each other,
and then he cast down his eyes.

"Mom, I'm sorry," he said softly. "You're right and
I'm just..." He heaved a sigh. "No excuse. I could make a
million of them, but I won't. I'm really sorry."

She folded, as Eliza Whitney often did when he
showed the least bit of emotion. "Oh, Dane." She reached
for him and wrapped him up in one of her tight mommy
squeezes, like he was eight and had skinned his knee.

"I know this isn't easy," she whispered gently. "From
the change in accommodations to the change in...life."
She inched back. "You hate change, remember?"

He shrugged, not even attempting to deny that. "But
sometimes, it can't be avoided." He searched her face,
hating the wellspring of emotion that rose up in him.
Even with his own mother, it made him a little itchy. "I'm
really sorry," he said again. "Totally uncalled for and
you're right to get mad at me."

"I'm over it," she assured him, her gray-blue gaze so
warm and familiar. Her hair was different, though. It
used to be auburn and straight, but now it looked four
shades lighter and flipped around in layers. "Get comfortable, honey. Take a shower in the hall bathroom, change
into beach clothes, and come down to the tea hut on the
beach and meet...the ragtags."

He grunted. "Not going to live that one down, am I?"

"Maybe not." She laughed softly, forgiving him with

an ease few other people could attempt. "Relax, Dane. Take this little adventure one day at a time and it might not be the worst thing that ever happened."

He nodded as she stepped away and left him. When he turned to the bed, his head knocked a plastic snowflake. He flipped it away, fighting a smile as a melody took shape in the back of his brain. It was slow, ironic, and full of a weird sense of...expectation.

What would he call a song like that? He hummed it softly, then looked down at the violet and fuchsia rug under his feet.

Destiny awaits!

Yeah, that would work nicely for this song. He'd have to thank the first grader for the inspiration.

"Got all the names straight now, bro?" Olivia sidled up next to him, a glass of wine in one hand, a guac-covered chip in the other. Behind her, the setting sun gave his dark-haired sister a halo of gold and cast a warm light that only made her look more content than she obviously was.

"Why? Is there a test at the end of the night?" he countered.

"Could be, but I've never known you to get less than an A-plus on any test." She cocked her head, thinking. "But if you needed to know something about everyone, would you pass? Did you listen and ask questions?"

"Am I at socializing camp?"

"You could use a week of that." She grinned. "So, how'd you like Deeley?"

He looked past her at the well-built man with long hair and lion's eyes, currently holding the blond toddler with the way-too-appropriate name of Bash in his arms, chatting with a few of the guests.

"Seems like a good guy," he said.

"High praise from Dane 'man of few words' Whitney."

He gave a soft laugh, something Liv was always able to get from him with her irreverence and wit. "Kid's cute, too. What does he call you?"

"Wibbie," she said on a laugh. "It's how he says Livvie."

"He might as well call you 'Mommy,' the way you take care of him."

Her eyes flashed. "I hope he does, someday. You know what happened to Bash's parents, Dane. One died with Deeley on a Navy SEAL mission, and his mother was in a tragic accident. Deeley's the official guardian and I think, once we...you know...get permanent, we'll adopt."

"Get permanent. Does that mean get married? Why not just say so?"

"'Cause he hasn't formally proposed, but we're talking about the future and our life together and..." She shot him a dirty look. "Quit judging, bro. He's the greatest thing that ever happened to me."

He had to force a smile and nod, but not because he wasn't happy for her. He was. And not because he was jealous, because nothing about her life appealed to him. But because...

"That was fast," he murmured. At her look, he added, "I mean, didn't you just meet him six months or so ago?"

"Or so," she said, her voice taut. "Fast, by whose timeframe?"

"Dad's," he said softly, regretting the word the minute he let it slip out. But he was always honest with his sister, and he didn't see any reason to change that now.

She choked softly. "Excuse me?"

"I mean..." He shifted from one foot to the other, not sure exactly what he meant and, good God, he hated conversations like this.

"Tell me," she urged. "What did you mean?"

"Nothing, Liv. It's just that you and Mom..." He stole one glance down to the boardwalk where his mother stood way too close to Miles Anderson. At her feet was a black and white dog gazing up at her with the same smitten look that was on the guy's face.

Dane had met Miles earlier, had a brief and meaning-less conversation and might have accepted an invitation to go out on the guy's boat. After that, Dane made a beeline for the bar before he said something else that hurt his mother's feelings. He'd done enough damage for Day One.

"Me and Mom what?" Olivia pressed. "What does that mean?"

"Come on, Liv. You've both...recovered. Quickly. That's all."

"Maybe you should stick around and recover with us," she said, her eyes, that same silvery color as their mother's, tapering to slits. "Mom said you're already talking about leaving."

"Well, the housing situation is troubling and..." His voice trailed off as he caught sight of a woman who just came to the beach. And he couldn't even remember what he was saying.

She was tall, elegant, and toned. Long black braids fell down to her waist and her dark, dark skin looked burnished by the sun. She wore a bright orange floor-length dress with skinny straps over shoulders so smooth and polished, it was like Michelangelo had carved her from onyx.

Hanging around her neck in some kind of baby carrier was a sleeping infant who he thought couldn't have been more than a few months old.

"Asia," Olivia whispered on a soft laugh.

"Excuse me?"

"That woman you're drooling over. Her name is Asia Turner, that's her baby, Zane, and she's one of my closest friends."

He wanted to deny the drooling, or make some kind of noncommittal comment, but all he could do was...yeah, wow.

"She's gorgeous," he muttered. "And obviously taken."

"Nothing is obvious, you left-brained deducer. You're looking at one entirely independent woman who, in her mid-thirties, decided to take matters into her own hands and went and got herself a baby from the sperm bank."

He blinked in shock. "She's...how old?"

"Thirty-five, maybe. So she's got you by seven years, but she's young at heart and one of the best women I know. Plus, you're a rock-solid twenty-eight going on forty-four. The only problem, I mean, besides the fact that you're so anxious to take off? She's a wee bit of a man hater."

He dragged his gaze from the new arrival and looked at his sister. "Why?"

"That is her secret, and one she's keeping. But...she's on her way over. Maybe you can be the one to change her opinion of the Y chromosome."

Before he could respond, the woman in question practically floated over, moving with grace and purpose.

"Dane Whitney," she said, extending one long-fingered hand that looked like it was made to play the piano. "I've heard so much about you from your mother and sister." She gave him a wide, bright smile, her dark eyes dancing. "I'm Asia Turner."

"Asia." He shook her hand and held it maybe one second too long because...*dang*. She was even more beautiful up close.

"My brother's speechless," Olivia quipped.

And he'd kill Liv later. "Only because your son is so... tiny," he said, looking down at the baby, hoping he'd saved himself. "How old?"

"Not quite six months," she said, stroking his head

with a light, loving touch. "This is Zane." She looked up and winked. "Rhymes with Dane. Which is...insane."

He cracked up. "You should write song lyrics, Asia."

"Well, I do write poetry."

"Really?" He lifted a brow, interested.

"These days, it's more like nursery rhymes than true poetry." She gave the baby's head another light stroke. "All about little Zee, who is as cute as he can be."

Dane laughed softly at the rhyme. "You call him Zee?"

"I do, but don't tell my mother." She pointed her thumb over her shoulder at a turbaned older woman he remembered meeting earlier, along with a bald guy who waxed on about Theodore Roosevelt once living here.

"Roz doesn't believe in nicknames," Asia continued. "Or too many feedings. Or picking up a baby when he cries. Or letting him sleep in his mother's bed." She let out a noisy sigh and looked at Olivia. "I don't think I can take much more," she whined in a whisper.

"Are you living with your parents?" Dane guessed.

"I was living up in Ohio, where I had Zee, but it was a trifle overwhelming being a single mom. So I let my mother talk me into moving here, and I love it. I work remote in executive recruitment, so it's super easy. There's only one catch." She rolled her eyes. "Roz Turner is a control freak, who has a totally different parenting style. It's starting to make me cray-cray."

She sang the last few words, making him laugh, and appreciate the way she effortlessly hit the notes.

"Well, if it makes you feel any better," he said, "I'm moving into Disney World on the beach."

"Ah, yes, Harper's room. Yeah, I heard the whole plan to live with your sister fell apart."

Olivia shrugged. "Unless he wants to share a room with Bash."

"I have an idea!" Asia exclaimed, her voice rising enough to stir the sleeping child. "Let's get a place together."

He drew back, not sure he'd heard right.

"I've been peeking at the Sanibel rental market," she said, glancing over her shoulder as if her mother might hear her. "One-beds are astronomical. But a two-bedroom with a roommate? Affordable...sort of. We could split the rent, or I'd even pay more because of Zee. What do you think?"

All he could do was stare at her. Move in with her? After knowing her for less than five minutes? His computer brain, even with some of the critical gray matter flattened just by looking at this woman, slid into its usual decision-making process of pros and cons.

Con: he'd have to commit to staying longer than he might want to. Pro: he was looking at her. Con. Con. Con?

Nope, no other cons. And the pro was nothing short of breathtaking.

"I think..." He glanced at Olivia, who wore a smug and satisfied expression that he knew so well and kind of hated. Just like the time she persuaded him go rock climbing when he was ten and he wanted to cry until he got to the top of the wall and pronounced himself the king of the world.

"I think that sounds amazing," he said, shifting his gaze to Asia's. "My only stipulation? Something on the first floor, because I come with a very big piano."

Her eyes sparked with humor and interest. "Easy. I come with a very needy baby."

"Maybe what he needs is music," Dane said.

She let out a whimsical giggle that sounded like a descending arpeggio in B minor. "You might be right, Dane. Let's start looking ASAP."

"I can't wait."

"Let me go break the news to Roz. She can't yell at me at a party. Well, not too much." She blew a kiss to them and pivoted, leaving him with Smug Face.

"What?" he demanded.

"Nothing," Olivia said, her eyes dancing with delight. "Just...welcome to Shellshocker Beach, dude. Be ready for anything."

He looked at Asia, the first real smile he'd felt all day pulling at his mouth. "I am."

Chapter Three

Olivia

"Sack of potatoes, incoming." Deeley made his way into the dimly lit room with a conked-out Bash draped over his shoulder. "One load of Sebastian Thomas Royce delivered to bed."

With the ease and grace that Connor Deeley did everything, he lifted the thirty-five-pound child from his back and gently lowered him to the toddler-sized bed near the window.

"I wish he was awake so I could tell him how good he was tonight." Olivia crouched down to pull the Velcro from his little sneakers, recoiling a bit when she pulled one off. "Also, he could use a bath."

"This kid can always use a bath," Deeley said dryly. "But if you wake him, he's all yours."

Olivia smiled up at him. "He *is* all mine," she said softly. "And I'm not complaining."

Gazing at her for a long moment, he dipped down to get face to face. "Let me put it this way—if you wake him, then we don't get to be alone and discuss every little thing from tonight's party. Like..." He leaned in and kissed her lightly. "How beautiful you were. Are."

She smiled and took another kiss. "Was I? Because I

felt gross all night. Hot and tired and, was it just me, or did the shrimp cocktail taste a little off?"

"It was just you." He kissed her again. "Are you hungry? I can make you a chicken salad sandwich if you didn't get enough to eat tonight."

"Not hungry. At least not for food." She returned the kiss, letting it deepen. "Okay," she whispered as they drew apart. "I'll let him sleep a tad dirty. Does that make me a bad mother?"

His whole expression softened. "Ah, Liv. You are the best mother in the world, especially considering—"

She quieted that with a fingertip to his lips. "Remember our deal? Bash is ours, we are a family, and it doesn't need to be discussed anymore."

"I know, but I just want you to know that there's nothing you do that I take for granted. I love you so much, Livvie."

Next to them, Bash murmured in his sleep, turning over and finding his thumb. They both stared at each other, bracing for a cry. After a second, he drifted off again.

"Whew. Close call," Deeley joked.

"Let me get him undressed," she said. "I can do it without waking him. You pour me some of that amazing lemon balm tea Teddy sent me home with, and we'll talk."

He pushed up, and as he did, he reached into the pocket of his cargo shorts, scowling at the phone he pulled out. "Another one?"

"Another what?"

"I keep getting these texts from a number I don't know, a woman named Jenny Brennan. I've never heard of her and all she'll say is it's urgent, can I call her back. Think it's spam or marketing? She's texted four times since this afternoon."

"Where is she?"

"No idea. Area code is 6 1 2."

"Minneapolis," she said without thinking. "Promenade had an office there. It's an hour earlier there. Why don't you call her back?"

He gave her a weird look she couldn't interpret. "I don't know. If it's so urgent, why not leave a voice mail?"

"Maybe she's an ex."

He gave a dry laugh. "Never knew a woman named Jenny, I swear."

"A connection from the Navy? Or maybe..." Her voice trailed off as she finally interpreted his look. "A relative of Bash's."

Her heart dropped as they stared at each other. The distant relatives were out there, she knew it. The closest ones they'd been able to track down had zero interest in taking the guardianship of Tommy and Marcie's orphaned two-year-old son. Although the law said family had priority in situations like Bash's, he didn't seem to have any that wanted him.

That was just fine with Olivia and Deeley, because now, they couldn't live without this kid and adopting him as their own was going to happen without a doubt. Unless...

"No relatives were in Minneapolis," she said, rooting

around for a reason that the call could be about anything else. "No connection to Tommy or Marcie's families in the state of Minnesota that I recall."

He nodded. "You're right. And we've been in touch with any possible branches of either family, but there are still notifications out there, and will have to be for the first year or until he's legally adopted."

"Call her back, Deeley."

He nodded. "Yeah. I want to put it out of my mind, and..." He bent over for one more kiss. "Get us that tea. Unless I need something with a little more kick in mine."

"Don't worry," she called softly as he walked out.

While she undressed Bash and managed to get PJs on him without waking him, she listened for Deeley's voice, but he'd gone out to the patio to make the call.

It could be anything, right? They'd done their due diligence and Bash was theirs to keep and raise. On a slow sigh, she stroked his blond curls and watched his lashes flutter in contentment.

No one could take him now. It would wreck this poor kid to have one more upheaval in his world. He'd finally learned how to understand the word "no" after his mother had spent the better part of his life letting him do whatever he wanted. He was off his all-sugar diet and went to bed at a normal hour every night.

Even better, he was developing respect and patience and had the kindest heart.

Best of all, he laughed all the time, which made Olivia believe that he was finally secure. And that made her happier than anything. It made her feel secure, too, here in her makeshift family with the world's greatest guys.

"I love you, Basher," she whispered, leaning close to plant a kiss on his warm skin. "Sleep tight, little man. Tomorrow is another wonderful day."

Just as she pushed up and walked into the hall, she heard the sliding glass door close and latch. Heading into the kitchen, she found Deeley bracing himself against the counter in the dark, the phone in front of him, his broad shoulders rising and falling with a tense breath.

"Who was it?"

He didn't say anything for a minute, long enough for her eyes to adjust to the dim light, so when he turned, she saw the answer in his pained expression.

"Jennifer Brennan," he said softly.

"Who's that?"

"The daughter of David and Susan Callahan, and Susan's mother, Jennifer's grandmother, was a lady named..." He screwed up his face. "Evelyn Royce...Berg-well. I think. Married name. Anyway, Evelyn was the estranged sister of Brian Royce, who was Tommy's grand-father...or Bash's great-grandfather."

Her head felt like it just went underwater and stayed there, making his words almost garbled and the complex relationships impossible to understand. All she needed to know was this Jennifer person was a distant relative of Bash's.

"And?" she asked, her heart already crawling up to her throat.

"And she and her husband, Will, are coming to Sanibel Island—"

She gasped and he held up a hand.

"To meet him," he finished. "Just to *meet* him. Or so she says."

"Meet him? He's not even three. There won't be sparkling conversations and get-to-know-you dinners. Can't they do a video call and see he's thriving? I mean, if they're worried?"

He shook his head, then tunneled his fingers into his hair, pulling it back. "She just said meet him. Nothing else."

Olivia pulled out a chair and dropped into it, staring at him. "Why didn't her name show up when we searched for relatives?"

"She said she hadn't had anything to do with that side of her family since she was a child. But they had some big family fallout way back in the sixties. I don't know. A lot of married names, decades past, and people lost."

"How did she find out about him?"

"She said she was searching online for something and put in her grandmother's maiden name, which is Royce, and found the legal notification about Bash. I don't know exactly how, but..." He shook his head, his whole being vibrating with frustration. "Anyway, they're coming here but didn't say when."

"A surprise visit?"

"She just said they'd be planning a trip 'soon' and would be in touch. She wanted to talk and confirm that he was being taken care of, and find out what happened to his parents."

"Did you tell her?"

He nodded. "Of course. There's nothing to hide. I also told her Bash is being well cared for by us and that he's a happy, healthy, wonderful little boy."

"Do you think they'll want to take him?" Her voice cracked at the possibility.

"I couldn't tell."

"Was she nice?"

He shrugged. "She was friendly, but direct and intentional. Didn't *ask* if she could come, if you know what I mean. And we have to remember that blood likely trumps friendship in guardianship issues when both parents are dead, unless we have to go to court and fight for him."

"Which we will," Olivia said without hesitation. "We will fight so hard for him, I'd...I'd...die for him."

His face crumpled as he reached for her, pulling her up from the chair and against his chest, his embrace so strong it nearly took her breath away. "Livvie. I never loved you more than I do right this minute."

She closed her eyes and let the words wash over her. "Oh, sure you have," she whispered lightly, trying not to fall apart.

But he inched back and looked into her eyes. "No, I haven't. You love that boy like he was your own."

"So do you," she countered. "And that's why, whatever happens, we can't lose him. I don't even want to think about what moving again would do to him. A new family? A new house? Minneapolis?" Her voice rose with every unimaginable word.

"Shhh." He rubbed her back, but she could feel he was wound as tight as she was. "She didn't say anything like that. Only that she really regretted that there was this family split—which I am clueless about, honestly."

"Tommy never mentioned anything like that?"

"Nothing. Never talked about his family much. And this woman, this Jenny Brennan, said that her grandmother—the one who had the split with her brother, Tommy's grandfather—died recently and now she wants to fix things."

Olivia scowled at him. "By visiting a toddler who is... are they cousins? Second or third? Her grandmother is Bash's...great-aunt? Maybe great-great? Twice removed or something like that?"

He managed a soft laugh. "Something like that."

She leaned back, shaking her head. "That is a stretch, Deeley. I mean, is there some DNA overlap? A strand or two, sure. But does that mean she can swoop in and take Bash as *family*?"

"I don't know. Like I said, she said, 'We want to meet him,' a few times, and that's all. She didn't say why. I couldn't exactly say no."

"Did you give her an address?"

"Not home. I told her I worked at Shellseeker Cottages, and she has my cell number. She should call before they leave."

Her eyes widened. "Or maybe they're going to come

anonymously or make a surprise visit—to catch us doing something wrong or see how Bash behaves."

He grunted at the very idea. "That could be hit or miss. But maybe it's totally innocuous. They want pictures or she's writing up a family genealogy."

"Or maybe they can't have kids and want ours, or the dead grandmother has a stipulation in her will that they mend the family rift to get her millions."

"Livvie." He managed a laugh. "That's only your family with the secret wills."

She lifted a dubious brow. For a long moment, they just stood there in silence, holding on to each other, as connected as two people could be.

"This could be it," Olivia muttered, putting her hand on a stomach that suddenly felt as unsettled as it did after the shrimp.

"This could be...what?"

"The other shoe. The next crisis. A new problem that the universe sends to keep us apart."

"Not following you."

She shrugged. "I was talking to my mother about it on the way to the airport. About how it feels like every time we get close to true happiness, contentment, and where we ought to be, something goes wrong. Maybe we weren't meant to be together, Deeley."

His whiskey-gold eyes flashed in the dark. "Don't ever say that again as long as you live."

She wanted to laugh at how serious he was, but he wasn't joking. "I just worry that there's going to be another...thing."

"Then we'll beat that thing, no matter what it takes." He tightened his hold on her and lowered his face to hers. "Skip the tea and stop fretting, Liv. And let me show you exactly how together we're meant to be."

She didn't fight that, but accepted his kiss with a sigh of surrender.

THE NEXT DAY, Deeley agreed that they should go directly to Miles Anderson for an assist. A skilled private investigator with an uncanny ability to dig through the internet and piece together a person's life, Miles could tell them more about Jennifer and William Brennan than they could ever figure out on their own.

They made plans to see him later that morning, so Olivia and Bash went with Deeley to Shellseeker Beach to drop him off for an hour with Eliza.

"See 'Liza?" Bash asked from his car seat in the back when Deeley turned onto Roosevelt Road and the three-story beach house was visible.

"Yes!" Olivia turned to smile at him and reach out her hand. "Eliza is going to babysit you for a little while."

His big blue eyes danced with approval, punctuated by slipping his beloved thumb in his mouth. Olivia frowned and waved her finger a tiny bit. "No thumb, Bash."

He closed his eyes and sucked harder.

"I thought we were going with Dr. Osborn's advice," Deeley said. "Not to fight it while he's adjusting, right?

He said it's only really a problem when permanent teeth come in."

Olivia sighed and turned back to face the front. "I know and I like that plan, but lots of people say to break the habit as young as possible, so it's easier when those permanent teeth are there." She waited a beat and added, "Also, it looks like we're not on top of things."

His eyes shuttered at the words. "You really think they're going to drop in and do some child-rearing inspection?"

Yes, she kind of did. "I don't know what I think," she said instead. "But I'll feel better after we know a little more about them. I'm sure Miles already has their home address, family history, personal bank records, and has hacked their email."

Deeley gave a dry laugh. "He doesn't do anything illegal. And what's legal will probably not tell us why they're coming and what they're planning to do."

"But it might tell us what kind of people they are."

He nodded, not terribly talkative this morning, and parked his truck in an open spot in the Shellseeker Cottages lot.

"I'm going to run down to the cabana," he said, jutting his chin in the direction of the beach rental business. "Noah's got this shift, but I want to let him know the jet skis are coming in this week and we need to set up a rental system."

"He's really working out well for you, isn't he?" When Deeley had gone up to North Carolina last month, Noah Hutchins had jumped in to help with the beach rental business that Deeley had been building for more than two years. Now Noah was at the cabana as frequently as he was at the tea hut he managed, and Deeley had been able expand the business. More because he was no longer supporting Bash's mother than the fact that he had Noah.

"He's been great," Deeley agreed. "He really gets the business and by giving him some hours, I feel like I have so much more time to buy new equipment and build things up. Without having to give a huge chunk of my income to Marcie, that second rental operation isn't out of reach."

"I'm glad you have Noah and I have Ileana. That way, the you-know-who's won't think we put Bash in daycare too often, but that he gets quality time with us."

He shot her a look. "You're too worried about what they think."

"You're not?"

"Yeah," he admitted. "I am."

A few minutes later, they were on their way down the garden path at Shellseeker Cottages. In front of them, the Gulf of Mexico sparkled to the horizon, the wide beach dotted with tourists bent over to find the treasures of Sanibel in the sand.

Each holding one of Bash's hands, Olivia and Deeley let him swing between them, stopping twice to ooh and aah over the "flutterbies" flitting over the lantana plants.

As they came around a huge cluster of live oaks and palm trees, Olivia stopped dead in her tracks at the sight of her brother, sprawled on his back on a stone bench, his eyes closed and huge noise-cancelling headphones over his ears.

"Hey, maestro!" She poked him and he leaped up, startled.

"What the—" He yanked the headset off and glowered at her.

"Careful, kiddie ears," she reminded him. "What are you doing out here?"

"Waiting for Asia," he said, a hint of a smile pulling at his lips just saying her name. "Gonna start our house-slash-apartment hunt." He nodded at Deeley, who was still holding Bash's hand. "Morning."

"How's it going, Dane?" Deeley asked.

"'Sokay. I especially loved the fairy lights while I tried to sleep."

Olivia snorted. "Makes for sweet dreams."

Deeley smiled and gave Bash's head a playful rub. "Be good, Basher. See you in a bit."

But Bash's attention was snagged by another butterfly, and he toddled after it.

"I'll be back in ten," Deeley said to Olivia, giving her a kiss. "Then we can go see Miles."

"Cool." When he left, she perched on the edge of the stone bench, one eye on Bash, the other on her brother, who looked slightly less tense than he'd been yesterday.

"Where's Mom?" she asked.

"I think she and Teddy are in the tea hut brewing up...something."

"Tea, most likely," Olivia cracked. "So, did you call the piano transport company and delay the shipment?"

"Not yet. I can call by the end of today. I'm waiting to see what we find for possible living quarters."

We. Dane and Asia. Talk about an interesting match. "So all it took to make you back off your plans to leave was the possibility of moving in with Asia? Pretty sure she meant as platonic roommates there, Romeo."

He frowned at her. "I know what she meant. Honest? I don't want to drag myself back to California where I have no more legit housing there than I do here. I'm on this rock, so I'll probably stay. And I want that piano here."

"There are other pianos in the world, probably some right here on Sanibel Island. Have you looked?"

"That one is...the one I play. It's special."

"Why?" she asked.

He looked at her for a long time, a little storm brewing in his eyes. "It's not important," he finally said.

"Sounds pretty darn important to me."

"Fine," he said. "I'll tell you. Ever since I got that piano, I've written amazing songs. Best of my life. And, for the first time, I could see my path, and I felt...I felt...I don't know..."

"More connected to Dad?" she guessed.

His nodded a silent admission. "And life and music and what I want to be doing with both," he added.

"I get that," she said softly, putting a hand on his leg. "I don't think it's the piano as much as the frame of mind, but I get it." She pushed up, adding a sisterly kiss to his head. "But Dad would tell you to, 'Get a haircut, son,'" she teased in a low voice, making him smile.

"It's my rock-star look."

"You're a cutie, *Dave*." She jabbed his shoulder. "And I hope you find the perfect place on a ground floor that's full of light and joy, and you and Asia and Zee live happily ever after."

He rolled his eyes. "Shut up."

"You think I don't know when you have a crush? You looked at her the way you used to look at Emily...Snicker-doodle or whatever her last name was."

"Snickenhoff." He gave in to a slight smile. "She was special."

"Like your piano." She pointed a playful finger at him, knowing there had been a time when he'd grab that finger and pull hard to make her stop teasing. "Told ya. You can deny it all you want, but you like Asia."

"Nothing not to like," he answered amicably.

"Except she ain't gonna be easy." Not that any girl came easily to Dane. He'd never been a player and had been tongue-tied around most females growing up. Obviously, that had changed, but he wasn't a flirt.

He looked up at her, a familiar glint in his eyes. Like when they'd both pick up a Wii controller and brace for a to-the-death game of *Super Smash Brothers*. And he *always* won.

"Wait. You think you have a shot?" She gave him an incredulous look.

"Thanks, Liv. Your confidence in me is so encouraging."

"No, I mean...I guess, maybe. But she thinks men are scum, trouble, and not worth her time."

"I'm not looking for anything but inspiration," he said. "And she's definitely that."

"Well, you've been warned," she reminded him, standing up to end the conversation. "I gotta find Mom. Good luck today."

"Thanks."

She called Bash from the butterflies and took his hand, heading off to the tea hut, where her mother and Teddy were head-to-head at one of the rattan tables, deep in conversation.

"Livvie!" Mom waved her over, rising to reach her arms out to Bash. "Good morning, handsome," she called.

"'Liza!" He pattered over to her, reaching up for a hug.

Teddy joined their group hug, the vignette sweet enough to make Olivia slow her step and just take them in. Eliza, like a grandmother, and Teddy, like a great-grandma, doting on a child who was...*like* hers.

Olivia made a mental note to get the Brennans right here to see that Bash had a village of love around him. Would that matter to them?

"What's wrong, Liv?" her mother asked, looking up.

Of course Eliza Whitney could sniff the first scent of trouble in Olivia's world. How did she do that?

She gave her head a nearly invisible shake and sneakily pointed to Bash to communicate that she didn't want to talk about it in front of him. Teddy saw that, and was up instantly.

"I have some lemonade and a cookie with your name on it!" she announced, taking his hand.

Olivia shot her a grateful look, then added, "Just one cookie, Bash." When they walked away, she slid closer to her mother and dumped everything she knew about the Brennans and their upcoming visit.

After she finished, her mother let out a sigh, taking her hand. "You have to stop," she said.

"Stop what? Stop worrying about what they want?"

"Yes, and stop clinging to the fear that you're going to lose him or something else is going to happen to break up you and Deeley. At the risk of sounding like the worst possible cliché, what will be, will be, Liv." She leaned in closer. "In other words, you can't fight everything and everyone. You have to live through this year until the guardianship is sealed."

"Or he's legally adopted."

"Can Deeley do that before the year is up?"

"We can start the process, which might take time. Still, we didn't think there was any rush. We hoped Bash would be a little older and understand the importance of it." She crinkled her nose. "Deeley wants to be more settled—and yes that is a euphemism for married—before we adopt him. At least, that's what we've talked about."

"Well, if you're going to spend every day frantic about losing him, then you should get married, start the adoption process, and make it all legal. That's what you want, right?"

"Yes, but not rushed because we have to. I want to plan something special and make it amazing. Don't you want to be a mother of the bride and all that?"

"I just want you to be happy and secure and not walking on guardianship eggshells."

Olivia nodded, unable to disagree with that. "Well, step one is to go meet with Miles today. I think he'll be able to shed some light on what we're dealing with on these people. Then step two is to wait for word from them...or a surprise visit when they announce..." She groaned. "They want him."

"Can they just do that? Isn't there a law to protect Bash?"

Olivia nodded. "He's legally under Deeley's guardianship. But if it goes to court, they have a powerful argument in that they are blood relatives."

"Great, grand, and several times removed," her mother said, rolling her eyes.

"True. But it's scary."

At the sound of Bash's high-pitched giggle, she turned to see him holding a plastic tumbler of lemonade in one hand and a cookie in the other, gazing up at Teddy with nothing but love.

"Look how happy that kid is," Mom mused. "Who could take him from all this?"

"Someone mean and heartless and cruel. Or certain that we're all wrong." Olivia pushed up and, on the way, dropped a kiss on her mother's head. "I'm going to go see your boyfriend and see if we can find—"

"Shh!" Mom warned, looking past Olivia. "Don't let Dane hear you call Miles that."

"Why? You're dating the man. It's just a matter of semantics, right?"

"Semantics that could really upset your brother."

"Did you talk about it?" Olivia asked.

"Dane? Talk? No. He bottled it all up, took a night walk on the beach, and went to bed."

"Oh, that boy. And this one." She helped Bash into the chair next to her, giving him a kiss. "That looks good." She pointed to the cookie.

He held it up. "Wanna bite, Wibbie?"

She whimpered with love and pulled him into her. "No, baby Bash, but I'll take a kiss for luck." She put a peck on his head and stood up. "Take good care of him."

"We always do," Teddy assured her.

She blew them kisses as she walked away, wondering if Jenny and Will Brennan had the amazing, wonderful, loving "community of caretakers" that she did. Highly, highly unlikely. She hoped.

Chapter Four

Asia

T his was a massive step forward. Massive. Not only was Asia ready to truly be a single mom, living without an assist from her ever-helpful but always over-bearing mother, she was seriously considering living with a *man*.

Not *living with*, obviously. That would never happen in her lifetime. But co-existing in the same domicile as roommates. And even on the most amicable and surface level, that would require Asia to trust the guy to some small extent, and that was the true massive step forward.

But if she didn't find a roommate, she'd die of asphyxiation. She loved her mother, but she needed air and space and the ability to make a decision that wasn't second-guessed. Her mother had an opinion on everything from the color of his socks—*"They have to match, Asia!"*—to his shortened name.

"Zee isn't a name, Asia! It's a letter."

That left few choices. Her job as an executive recruiter was completely remote, handled entirely by phone, video, and computer, making it easy for her to live anywhere. She didn't want to be alone with her baby; she loved having family nearby. Close, but not completely up in her business with the critical eye of a woman whose middle name should be Judgment.

Plus, Asia had fallen pretty hard in love with the Sanibel life. It suited her laidback, warm weather-loving self.

That left one option—to find the perfect roommate until she could afford to live alone. She'd looked at some local Facebook pages for female options, but no single women wanted a baby around, and she could understand that.

She was starting to consider how deep she could dip into her savings when the good Lord dropped Dane Whitney on Shellseeker Beach and gave her the answer she needed.

She could be friends with a man, right? Roommates and casual acquaintances? Of course she could.

She wasn't *that* destroyed by her past.

So, with baby Zee in one arm and a list of potential rentals under the other, Asia had packed up her car, picked up her new pal, Dane, and now she was driving them toward a small neighborhood near the lighthouse to start with the least expensive two-bedroom option they could find.

As they chatted about life, jobs, weather, and families, she tried to size up this relative stranger she might very well call "roommate" soon. She'd heard bits and pieces about Dane from his sister and mother, and knew he was a brilliant and logical twenty-eight-year-old computer engineer—those descriptions had become attached to his name in her head—and that he'd left an impressive tech job to follow his passion for composing music.

That surprising decision alone made him interesting, along with the fact that he seemed to hold back his feelings much more than his sister or mother. Those two wore their emotions for the world to see; Dane didn't show his cards too easily.

Livvie had shared that Dane had been very close to their father, and that he'd taken their dad's death a year ago pretty hard. They all had, but Dane, Livvie said, seemed to utterly change after that.

He also wasn't a try-hard. He seemed chill and comfortable, and she liked the way he jumped at the idea of being roommates with a stranger—and her baby. Maybe he was desperate to get out of Teddy's place, but it still showed an adventurous spirit that she thought would be a good influence on Zee.

Not that her six-month-old would be heavily influenced by anyone at this age. But a man—any man at all—would have some kind of subtle, undeniable impact on her son, and she wanted that to be all positive, strong, and good.

"Here it is," Dane said, gesturing to an older two-story complex just off the main road, lowering his sunglasses to get a better look. "I think the cons might beat the pros on this one."

"Is that how you make every major decision?" she asked, glancing at his profile instead of the apartment, which looked...ugh. Like it probably had mold.

"Major and minor," he said. "It's the logical way to make a decision."

"But some do have to be made by the heart. Surely walking away from your job to pursue music had more cons than pros."

He turned to her, and she noticed that his eyes looked green in the bright sunlight. She could have sworn they were a light brown. "There were no cons that could rival my sanity. Sometimes the pro list is short but carries more weight. I always do weighted pros and cons."

She laughed at how serious he was, taking another moment to study those green—yes, green—eyes before turning to the apartment.

"What's the weight on mold?" she asked. "Because I have a feeling this place might have some."

"I'm not allergic, but I sure wouldn't want that little guy breathing any." He tipped his head toward Zee, where her baby snoozed in the back-facing car seat. "Or you."

She smiled, touched by the consideration. "Good, 'cause if we're weighing things, my baby's health is heavier than anything."

"And my—"

"Piano, I know," she said on a laugh, clicking her seatbelt latch after parking. "The whole list is first floor. Come on, let's look at it and sniff around. But not too hard." She waved her hand in front of her nose. "Those mold spores can be wicked."

"I can go in alone and you can wait with the baby."

"You're thoughtful, but I'd like to see it, too. Maybe we'll be pleasantly surprised."

He looked like he doubted that. A few minutes later, she had Zee wrapped up in a carrier around her chest, awake but calm as always.

"Does he ever cry?" Dane asked as they walked toward the rental office.

"He's trying to impress you," she joked. "That way, you'll want him as a freeloading roommate."

"I'm impressed," Dane said, a sparkle in his eye that showed her that for all his seriousness, there was definitely some humor there, and if they were going to be roommates, she'd need that.

The woman in the office greeted them warmly, and let them take the key and look at the unit alone, which Asia appreciated. Dane led the way, following the numbers until they got to the dingy beige door of Unit 106.

She let out a moan even before he unlocked the door.

"Wait out here?" he asked.

"No, we'll go in, but my expectations couldn't be lower."

And, even with the lowest possible expectations, the unit disappointed. Dark, small, with a musty scent, the place couldn't have been more unwelcoming. She stayed in the living room and held Zee while Dane checked out the two bedrooms and one bath, and came out looking as disinterested as she felt. Thank goodness.

They barely stayed five minutes, returned the key, and headed back to her car. In fact, it took longer to get

Zee in the car seat and latched up than it had taken for
the apartment tour.

"Okay," Dane said, picking up the printout she'd left
on the console between them. "Scratch this one. Next is a
townhouse, I see. Based on that map, it looks like it's not
far from my sister, right?"

She nodded, her gratitude for this man growing every
minute. "Thank you," she said softly. "For not being, you
know..."

"Ready to take the first dump we find?" he guessed.

"Just not insistent that I give it a chance. I just want
you to know I appreciate that in a—" She caught herself
before she said *man*. "—in a potential roommate," she
finished.

"Asia, we're doing this little adventure together to get
us both into better living situations," he replied. "I'm not
going to force-fit you and Zee, or myself, into something
that would make us miserable. That place was gloom.
We're in the Sunshine State, much to my dismay, so let's
at least have some of that."

"Yes," she agreed. "Sunshine is high on the pro list."
As she started up the car, she glanced at him. "Why to
your dismay? Don't you want to be here?"

"Not particularly," he said, tugging at the seatbelt on
his chest as if it pressed too hard. Or the conversation did.

"Why not? It's paradise and your family is here,
unless there's a reason you need to be in L.A. or Nash-
ville or New York."

"No, my business—not that it's any 'business' yet—
can be done anywhere. I'm going to write songs and try to

sell them. With my piano for composing, I can produce high-quality output with computer software, which actually supplies the other 'musicians,' if I want a band or symphonic effect."

"I placed someone at a record company last year," she said. "As a recruiter, I get to talk to people in every imaginable industry. He was in accounting for a label called..." She dug into her memory. "Soulshifters?"

"Great R&B," he said. "Not what I write, but fantastic music."

"What exactly do you write?"

"I don't know what you'd call it. Symphonic soft rock with a side of...melody."

She cracked up. "What station is that on?"

"Yeah, it might be *too* groundbreaking, but I know what I like. Think movie scores with lyrics. And I can write pop. I don't have anything against pop, it's just that it's a little more challenging for me."

"Do you write the lyrics, too?" she asked.

"I try, but I'm much stronger in music than lyrics. I hear melodies constantly, which can make me look like a crazy person when I'm trying to transpose one into a line of actual music while I'm walking down the street."

"Did you inherit your mother's gorgeous singing voice?" she asked. "I can't believe Eliza was on Broadway."

"I wish, but my voice is mediocre at best. Not only does she have a beautiful voice, but my mother has always had a way with lyrics. When I was growing up, I'd play the piano and she'd sit next to me and just...make up words. Before you knew it, we had a song."

"Look at you with the big fat smile on your face." She nudged his shoulder playfully. "Why on Earth *wouldn't* you want to be in the state where that lady is, the one who wrote your lyrics?"

"I don't know," he said, turning to look out the window.

"I mean, she's certainly not the hovercraft *smother* that mine is," she added, liking that the nickname made him laugh. "I adore your mother. Everyone does."

"Everyone." He dragged out the word with just a little bit of something she couldn't quite interpret.

"What does that mean?" she asked. "With all that...subtext?"

"Subtext?"

"Come on, music man. Spill your real feels."

He laughed, throwing a look at her. "My real feels are I can't stand it when people call them 'feels.'"

"Or you can't stand talking about emotions. Don't lie. I already know this from your darling sister, who is one of my best pals."

He looked skyward. "Great. Well, don't believe everything Livvie says. Sisters are..." He turned to her. "Do you have one?"

"I have a brother up in Ohio."

"Do you believe everything he says?"

She laughed. "Nothing at all."

"Then don't believe everything Liv says about me."

"But you don't like talking about emotions, am I right?"

He considered that. "I prefer to put them to music."

"Fair enough. Do I turn here?"

He shifted his attention to the GPS, tapping the screen to zoom in. "Left at the next intersection. No light there."

"There are no stop lights on Sanibel Island," she told him. "Protects the sea turtles at night, allows for better viewing of the night sky, and it's prettier. Now, what's not to like about this place, Dane Whitney?"

He smiled. "You're relentless, I see."

"I've been called worse," she conceded. "Come on, I need to know if you're going to bail in two months and leave me high and dry for a roommate. What don't you like about it here?"

He sighed as she made the turn, obviously not a man who answered questions without thinking.

"I haven't been here long enough to form an opinion," he finally said. "But my mother and then my sister decided to move so...abruptly."

"You didn't live near them, did you?"

"No, I was in Silicon Valley, which is in Northern California. My mom was in L.A., and Liv was up in Seattle. We were in the same time zone, though."

"But not close enough to miss them when they moved," she pressed. "Then why does it bother you so much that they have?"

"It doesn't..." His voice trailed off and she waited while he gathered his thoughts, taking a good, long fifteen seconds to do so. "It's a big change so soon after my dad died. I always heard a widow should not make any major decisions for a year or two after losing her spouse."

"You *heard* that?" she challenged. "Water cooler talk at the tech firm where you worked?"

He chuckled. "Okay, I googled it, but it makes sense."

"To who? Not to your mother, who, for the record, seems very, very happy here."

He studied the phone screen. "Next right and it'll be on the left."

"She is, you know."

"Oh, I know. I hear about it all the time. Livvie's in love. Mom has a new purpose. And a man, so—"

She tapped the brakes at the townhouse units, stopping before she pulled in. "You don't want your mother to be happy?"

He closed his eyes and she knew at that minute, she'd gone one tiny bit too far. She braced for his reaction, the flash of anger, the flared nostrils, the harsh tone. Her whole body squeezed in anticipation, and she was furious with herself for pushing.

"That's not it at all," he said, so softly she barely heard the words. Then he looked at her and his eyes— which were light brown again—were filled with sadness. "I just miss my dad a lot," he confessed in a ragged voice. "And when I see her with, uh, Miles, then I miss my dad more than I expected to."

"Oh." She breathed the word, a mix of relief and awe and genuine admiration for such honesty, especially from someone who didn't love the feels. Without thinking, she put her hand on his arm and added some pressure. "That's so understandable and...and real. I'm sorry I pressed you on it."

"No, it's fine. You do have a right to know if I'm going to stick around if we become roommates. I'll..." He took a deep breath. "I'll let you know for sure before we sign anything."

She was surprisingly sad that he was even considering leaving, but she nodded and turned to the building. But she didn't really see it. She was too focused on all the emotion rolling through her.

Speaking of feels, she was suddenly drowning in them.

It had been a long, long time since she felt the tiniest bit of trust toward a man. A long time since she didn't live a little scared, a little wary, and a lot uncertain of what or who to believe.

But this man was...kind. Hurting. And so very honest.

She'd forgotten men like that existed.

"Looks better than the last one," he said, peering past her at the building.

"Anything would look better than the last one."

He chuckled, thinking she was talking about the apartment. She wasn't.

Chapter Five

Olivia

A minister? Will Brennan was a Presbyterian minister with a flock who adored him, a wife who ran a food bank, and three kids between five and twelve, each one cuter than the next?

Olivia practically groaned in misery.

"Are you sure that's the right Will and Jenny Brennan?" she asked as she studied the Facebook page over Miles's shoulder. Jenny was blond, maybe early forties, with sharp blue eyes and a catalogue-model smile. Will had a beard and wore Hawaiian shirts, with a kid on his hip in every picture unless he was holding tools at the latest Habitat for Humanity building project.

"They're...saints," she murmured.

"That should make you feel better," Miles said.

Except...it didn't. They were perfect, loved children, and probably longed to adopt the orphan in the family.

"Did you find anything else? A good church scandal or a pending divorce? Maybe one of them broke the law once? Parked in a handicapped spot or didn't recycle?"

Miles chuckled and shook his head. "Nothing. And, honestly, Liv, except for their address—and yes, they own their house with no mortgage—"

"Of course they do."

"You could have done this search yourself in about ten minutes," he finished. "There are no secrets here, not as far as I can tell. This couple is straight as an arrow, pillars of the community, and seem like nice enough people."

"Just what I was worried about," she said, rounding his long monitor-covered desk to thump down onto the sofa between Deeley and Tinkerbell, Miles's dog. Tink made space for her, but Deeley put a loving arm around Olivia's shoulder.

"I'm not sure I agree," he said. "If the family is that good, then these people have good hearts and a strong moral compass. They'll see that Bash is in a great place and...and...they'll be happy about that."

She wasn't so sure. "Or they could see a kid who isn't legally adopted being cared for by two people who have known each other less than a year—and are living in sin, mind you—not to mention that Bash's totally unfit mother ran off to Vegas with a virtual stranger and left him alone. On paper, it isn't ideal."

"Paper isn't reality, and his mother's issues are ancient history," Deeley insisted. "He's well-loved and well-cared for. And they didn't say a word about taking him or trying to take him. They want to meet him. Maybe they want to...baptize him." He lifted his brows. "We could do that, if that's what they wanted, right?"

"Of course! I'd want to baptize him. We could do anything to keep him, but..." She turned to Miles. "What do you think? You are so good at sussing out people's evil motivations and dark histories."

Miles smiled at the compliment. "I think these are upstanding citizens, and Jenny's story holds true. I couldn't legally hack anything too deeply personal, but I got a surprising amount of information from her Facebook history. You can see that she's recently become online friends with people with the last name of Royce, which tells me she's been looking into her family connections. There are pictures of at 'Grandma Evie's' funeral, and the name Royce appears in the family line."

"And that was enough for her to hunt down Bash."

"She didn't know he existed," Deeley said. "She stumbled onto the notification that we're legally obligated to post."

"Which means that notification process works," Miles said. "You want her to know about Bash now, not later. The sooner you meet this woman and get the relationship squared away, the better you'll feel, Liv."

She nodded glumly. "I'm not going to feel better until Bash is ours, legally and officially."

"He is yours legally," Miles reminded her gently. "Well, he's Deeley's. You have been through some pretty big legal hoops the last few months, and someone, even with the same DNA, cannot just pounce on Bash and take him home without a court order."

She grunted at the very idea, but the words did lift some of the pressure off her chest.

"A court order for what?" Deeley asked.

"To contest the guardianship," Miles said...and the

pressure came back. "Or they could seek a kinship adoption based on family ties. But I don't know what their reason could or would be."

She knew what—the fact that Deeley and Olivia weren't married or that they rented and didn't own their house. Or maybe because Deeley was digging out of debt, or she was in pretty deep on the store. Perhaps the Brennans wanted to raise Bash in their church, and would take issue with the fact that Olivia and Deeley hadn't stepped foot in one for a long time.

She writhed around on the sofa, stilled only by the strong arm of her man around her.

"Look," Deeley said. "We got what we came for. We know a little bit about them, so when—and if—they come to Sanibel, we're going to be warm and friendly and show them how much we love Bash. That's it. That's all."

But was it? "At least we know what they look like in case we spot them sniffing around Shellseeker Beach."

Deeley pushed up and glanced at his phone. "Oh, sorry. I'm getting a call from Noah about a rental issue. Gimme a sec, okay?"

"Of course," she said, reaching for Tinkerbell's soft black and white head. The Boston terrier mix looked up with the same skepticism Olivia expected to see in Jenny Brennan's eyes when they met. The look that said she was a sin-living, kid-stealing, non-house-owning mess.

"What's wrong, Tinkie?" she asked softly.

"She sees you, she expects her beloved Eliza," Miles said on a laugh. "We're both always happier when she's around."

"Who isn't?" Olivia looked up at him, shaking off her self-absorption to eye the man who'd made tremendous headway in the Great Quest for Eliza's Heart.

"I know who's not happy that *I'm* around," Miles said with a mirthless smile. "Your brother. Or am I imagining things?"

The question touched, and saddened, her. She'd truly hoped that Miles had no idea that Dane was fundamentally opposed to his relationship with their mother.

She sighed and smiled. "You know, Miles, someday your capability for figuring out what motivates people is going to get you in trouble."

He laughed. "It does pay the bills, but..." He lifted his brows. "I'm not wrong, am I?"

Uncomfortable with the subject, she rubbed Tink's head and leaned in to whisper, "Help me out here, doggo. Please do something so cute it changes the subject."

"Livvie," he said. "Think of it this way. I'm asking for *your* advice and help for a change. What can I do to improve the situation? Other than the usual—take him out on the boat and make him fall in love with Sanibel Island."

But how would that make her brother accept and embrace Miles and Eliza as a couple? She looked hard at Miles, trying to come up with the best answer.

"I guess you need patience with him, and he needs time to see what all the rest of us see. That you're amazing and good for my mom and she's content again. How could he want anything but that?"

"Because I'm not his father and if I'm with Eliza,

then I'm replacing your father." He smiled, making his green eyes dance. "And believe me, I know enough about Ben Whitney to not even try and compete."

His humility touched her, and made her like the man even more. "It's not a competition, Miles. You're different and wonderful in your own way. And I say that as one of the biggest Ben Whitney fans who ever lived."

He sighed. "That's kind, Liv. And I appreciate it. After all, we're coming up on the one-year anniversary of his death."

"I know. We all know. It's looming."

"Not looming," he said. "I'm looking forward to passing that mark. I know it's been a...a milestone, I guess, for Eliza. I know she's going to feel better about having a relationship with me once she thinks a 'proper' amount of time has passed."

Olivia nodded, well aware of her mother's timeline, and, like Miles, hoping that once they passed it, Eliza could let herself truly love again.

"I'm just not sure if Dane being here is a setback or something good for her," Miles said. "So that's why I'm asking. Is there anything I can do to smooth things over or gain his trust? I really want him to stay here, because family means so much to both you and Eliza."

"Oh, I don't think he's leaving," she said. "He's apartment hunting with Asia Turner right now."

Miles's brows shot up. "Really?"

"As roommates," she clarified. "They just met last night."

"Well, that bodes well for him staying." He shrugged.

"And gives me more incentive to get to know him and build a relationship with him." He waited a beat and added, "Do you think that's even possible?"

"Right now, fresh out of the gate on Day Two?" She shook her head. "But that doesn't mean you can't or won't. Just understand that he's still grieving, he's guarded, and he isn't comfortable talking about touchy-feely things. He's very logical. Appeal to that, and he'll trust you."

He nodded and gave in to a slow smile. "Well, there's nothing all that logical about how I feel about your mother," he said. "But it couldn't be more real."

"Oh, Miles." She stood and so did he, coming around his desk to accept the spontaneous hug she offered. "I'm so happy she found you. That we both did." She added a squeeze. "I've got your back and will be doing all sorts of pro-Miles PR on the home front."

He chuckled. "Thanks, Liv. And I've got yours. If the Brennans need character witnesses, I will sing your praises to the moon and back."

The words touched her heart, eliciting one more tight squeeze of gratitude. Dane was a moron for not seeing that, in the grand scheme of life and death, they'd been blessed with this man. No, he wasn't Ben Whitney, but he was as awesome in his own way. Somehow, she'd get her brother to realize that.

WORK WAS a welcome distraction that afternoon for Olivia. After Ileana left, Sanibel Sisters kept a steady flow of customers, almost all of them buying something from her gorgeous displays of elegant and casual women's clothing. Most needed enough help in the dressing area that she didn't have time to dwell on what she'd learned about the Brennan family or their pending visit.

There wasn't anything they could do at this point, just wait and hope and—

"Oh, you're here."

Olivia turned at the sound of a man's voice coming from the back office, a sound that at one time would have surprised her. But she was long used to drop-by visits from Abner "Buck" Underwood, who owned the bait shop next to Sanibel Sisters, and had grown to be a very important part of their ad hoc family.

"I just came from Cami's place," he said, striding into the store in his usual faded jeans and flannel shirt.

With his six-foot frame and shock of white hair, this seventy-five-year-old always seemed so out of place in the feminine explosion of fabric and color that was the boutique. But he'd worked his way into the place with one Southern-accented compliment after another directed at Camille, and moments before her emergency heart surgery a month ago, he'd proposed.

And every day, Olivia liked him more. "How's she doing today?" she asked.

"Up and about, taking her meds, eyeing her high heels, and itching to get back to this instead of being your silent, sick partner." He gave a grin that crinkled the network of lines on his face. "She sends her love."

"And I graciously accept her love, but am shocked she has any left over after all she showers on you."

He beamed at her. "And I am enjoyin' every minute of it. As a matter of fact..." He glanced around and noticed that there was only one customer, way in the front of the store checking out the newest arrivals. "I need to ask you a very big favor, Livvie."

"Sure. What do you need?"

"I want to marry Cami."

"I know," she said on a laugh. "Your bedside ICU proposal is the talk of Sanibel Island."

"You know I hate to be fodder for those gossips."

She nodded. He hated it so much that no one— including Teddy, who'd lived on Sanibel her entire life— knew that Buck was a multimillionaire who'd made his fortune buying and selling strip centers like this one.

"So, that's why I want your help on a little surprise I'm planning for Cami."

"Sure, whatever I can do."

He nodded toward the customer coming closer, who held a tank top and one of the new chain belts Olivia knew would sell well. "You take care of this lady. I'll wait in the back."

After she rang up the sale and chatted with the customer, Olivia walked to the back office to find him patiently waiting in an extra dressing room chair, his lanky frame out of place even here.

"What can I do for you?" Olivia asked, leaning

against the doorjamb so she could talk to him but still be available if someone came into the store.

"I want to marry Cami."

She laughed. "I *know*."

"I mean I want to marry her...now. If not now, then soon. Very soon."

She blinked in surprise. "Aren't you two planning something for when Camille gets clearance to travel so you can take a honeymoon?"

"Pffft." He flipped a weathered hand. "We don't need that. We're old and days are short. I just don't want to wait to make the woman my wife."

"Oh." She put a hand over her heart. "You're so romantic, Buck. Why don't you just tell her you want to speed things up?"

"Because she wants everything to be perfect."

"I get that," Olivia said on a laugh. "I'm kind of waiting for the same thing."

"Well, nothing's perfect in life, least of all some fancy to-do with a bunch of people I don't know or like. I just want a small group on the beach at sunset."

"Nice."

"And I want to surprise her."

Olivia's jaw dropped. "Not sure that's nice. Especially for a woman who just got a new heart valve. Surprise her for her own wedding?"

"I think she'll be more relieved than anything," he said. "And once she's my wife, I can stay with her all night and make sure she's okay. As it is, I'm texting her every hour."

"Buck!" She cooed his name. "You are so sweet. And you know Claire's been staying with her almost every night, and my mother, too."

"I should be with her," he said with authority and strength. "She's my woman. But I will not mire her in one ounce of scandal, so I'm not spending the night, even in the next room." He leaned forward with a plea in his eyes. "Livvie, she'll be so much happier when we're married. Help me make it happen. Get her in a pretty dress, tell her there's something going on at the beach, and then, I guess at the last minute, you can break it to her. Once she catches her breath, I guarantee you she'll be the happiest bride in the world."

It was downright swoon worthy. "Okay," Olivia said, unable to say no. "When, where, and how do we do this?"

"I'd like it to be in this month, the twenty-sixth? That's a Saturday. She has her clearance appointment the day before that."

She nodded, thinking about the dates. The twenty-fifth was the anniversary of her father's death, and she and her mother had talked about doing something special, maybe letting his ashes go. "I think we could do that."

"All I want is for you to gather some friends and family at sunset on Shellseeker Beach. Maybe in that gazebo? I think she'd like that."

"And your family?"

He shrugged. "My family is all Polly's folks," he said, referring to his late wife. "And while we've done some fence mendin', they don't need to be there. I got a couple of buddies to invite, a small thing. Maybe you can help me figure out food and some decorations, nothing fancy. A little music, some champagne. Maybe find the right man to marry us, and a cake."

That all sounded like a lot more planning than he realized. "Are you sure you don't want to give her more time to—"

"Not a minute," he said. "We'll have the rest of our lives to get used to the idea, and at our age, that ain't decades. I have no idea how to pull something like this off, and I'd talk to Claire, but I know you so well and... Can you help me, Liv?"

How could she not?

"You know, that sounds really perfect," she said, but still wanted to run it by her mother. "Can I talk to Eliza and Teddy to make sure there's nothing planned on Shellseeker Beach that day? And I would want Claire involved, since they are a close mother-daughter duo."

"Yes, please. But no delays. We got a combined age of a hundred and forty-six, Liv, and this isn't a first for either of us." He let out a sigh. "But it's gonna be the last and I want to hold her all night long as soon as I can."

She needed the doorjamb to hold her up, since the words made her a little dizzy.

"Let me enlist the crew from Shellseeker," she said. "We can make this happen."

"But not a word to her," he said, pushing up. "She'll try and talk you out of it."

"But Buck." She eyed him. "You're *sure* she wants this? I mean...a surprise wedding?"

"I am, but if it would make you feel better, you talk to her and make sure marryin' me sooner rather than later is what she wants. Don't tell her a date or time, but you see if she doesn't look as happy as I am. If you have any doubts, then I'll back off and we can just stay engaged until she's ready."

"Deal." Olivia nodded, and turned when she heard the door to the store open, brightening when she saw Asia and Dane walking in.

"You go handle your customers," Buck said. "We'll talk. I'm right next door." He gave his signature tip of an invisible hat, and slipped through the doorway that connected their two places of business.

"If it's not two of my favorite people," Olivia called as she spun around to greet them, but she stopped mid-step. "Who don't look happy."

"Hey, Liv." Asia glided into the store, both arms around a crying infant who was almost always attached to her via a baby sling. "We have one more place to see, but needed air conditioning and...a nursing break. Can I use your back room?"

"Of course! You know there's a chair in the ladies room. Go relax." She eyed her brother, who stood in the doorway looking almost as awkward as Buck had.

"This is really nice, Livvie," he said, looking around with a mix of awe and...fear. "Girlie."

She laughed. "It's a women's clothing boutique, numskull. Girlie is our stock-in-trade. Come on in. The clothes don't bite and you look like you could use a rest." She gestured toward the small grouping of French

Provincial-style seating that Camille had lovingly created in the spacious area outside the dressing rooms. "I have some bottled water in the back."

"Good, because, dang, it's hot."

"It's glorious," she countered. "Wait until July. That's hot. This is what people want. Most people, anyway. Sit."

He dropped into the chair and she slipped into the office to grab cold bottled water. When she came back, he had his head back, eyes closed, and a face that looked...unhappy.

She put a light hand on his shoulder, making him sit up. "Did this apartment share turn out to be not a good idea?" she guessed on a whisper. "It's not cool with Asia?"

"Oh, it's...cool." He twisted the cap. "She's fantastic." He practically sighed the word, then took a long, long drink.

Perching on the seat next to him, she leaned forward. "So what's the problem?"

"We can't find a place to rent," he said.

She made a face, knowing exactly how tough that market was in a tourist haven like this. "I thought it would be easier to find a two-bedroom on the first floor. Most people want to be high up."

"Two-bedroom? Easy-ish. First floor with piano access?" He closed his eyes and shook his head. "We could have a great place signed and sealed right now, but for my stupid piano."

And just this morning, it was magic. "You said the piano's fine with Jake in California," she said gently, always able to gauge when she could torque her brother. Not now, for sure. "Why don't you leave it there and—"

"I can't!" he barked, then instantly held up a hand in apology. "I won't. Also...Asia."

"What about her?"

"She's so..." He glanced toward the back, as if he didn't want her to hear what he would say next. That just made Olivia lean closer.

"She's so what?" Picky? Feisty? Sassy? What *was* she?

"Awesome," he said on an exhale of utter awe. "I hate to keep disappointing and frustrating her. But we've gone to two places that were supposed to be first-floor units, only to find out when we got there that they weren't. Or not available. Something. Anyway, they had other places that were perfect, but would take an act of God to get a piano in."

"So you just have to keep looking."

"It's not that big an island, Liv."

"Captiva? Pine Island? The mainland?"

"That's not where she wants to be," he said, giving her the distinct impression they'd been talking—and talking a lot—on their search today. "Roz is a little too controlling but Asia still wants to be close enough to feel secure and have backup when she needs it."

Olivia looked at him for a long moment, silent as she thought about the small island geography geared to vacation rentals. She knew firsthand how few long-term rentals there were.

"I really want her to be happy," he muttered. "She deserves that."

Her eyes widened as his words hit her.

"What?" he asked. "I still want it, but...why are you looking at me like that?"

"Nothing. It's just...you *really* like her, don't you?"

"As a *friend*," he said so quickly she kind of wanted to make a "you doth protest too much" joke. "And we both like the idea of a roommate. It takes care of so many problems, but it might not work out for either of us."

"Then you'd leave?" she asked, unable to keep the disappointment out of her voice.

"I don't know, Liv. Probably not."

Probably not was a step in the right direction. Did she have Asia to thank for that?

Some new customers came in and while she took care of them, Dane finished his water, and Zee finished his lunch. After the ladies left, Olivia found Dane and Asia next to each other in the waiting chairs, both of them laughing softly over something. Dane had found the water for Asia, and Zee was sound asleep in his mother's arms.

Wasn't that a cozy image?

"So, where's the next place?" Olivia asked, taking a seat on the sofa across from them.

"Captiva," Asia said. "It's a small duplex, not far from the beach, but way up in our budget. And kind of far, especially when there's a lot of traffic."

Dane flipped his empty water bottle and looked at Asia, that old crushed-out look on his face. No one else would notice except his sister, but it sure made her wonder how this roommate situation would go down, should it happen at all.

"Let's go back to the place on Wooster Lane," Dane said.

"It's the second floor," Asia replied. "We have a deal, Dane. If I bring baby Zee, then you bring baby grand."

"It's actually a legit grand," he said. "But that Wooster place was perfect. Two big bedrooms, both with ensuites and a powder room. And the balcony was screened in."

Asia's head tipped to an angle as she regarded him. "First floor's a weighted con, Dane, and we're not compromising."

Did she just say...*whoa*. For a few heartbeats, while they just looked at each other silently, chills danced up Olivia's spine.

Dane stood up and nodded. "Then we better go see place number...eight?"

"Nine." Asia laughed as she stood gracefully without even jostling the baby. "I thought you were like some sort of math genius."

"It's the heat. Sweat the IQ right out of me."

Laughing together, they said goodbye and headed out, leaving Olivia a little speechless at what she just witnessed.

And Buck wanting a surprise wedding?

Something was in the air on Sanibel, and it wasn't just periwinkles and sunshine.

Chapter Six

Eliza

S he didn't have to go over to Miles's house an hour before they set out for the sunset cruise on *Miles Away*, but Eliza couldn't wait another hour. She'd made up an excuse that Miles needed help getting the food and drink together, which anyone could see right through if they'd been on enough of these cruises.

Miles had entertaining on his boat down to an art, and the only help he usually accepted was from Deeley for the heavy lifting in getting the boat ready. But Deeley and Olivia were on their way to Teddy's to drop off Bash for the evening, so Eliza claimed she had to go help Miles. She suggested Dane come over later with Deeley and Olivia, and he seemed fine with that.

As fine as he ever seemed when the name Miles Anderson was mentioned, that was. Teddy, of course, knew exactly why Eliza was slipping out early.

"Have fun," Teddy had whispered with a kiss when she said goodbye to Eliza. "Don't let anyone get in the way of your happiness."

Eliza clung to the advice, letting the words play over and over in her head while she drove the short distance to

Miles's lovely canal home not far from the lighthouse and the bridge to the mainland.

Who would have thought her very own son might get in the way of her happiness? Not that Dane had said or done anything in the few days he'd been here. He seemed fairly consumed with the idea of finding a place to rent with Asia, but they'd struck out on that front, left to wait for more properties to hit the market in a few weeks.

No, her son hadn't said a word about Miles, and maybe that was what was bothering her. She knew he had issues and didn't want them bubbling under the surface. But something was bubbling.

Olivia seemed to think it was a crush on Asia. Teddy was convinced it was the impact of a life change and sneaked extra crystals into his room, which he just accepted as part of the Disney décor.

But Eliza was certain the core of Dane's tension was Miles, and that's why she was stressed about how this Whitney family cruise would unfold tonight at sunset.

One thing she knew for certain—Miles would be a gentleman, always kind, thoughtful, wise, and classy. That just made her hit the accelerator harder to get to him even sooner.

And it still wasn't a year since Ben died.

She tamped down the guilt, having gotten quite adept at ignoring that sensation, and turned into his driveway. She felt her whole body get lighter when he opened the front door and let Tinkerbell come bounding out, ready to pounce.

"Tinky!" Eliza climbed out and reached down to love

on a dog who'd stolen her heart almost as completely as her owner. "There's my beautiful girl."

"And there's mine."

She looked up, not sure if Miles meant for her to hear that, but he didn't look the least bit shy about his feelings. Oh, dear. How would that go over tonight? If he held her and kissed her, as he had in public on a few—very few— occasions, would that upset Dane?

Normally, she wouldn't care. But now she was straddling a chasm between being a mother and a woman and didn't want to fall.

She buried her head against Tink's fur for a moment, then straightened and smiled at Miles.

It wasn't difficult to smile at this handsome man in the prime of his late fifties, his salt-and-pepper hair clipped short, like his close-cropped beard. Eyes the color of one of Teddy's jade stones always warmed when his gaze landed on her, making her feel things she hadn't felt in many, many years.

Yes, she'd loved Ben with every fiber of her being. But the last few years of their lives together had been consumed by his sickness, and heated gazes, casual touches, and almost all their intimacy had been stolen by his cancer.

Miles stretched his arms out in greeting, accentuating his tall and fit frame, and she went right into his hug, which was starting to feel very much like home now.

"I love this idea," he whispered, tipping her chin to look into her eyes. "I can't tell you how happy I am to get a few minutes alone with you."

She sighed deeper into his arms. "Same. A thousand times the same. And I'm happy to help you make that fabulous artichoke dip."

"Done. And so's the rest of the charcuterie board. Plus some salads and cold chicken. The boat's gassed up, the seat covers are stowed, and ice is in the coolers."

"So what do you need me for?"

"This." He lowered his face and gave her the lightest, sweetest kiss, just enough to make her knees weak. She returned the kiss with a little more pent-up fervor, so deeply happy to be with him again.

"Eliza," he whispered. "Are you okay?"

She laughed. "I can't kiss you back?"

"Oh, you can. But you're normally more restrained."

"I'm normally not under the microscope of a disapproving son." She slid her arm around his waist and walked with him into the house, smiling as Tink led the way.

"It's not fun having Dane here?"

"It's not *not* fun," she said as they stepped inside the cool entryway, his home feeling so familiar and comfortable now. "I'm just hoping tonight goes well."

"You and me both." He gestured toward the wide-open sliding doors that led to the back lanai, and the dock behind it, where his thirty-foot fishing cruiser bobbed. "Do you want to board early?"

"You really don't need help in the kitchen?"

"All I need is you." He took both hands and guided her out to the sofa outside. "And maybe some advice on how not to feel like a kid about to meet my sweetheart's father."

Sweetheart made her smile. "Well, you already met my father. Did Dutch scare you?"

"Mostly, he amused me," he said. "But you weren't in the picture, E."

She settled in next to him, leaning into his strong body for the warmth and support she always got. "You were the one who told me about how the death of a father affects a man," she said.

"It really does. It changes him. But we're not talking about Dane's father's death, we're talking about his mother's love life."

She looked up at him, holding his gaze. "*Love* life, huh?"

"Don't be coy, Eliza Whitney. You know where I'm going with this."

Oh, she knew. He'd confessed well over a month ago that their relationship—however new, chaste, and slow—was long-term for him. He actually used the M word, and said he wasn't playing for fun.

And while the idea of marrying anyone at all was utterly unthinkable, still, the knowledge that Miles was serious had somehow broken down yet another wall around Eliza's grieving heart.

She trusted him, plain and simple.

Would she marry him? She never wanted to marry another man, and it was only a year since she'd buried the man she'd loved with her entire heart, soul, and body. She wasn't ready to go there on any level, but that didn't keep her from thoroughly enjoying every minute with Miles.

And speaking of one year... She turned and looked up at him, suddenly knowing he was the one who could advise her on her latest problem.

"So, Buck wants to marry Camille," she said.

"I've heard that news."

"He wants to marry her on February twenty-sixth in a surprise ceremony on Shellseeker Beach. In the gazebo."

He choked softly and inched back. "A surprise wedding? That's a new one on me."

"I can understand why he wants to, since he's a man who doesn't like to wait. And," she added with a smile, "he won't spend the night at her place until it's legal."

"So also a man of good morals," Miles said.

"I know, and we can do it at the resort that day, except..." She bit her lip and hoped it was truly appropriate to ask his advice. He was such a wise man, and had never steered her wrong. "That's the twenty-sixth, the day after the anniversary of my husband's death."

"Ohhh." He nodded, considering that. "How do you feel about that, E?"

"Not sure I'll be up for a wedding the next day," she said on an honest sigh. "Livvie thinks it would be good to replace the sad memory with a happy one that weekend. I haven't breathed a word to Dane, who'll probably have a cow."

"But it's your decision. Were you planning to sort of... hole up all weekend?"

"No, not really. But that day? Friday, the twenty-fifth? I've been thinking we could take a few of Deeley's kayaks out and..." Her voice grew thick.

"Ashes?" he asked on a whisper.

She nodded.

"You could still do that, E," he said gently. "Maybe in the morning? Then have a whole day to remember and recover. The next day, replace it all with an event that's more hopeful and happy."

Her heart shifted around in her chest. "Do you think that would be appropriate?"

"Yes," he answered on a soft chuckle. "There are no rules, just what makes you and your kids comfortable."

She looked at him for a long time, slipping closer and closer to him, which seemed wrong as she discussed her late husband's ashes. Her eyes shuttered with a mix of shame and disbelief.

"Hey." He put a finger under her chin and tipped her face up, forcing her eyes back open. "You had the love of a great man, and nothing will ever dull his memory. You should celebrate his life. That doesn't mean your life, or your kids' lives, or those of your dear friends, should end. And nothing will remind you of that more than watching Camille and Buck exchange vows."

"You really think so?" she asked.

"I know so. And, E, if you want to take my boat for the day for your excursion, it's yours. I'm sure I can give Dane a lesson or you can drive it. No kayaks. And no Captain Miles," he added. "Just you and your family, privately. I can teach him tonight, as a matter of fact, without saying why."

She closed her eyes again, this time because there were tears stinging her lids. Tears of gratitude and affection and hope. "Miles," she whispered. "Thank you."

She dropped her head onto his shoulder and sighed, unable to find the word to describe what she was feeling.

Well, she knew the word...but she wasn't ready to use it. She might never be, but she knew he'd wait anyway. And that only made her feel it more.

TEACHING Dane to drive the boat was a stroke of genius on Miles's part. Eliza's son arrived with Olivia and Deeley, carrying just enough of a chip on his shoulder that it was noticeable—at least to his mother. He gave pleasant nods while getting a quick tour around *Miles Away*, showed mild interest in the swivel fishing chairs and Deeley's suggestion that they throw out a line later. He barely knew what to do with Tinkerbell, despite the dog's best efforts to make a new friend.

Quiet by nature, Eliza would have classified Dane as being borderline sullen tonight, but he did share how frustrated he was by the housing hunt, and that almost explained his mood. Essentially, he wasn't rude, but he hardly touched the charcuterie board or salads, nursed a half-glass of wine, and spent a good part of the first hour staring at the horizon, silent.

But Miles wasn't a man to give up easily, and once

they were out a mile or so, he put a hand on Dane's back and gestured toward the helm.

"Would you like to take us out a bit?" he asked.

Dane almost bristled, but the lure of driving a boat of this size and quality won, and he nodded, following Miles to the captain's chair, interested and intrigued by any machinery.

"Ah, the lure of an expensive boat." Eliza whispered, leaning close to Olivia on the banquette. "It melts the most determined man's heart."

"What's he determined to do?" Olivia asked under her breath. "Make us sorry we invited him?"

Eliza snorted softly, holding her wineglass to her lips to cover her mouth. "I talked to Miles," she said. "He was wonderfully encouraging. He thinks we should take the opportunity to see the weekend differently, and..." She turned to face her daughter. "He offered the boat."

She frowned. "For a drive-by at the wedding?"

"For us to take out that Friday morning, which is why he's teaching Dane to drive it."

"To take out..." Realization dawned, making Olivia sigh. "For the ashes. Oh, wow. That's wonderful."

"You think so? Would you be all right with that, Liv?"

"Would Dad? Did he want the Gulf of Mexico? Has he even ever been here?"

"We went to Padre Island in Texas once when you guys were little, and we left you with my mother. To my knowledge, that was the one and only time he'd been to this particular body of water." She held up a finger to quiet whatever Olivia was going to say. "He left no instructions, Liv. He wouldn't talk about it."

The truth was, even right to the end, Ben refused to discuss their lives after he was gone. No last requests made, no deathbed promises elicited, and he certainly didn't give Eliza "permission" to love again. If he had, this would all be easier.

"This way he's close to me," Eliza said. "I know he was a New Yorker and a Californian, but I'd like to think of him as right here, on our horizon, sharing our sunsets."

Her eyes misted. "Mom, I think that would be wonderful. Will Dane agree, or don't we care?"

"We care and—"

"Whoa!" Dane exclaimed as he glided the throttle forward just enough to almost spill their wine. "Sorry," he added on a laugh. "Just getting the hang of this. Man, I've never driven a boat like this."

"He'll do it," Olivia said. "I think Miles is creating a monster."

Eliza watched the two men talking. Well, Dane was nodding, listening, and learning—with lightning speed, as he did—while Miles patiently explained the various gauges and dials around the helm. A natural quick study, Dane was cruising them into the Gulf in no time.

All in all, the evening was lovely, even though Miles hadn't so much as touched Eliza's shoulder or shared one long, affectionate glance. But she knew that was out of the utmost respect—and maybe a little fear—of Dane.

Deeley had gotten some fishing gear ready, but came back to sit next to Olivia, putting a loving arm around her as they talked. She filled him in on the plan for Camille's wedding, and held on to their glasses while Dane kicked the engine high enough to create a wake and get the hang of the boat.

Afterward, when they dropped anchor, Eliza was certain that at least some of her son's wall had been taken down as he asked a few questions and finally finished a glass of wine.

"So tell me about your music, Dane," Miles said as he opened another bottle. "Eliza says you're a composer. Any particular genre?"

"Well, not country," he said. "And not what I guess you'd call classic soft rock. I compose symphonies, too, but I know there's not a lot of money in selling a symphony. I've been trying to stretch into something a little more mainstream, but it's a crazy competitive market."

"He's a fantastic songwriter," Eliza said, unable to keep the compliment in. "He gets three notes in his head, and before you know it, there's an opening, a chorus, a bridge, and a melody I can hum for days."

"Really? You should stop into Little Blue's on open mic night," Miles said. "I've heard some amazing acts there."

"I'm not that much of a singer," Dane admitted. "That's my mom's department."

"She does sing like an angel," Miles said, putting a hand on Eliza's leg for the first time all night. "They have duo acts, and some instrumentals."

"Sounds...interesting," Dane said, sounding a little uptight again. "When is it?"

Miles must have noticed, because he casually removed his hand and started to pick up the trays for cleanup. "Once a month, I think. Maybe the second Tuesday? I'm not sure, but you should check it out. In fact, you can go in the place and play the piano he's got," Miles told him.

That got Dane's attention. "Really? Do you have to book ahead, or can you just walk in and play?" he asked.

"Walk in. The place is called the Little Blue Heron, right down near Wulfert Road, but no one ever calls it anything but Little Blue's. The owner played professionally, I think, and he lets anyone play the piano. It's a mellow crowd, lots of locals, very low-key. But once a month, it's packed, and the open mic performances are excellent."

Dane's brows lifted. "I wouldn't mind getting my hands on a piano. I'm itching to play and not sure when I'll get mine."

"Give up the piano, you dingdong." Olivia lifted her head from where she had it nestled against Deeley's shoulder.

"Mind your own, Liv."

"I'm serious. You're going to end up living in a dump, or permanently on ice in Elsa's bedroom if you don't."

"I thought her name was Harper."

She rolled her eyes and dropped her head back. "I can't with him."

Eliza leaned forward. "He wants the piano, Liv. I don't see why he should compromise."

"Unless Asia finds a perfect one-bedroom and skips the whole roommate thing." Olivia pointed at Dane. "She's not the kind of woman who waits for what she wants, and she wants out from underneath the ruling thumb of her 'smother.'"

Instead of laughing at that, Dane looked like he didn't love that possibility, but in the waning light, a man who showed no emotions was even harder to read.

"I just need to play," he muttered. "I miss that piano."

"Stop into Little Blue's anytime," Miles said encouragingly. "Jimmy's a good guy, and I'm pretty sure that's a Steinway he's got."

"Whoa, okay." Dane nodded. "I might do that. Thanks for the recommendation, Miles."

Eliza felt like she could fist pump, that exchange made her feel so good. For the first time, she had real hope that these two men could like each other.

As the sun disappeared and Miles stood to pick up the anchor and head back, Eliza slipped downstairs to the head, humming to herself with the success of the boat ride.

Of course, it helped to have Olivia here, who kept everything lively and smooth, even though she seemed a little quieter tonight, and had a lot on her heart with the possible arrival of Bash's relatives.

All in all, a great night, Eliza thought as she dried her hands and slid the door open to step into the lower cabin, where Miles was waiting.

"Oh, it's all yours," she said, gesturing to the head.

"Not what I want." He reached for her, pulling her in for a hug. "I came for this."

Smiling, she obliged with a kiss and then drew back. "It's been a good night, don't you think?"

"Very." He glanced over his shoulder toward the steps that led up to the deck. "He's a great guy, E. I think he's had a good time."

"Thanks to you, the classiest guy on the high seas."

He chuckled at the compliment. "I love when he and Liv tease each other. It reminds me of my own kids."

"I'm optimistic," she confessed, looking up at him.

"And I'm..." His eyes shuttered. "Crazy about you."

Laughing again, she eased into another kiss, wrapping her arms around his neck and surrendering to the sweet sensation. Crazy. Yes, it kind of was. Maybe a little soon, but she liked him so much and this kiss was—

"*Ahem.*"

They broke apart like a couple of high school kids caught under the bleachers by the principal. Dane stared, scowled, and stood stone still on the steps.

"Oh, Dane," Eliza said, sounding as flustered as she felt. "Looking for the head? It's right here."

He just closed his eyes and shook his head, turning and jogging up the two steps to the deck.

Eliza and Miles stayed perfectly motionless except for the rocking of the boat under them. She broke the silence with a sigh.

"He'll be okay," she whispered. "It'll take some getting used to."

"I didn't mean for him to see that."

"We can't hide this, Miles," she said as irritation tightened her chest. "We're not doing anything wrong."

"But it's new to him. And..."

"And it hasn't been a year yet." She gave a wistful smile. "It will be soon enough."

"Let's keep our distance until then. In the meantime, you just be with your son. Talk to him. Let him get comfortable."

"What will you do?"

"Wait impatiently." He placed a light kiss on her forehead. "The bigger question is, what will you do?"

"What do you mean?"

"When it's been over a year and you're out of your official period of mourning. What will you do?"

Her smile wavered as she looked up at him. "I'll never not mourn Ben," she said softly. "But every single day, you're making it easier to be with you, Miles. I don't know what will change except that I might lose some guilt."

He nodded, understanding. "Let's stay focused on Dane now. Talk to him, and I'll...miss you."

She stole one more hug, knowing that when more than a few days went by without his warmth and strength, she would miss him, too.

Chapter Seven

Dane

I f the word seething meant gritting his teeth, staying silent, staring straight ahead, and fighting the urge to punch a wall, then Dane was Seething with a capital S. The engine was loud enough as the boat slapped over the waves that he could be silent on the way back to Sanibel. Once there and docked, he made a point of getting back in Deeley's truck, managing to stumble through a few awkward goodbyes and thank yous.

There was no way he was riding back to Shellseeker Beach with his mother. He had no desire to sit in the car with her, make small talk like he had all night, and not explode over the fact that...

She *kissed* him? Was it like Dad never even existed?

The minute Deeley pulled out of the driveway, Livvie swung around from the passenger seat to glare at him. "What's eating you?"

"Nothing," he lied, shifting in the seat of the cab to look out the window.

"Dane, come on." She heaved a sigh and looked at Deeley like he might help, but her boyfriend didn't say a word.

"Just let it go, Liv," Dane said.

"Let *what* go? What happened? One minute you were perfectly cool, driving the boat, talking about music, then wham!" She swiped her hand in front of her face. "Up goes the wall of impenetrable steel."

"Could you not be quite so dramatic?" he asked.

"Could you not be quite so petulant?" she volleyed back. "What happened?"

He sucked in a slow breath as Deeley pulled out onto the main drag, weighing the pros and cons of talking to her.

Pro: he'd vent. Con: she'd be on Mom's side.

"Is it Mom and Miles?" she pressed.

"You won't let it go, will you?" He groaned. "Does she ever let anything go, Deeley?"

"Officially staying out of this family feud."

"It's not a feud," Olivia insisted. "It's a legit question. You were fine, everything was cool, and then you weren't. Now you're doing your typical shutdown instead of talking it out. Talk. It's time to talk."

Unrelenting. That should be his sister's middle name. He waited a beat, then looked at her. "I just can't believe she's already...doing that."

"Doing what? Whatever you think she's doing, I can guarantee you, she's not."

He snorted. "Please, Liv."

"I'm serious," she said, turning again. "And you don't have to talk like a fourth grader who can't whisper the word *sex*. Which, I can tell you on good authority, she is *not* doing. They barely kiss."

"Didn't look like *barely* to me," he muttered.

"That's what this is about? You saw them kissing?"

He sucked in a breath. "Come on. Give it a break."

"You come on, Dane. For a genius, you're pretty darn stupid sometimes."

"It's not stupid to feel betrayed when I see my mother kiss a man who is not my father, who hasn't even been gone a year. Geez."

"Dane, listen to you!" She was fully turned now, with fire in her eyes, her shoulders locked in that fighting stance that came out when they argued or competed over a video game.

"She's a grown woman," Olivia insisted. "A widow, and he's a perfectly nice man and they like each other. Don't you want her to be happy?"

"Of course I do, but...how can she just forget Dad like that?" He loathed the pain in his voice, but try as he might, he couldn't cover it. Because this hurt. This hurt so much it nearly choked him.

"She didn't *forget Dad*. No one has, no one ever could. Do you have any clue what that woman has been through?"

He narrowed his eyes at her, his whole body tightening. "Yes, Olivia. I went through it, too. We all did. Years of illness, of worry, of doctors, and tests, only to lose him."

"But we weren't even living in Los Angeles the last few years," she said. "She bore the brunt of that mostly alone, and then, a month after he dies, her stupid talent agency fires her. They only kept her on because her husband owned a small studio and Nick Frye wouldn't work with any other agent. When Dad died and Nick retired, Mom was dispensable." She stared at him, letting that sink in. "Do you have any idea what that did to her? She deserves some happiness and she's found it at Shellseeker Cottages and with Miles Anderson. Period. End of story."

He couldn't argue with her, and not because she was right. Maybe she was, maybe she wasn't. That didn't matter. What mattered was something he hated—the churning in his gut, the ache in his chest, the hole in his heart that had been there since the day Ben Whitney died.

Where was his stinking piano when he needed it? That instrument had changed his life these past few months, and he longed to sit down and lose himself on it.

"Just drop me off," he muttered as Deeley rumbled his truck down the road that led to Shellseeker Beach.

"Dane." Livvie's voice was softer now, her eruption over, and next she'd reach for him and say she was sorry and beg to be pals again. Didn't her emotional roller-coaster get exhausting?

"Just let it go, Liv. I'm overreacting."

"No, no." She stretched her hand toward him. "I am. I'm sorry. I know this is all new to you and I just want you to see—"

"I see." God knows he'd seen enough. "Seriously, just...let me out. I'm going to take a walk or something."

Deeley pulled into the lot and stopped the truck, looking into the rearview mirror to catch Dane's eye.

"Miles is a good man," Deeley said softly. "I've known him since I got here. He's helped us all on many occasions, and he is tremendously respectful of your mother."

Great. Now they were tag-teaming him.

But Dane just gave a nod. "I know, and thanks for the ride. And…" He gave Livvie a tight smile. "The pep talk. I'll do better."

"Can I help?" she asked, making that apology face he knew so well.

"Help me get my piano into a place to live," he said. "I need to play music." It was the most honest thing he could say. With this many unwelcome emotions, writing a song that came from inside this well of pain was the only way to manage it all.

"I could take you down to Little Blue's," Deeley offered.

"Thanks, man. I'll just…take a walk. Bye, Liv. Thanks." He didn't wait for a long goodbye, but climbed out of the truck's cab as quickly as he could.

They all claimed this was such amazing weather, but even in February, the air was thick with an unfamiliar humidity. Not uncomfortable, just warmer and heavier than anything he was used to in California. And it smelled like flowers and salt and…*change*.

That's what he didn't like, he admitted as he strode toward the darkened beach. He walked under the stilted beach house where his Barbie room waited. Glancing around, he saw no sign of his mother's car, so at least he didn't feel obligated to go say goodnight to her. Maybe she'd stayed on with Miles to…

Don't go there.

He shook off the thought and walked toward the boardwalk, stopping to take in the blackness of the night beach. Only soft yellow lights from the cottages and the solar uplights along the path shed any brightness. He remembered Teddy saying they set it up that way to make sure the turtles could hatch in their season.

He liked the dark, happy that the moon was behind a rare cloud.

Holding that thought, he let some lyrics play in his head. Dark clouds. Beach at night. Moon on sand. And with that, the first few notes of a melody. A minor chord, a gentle trill, a—

The hum of his phone pulled him out of the reverie, making him realize he was nearly down the boardwalk and on the beach.

He considered ignoring the text, certain it was his mother, begging for a do-over or offering up an explanation or trying to make things nice. He loved her for that, just like he loved Liv for her blind defense of Mom, and her always-instant apology after she fried him with one of her speeches.

On a sigh, he pulled out the phone, his whole being feeling lighter when he stared at the text on the screen.

Asia Turner: *Found a great one! Townhouse with first floor entry, decent rent, 2/2 plus powder room! Fenced in backyard. Parking! Here's the link! Want to look at it tomorrow?*

He wanted to look at it now. No, he wanted to look at *her* now. To hear her lilting voice and easy laugh.

Instead of answering, he tapped the call button and it

only rang one time before he heard both those things.

"I'ma take this speedy response as a yes," she said on a sweet chuckle.

"Oh, is it okay to call? I didn't wake Zee, did I?"

"Nothing would wake him right now," she said. "And I'm glad you called. Did you like it?"

"I didn't open the link," he admitted. "I just..." He took a breath of the sweet-smelling air. "I don't suppose you're in the mood to do something completely spontaneous?"

She waited a beat, then said, "I guess it depends on what you have in mind."

"Going to a place called...Little Blue's."

"Now?" Her voice rose in surprise.

"Oh, yeah, Zee. That was dumb. I totally forgot you can't just up and get a drink at nine at night."

"Umm...yes, I can. Enter the *smother* who loves nothing more than a chance to babysit."

He felt a smile pull. "So, that's a yes?"

"It is. I've been to that bar and it's super chill. And, oh! There's a piano."

"That's why I want to go." And to see her, but he kept that to himself.

"You'll play? Wild! Where are you now?"

"On the beach in front of my mother's house. Without a car."

She laughed. "Gimme twenty minutes and I'll get you."

That smile got wider. "Perfect."

And for the first time in an hour or so, everything *was*

perfect.

LITTLE BLUE'S HAD A JAZZY, locals-only vibe that Dane liked the minute he walked in. Dimly lit and filled with the vague smell of beer and fried food, a smattering of tables and a long, inviting bar, the place felt utterly unpretentious. And off to one side, raised up on a black platform with a single light shining on it, sat an absolutely gorgeous Steinway baby grand that looked so out of place, he almost laughed.

They slipped into empty barstools that gave him a perfect view of the piano and the woman who'd surprised him by accepting the invitation. Both were staggeringly attractive.

"What'll it be?" A sixty-something bartender with a weathered face and long gray hair pulled back into a ponytail slapped two cardboard coasters in front of them.

Dane raised his brows in question to Asia. "Can you drink?" he asked, knowing she was nursing Zee.

"I can if I..." She leaned and whispered. "Pump and dump. But that is rare because...Roz."

He laughed. "No doubt she's opposed."

"And also not here." She turned to the bartender. "Rum and Coke, please."

He nodded, and looked at Dane, who asked for a Blue Moon on tap while Asia stared at the piano.

"Is yours that big?" she asked.

"It's um, bigger. That's a baby grand. Mine is grand."

She lifted her brows. "Does size matter?"

He laughed softly. "It actually does. All grands have good sound, but smaller pianos have less volume and sharper overtones. But that one? Wow. That's a flipping gorgeous instrument."

"What makes a Steinway so special?"

He thought about it for a moment, shaking his head. "That's like asking why is Zee better than any other kid."

"He just is," she quipped without a second's hesitation.

"Well, that just is." He angled his head toward the piano. "The best wood, thicker and more resonant. It takes a year to build one, they have the most stunning finish, and the sound is just...rich. Perfect, really."

She smiled at him. "You're glowing, Dane."

"Am I?" He stared at the piano. "I love mine, don't get me wrong. I have a connection to mine like no other, but that one is...wow. I can see the appeal of that instrument to any musician."

"Thanks," the bartender said, putting down the drinks. "I've carted that sucker around for years, and it's finally home."

"Are you Jimmy? The owner who lets strangers play?" Dane asked.

"Guilty as charged. Hey, I believe a piano is made for playing," he said, squinting hard at Dane. "You're not a tourist? I don't recognize your face."

"I'm visiting, but might be staying. We're looking for a place." He realized exactly how that sounded and was ready to clarify with a "just as roommates" addendum, but Asia didn't seem the least bit uncomfortable with the obvious wrong assumption. Instead, she tasted her rum and Coke and let her eyes flutter in satisfaction. A look that was...whoa. Pretty.

"So how'd you hear about this place?" Jimmy asked.

He opened his mouth to answer and hesitated, almost unwilling to say the guy's name. But he had to. "Miles Anderson."

That got a nod of recognition. "Good man, Miles. I guess you know he used to be JAG, which always impressed me. Haven't seen him in here in ages though. I heard he has a girlfriend," he added with a wry laugh. "That's why I stay single. Women'll suck the bar time out of you."

Dane slid a look at Asia, who shrugged.

"You're not in Kansas anymore," she teased. "Welcome to Small Town, USA, baby."

The other man took a breath like he was going to ask yet another question that Dane might not like, when Asia put down her drink and held out one of her gorgeous long-fingered hands to interrupt the conversation.

"Could he play?" she asked, tipping her head toward Dane. "This man is a virtuoso, a talented songwriter, and he's itching to get on that Steinway."

Dane snorted softly. "Not so sure about one and two, but yes to Door Number Three."

Jimmy swept a hand toward the stage. "Knock yourself out. I'll shut down the tunes when you start."

"Thanks." Something in his chest shifted, like a door unlocking with a snap. He held out his hand over the bar to shake Jimmy's. "Dane Whitney," he said. "And this is Asia Turner."

Jimmy shook both their hands. "Jimmy Thanos."

"Nice to meet you..." As Dane pulled away from the shake, he frowned, letting the name hit his unfailing memory. "Jimmy Thanos? Like...the keyboard player? For Square None?"

Jimmy's jaw loosened. "You must be a jazz fan. That's me, retired and living anonymously at Little Blue's."

Dane searched the guy's face, not really seeing the much younger keyboard player who could destroy a funky riff.

"I'm a fan of all music," Dane said. "But anyone who knows keyboards knows you. Jeez." Dane held up both hands. "I'm not sure I can play now."

"Oh, please," Jimmy said. "Like I said, that instrument is there to soothe the inner beast. It's a heck of a lot healthier than what some folks soothe with in here." He tapped the bar.

Dane laughed, and looked at Asia. "We're in the presence of greatness."

"Then impress him," she said, giving a nudge. "Can I come with and watch you play?"

"Of course." Grinning, he took a deep gulp of beer, then slipped off the stool, shaking his head. "Jimmy Thanos. Man."

Asia came right with him as they walked toward the stage. "Is he a really big deal?" she whispered.

"If you're into music. He's not a household name, and

Square None didn't have the lead guitarist of, say, Pat Metheny. But they put out some amazing music and..." He glanced over his shoulder at Jimmy, and the ponytail definitely made sense. "He's incredibly talented."

"Are you intimidated?" she asked, nestling close to him on the piano bench, the spotlight making her eyes spark like black diamonds.

"Not by him," he murmured, holding her gaze for just one second.

She smiled and touched a key, hitting a low D that instantly reverberated. "Play me something original."

Looking down at the keyboard, he felt the usual fire in his veins, the hum of anticipation for how the notes would come out, and the instant blank slate that freed his mind and mood.

He spread his hands and hovered over the keyboard, thinking through his repertoire, but the melody that rose to the surface was the one that had just teased him on the beach.

"Something brand new," he said softly. "Something I haven't even written yet."

"Oh." She breathed the response with just enough awe and wonder that he was inspired to start playing. "That *is* original."

From the first note, he felt better. He could sense the tension and anger that had built up on that boat ride floating away with each chord. He did what he always did—closed his eyes and let his fingers move through chord progressions and a melody that didn't make sense until...it did.

He played the opening, a few bars, a few more, then a simple chorus that sounded like...a sunset and water and a whole different ending to what had been a really good night until...until...until he ruined it.

He hit the next chord hard, releasing the frustration, then slid into the main melody again, just up an octave.

"Dane," Asia whispered next to him. "This is beautiful."

He turned to her, his fingers still moving as if they had a mind of their own. They did, actually. One that wasn't logical or rational or bound by pros and cons. His hands were moved by his soul and there, to his own and others' surprise, resided all of his feelings.

"What's this song about, Dane?" she asked on a whisper.

"Change," he replied without missing a beat.

"Good change? Bad change? Change of heart? Change of pace? Change of tune?"

He chuckled and flew into the chorus again. "All of the above." He turned to her, locked on her ebony eyes. "You're the poet. Write me some lyrics, Aje."

She smiled, maybe at the shortened version of her name, which was more familiar than he'd planned, but then, he hadn't planned any of this.

"Okay, but start me out. Opening line or two," she said, sitting a little closer as she got into it.

He closed his eyes and let himself drift back to that boat, down in that cabin, the punch of seeing his mother's fingers threaded into another man's hair.

"I don't like change," he admitted softly. "So when

someone else changes, I feel like I can't catch up."

The admission hung in the air, then fell like another brick in his personal wall.

Right then, he didn't care. He didn't even remember his mother kissing his father, not like that.

His fingers missed a note.

"I just want people to stay the same," he finally said.

For a moment, they didn't talk while he took the whole piece back to the beginning, playing with the opening chords over and over until he had a melody. Then the chorus, which wrote itself, then back to the verses.

Asia leaned in as he started the song from the beginning one more time.

"Looks like you've had a change of heart, a change of scene, and change of pace." She sang the words softly, hitting the notes with a surprisingly clear voice. "I'm looking for the old you but all I see is change on your face."

He wanted to laugh, or at least smile, but he just stared at her as he played. How did she know that's exactly how he felt?

She didn't attempt the rest of the verse, but looked like she was thinking.

"I told you lyrics are the hard part. Don't stop now. Here's the chorus. Go for it."

She took a deep breath and sang, "The more you want, the more I refuse to give..." She lifted her brows in question and he nodded to get her to continue. "The more you fight, the more I...want to live?" She shrugged off the rhyme with a laugh. "The more you run, the more I never move. The more you want, the more I refuse." She looked up at him, hitting the last line. "The more you change, the more I stay...the same."

His fingers stilled as her voice rang out, lasting just as long as the resonant G on the Steinway.

"Wow," he whispered.

"Not exactly Grammy-winning," she joked.

"But you...got it." He shook his head, in amazement. She got the song, the feelings, and his inner struggle with change.

"Let's do it again," she said, tapping her fingers together. "From the top!"

Laughing, he played through and she sang with even more confidence, changing a word here and there, holding his gaze, sharing the spectacular and unexpected moment.

When they finished, there was a smattering of applause and both of them just looked at each other, mesmerized by the moment, having completely forgotten there was anyone else in the room.

Asia threw her arms around him and squeezed. "I love it! We're writing a song together, Dane."

He laughed and slid off the bench before he did something really stupid, like hug her back and kiss her.

They were still smiling when they came back to the bar, and so was Jimmy.

"I liked it," he said. "You two should come in and do an open mic night. Next one's March tenth, I think."

"Well, we'd need a song we weren't just writing while

we're up there," Dane said, reaching for the beer that he needed now more than ever.

"Work on that one," Jimmy said. "You could win."

"Really?" Asia sat on her stool and lifted her drink, raising it in a toast that Dane met with his beer glass. "What's the prize?"

"You drink free one night."

They both nodded their approval.

"The only problem is I don't have a real piano to play," Dane said. "I'm waiting on mine to be delivered. I hope, anyway."

"Come here and play this one," Jimmy replied. "This place is a morgue during the day, and I don't even have staff."

Dane blinked at him. "Are you serious?"

Jimmy's brows shot up. "I'm a musician, man. I don't kid about things like that."

He glanced at Asia, who looked like he'd be nuts to say no. "Weighted pros, bro," she said. "You want to play and you don't have your piano yet. Got a con?"

"Not a single one." He turned to Jimmy. "Any afternoon?"

"Any and all. I'm always here." He stepped away to take care of two new customers and Asia and Dane toasted again.

And for a good long, satisfying moment, he could feel all his anger and frustration slip away, replaced by a feeling so good, he couldn't even put it into words. But he'd bet Asia could.

And they'd rhyme.

Chapter Eight

Asia

L*ooks like you've had a change of heart, a change of scene, and change of pace...*

Asia sang the words softly, the melody still crystal clear in her mind. But not the words, dang it.

"Then what?" she murmured, staring at her face in the mirror after she finished her makeup. Why weren't the words coming easily like they had with Dane?

Because she needed a notebook. Don't all songwriters use a notebook?

Stepping to the small desk in her room that had become her de facto office, she pulled open the bottom drawer in search of a notebook. She found one, but it was almost full of work notes, same with another.

There, on the very bottom, was one covered in red silk with a dragon on the front.

For a long time, she just stared at it, tamping down a curse.

She thought she'd gotten rid of every gift he'd ever given her. Every one. They all had the Asian theme, which he'd thought was so clever because of her name.

She'd thrown away a box of them—a Buddha, a ceramic lotus, a necklace with the yin-yang symbol, a kimono, chopsticks, a pagoda lantern, and so many paper fans. Tossing all that had felt good and cathartic.

But she'd missed this dragon notebook.

Very slowly, she eased it out and opened the first page. She'd opened this on a plane to London, she recalled, to write poetry. These words were clearly those of a besotted woman fantasizing about a ring.

That was the last time she'd written any poetry...until last night.

She almost tossed it back into the drawer, but instead, she tore out the page with a satisfying rip. Then she shredded that with her bare hands, fluttering fifty tiny pieces of her aching heart into the trash.

Swiping her hand over the now empty first page, she smiled, grabbed a pen and started writing her song.

Looks like you've had a change of heart, a change of scene, and change of pace...

I'm looking for the old you but all I see is change on your face.

Then what? "You want something new, shiny and gold," she whispered. "But...something something something is old."

Grunting at how frustrating it was to write a song without the music and that glorious piano, she snapped the notebook closed and headed downstairs. But the melody was in her head now and she was still humming when she came around the corner into the kitchen.

"My, my, my, your mother is happy today!" Roz sat at the table sipping coffee with Zee in his bouncer on the table. "Someone must have had fun last night. So much fun that my backup stash of pre-pumped bottles is down."

"I couldn't nurse him overnight, since I had a drink. So, yes, I had fun. And this little angel..." She bent over and kissed Zee's sweet, sweet head, getting a gummy smile that just broke her heart with joy. "Slept until six-thirty, which is amazing, and loved his bottle. Thanks for taking him while I showered and got dressed, Mama." She added a kiss on her mother's turbaned head just because. "Dane and I have a place to look at in an hour and I'm so optimistic this will be it."

The look Roz gave her wasn't nearly as sweet as the one she'd gotten from Zee. "You don't have to move, Asia."

"Again? We're discussing this again?" She walked to the coffee pot and poured a large mug, then took it to the table. Sitting down, she braced for the reprimand about the size of the cup. "*Coffee in moderation, Asia! What you eat, Zane eats, Asia!*"

But Roz was too busy playing a counting game with Zee's little toes, making him giggle.

So Asia decided to live dangerously and reached for the sugar.

"Seriously?" her mother said just as her hand landed on the ceramic canister on the table.

"And you wonder why I have to move," Asia muttered, pushing it away and opting for the bitterness of black coffee, which was still preferable to the judgment over every granule of sugar that could sweeten it.

"No, but I'm wondering about your spontaneous date last night," she said, lifting a brow. "I guess it was good."

"It was not a date. Dane is barely a friend, a possible roommate. Please, for the love of all that's holy, don't make this more than it is." Even though there sure were moments on that piano bench when she felt a flicker of something she really didn't want to feel.

She blamed the rum, the song, the bar, the... anything. Because *that* was not happening, not now, not ever.

"A mother can hope, you know."

She snorted. "You're hoping already? You've met the guy once."

"But I adore his mother and sister," she said. "Dane comes from a good family. He's great looking, and did you know his IQ is off the charts?"

She shot her mother a look. "You're joking, right?"

"I don't joke about things like a man's IQ or good looks."

"Okay, let's start with the fact that he's seven years younger than I am, currently unemployed, and not the *brother* you probably dreamed of for me."

Roz shrugged. "I don't care about race, and age is a number. And geniuses don't stay unemployed for long. I want you to be loved, Asia."

"Please, Mama." She gave her the most sincere look she had. Roz didn't always respond well to jokes or sarcasm. But if she thought Asia was hurting, she'd back off. And she *needed* to back off.

"Okay, okay. But..." Her mother shifted in her seat,

lifted her cup, then lowered it again, leaning in. "You do have to try again someday."

Asia's eyes flashed and she looked toward the door, where her father could walk in any minute.

"He's at Sanibel Treasures," Roz said. "I would never..." She blew out a breath and moaned. "Hardest thing in my life, you know. Holding your secret, knowing your truth, and not telling my own husband."

"Is there no conversation you can't have twenty times?" Asia asked, the last vestiges of her good mood floating away. "Because we've had this one enough. You *promised*. And this is officially the last time you can even refer to it in front of Zee."

"Zane is six months old. He doesn't know."

But he would someday. She looked at her son, sighing hard when she thought about the lie she would tell him. The same lie she told everyone, every single person, except one.

Oddly enough, Roz was the one she *should* have lied to. Her mother, like everyone else, should think that Zane Turner was a sperm bank baby, conceived by a thirty-four-year-old woman desperate to have a child. It was a good story, a respectable story. So much better than the truth.

But when push came to shove, Asia hadn't been able to lie to her mother. Like she had for her entire life, she gave up control and told her the truth, and some days she regretted it more than anything.

"All I'm saying is that you should give a man—"

"No!" Asia said sharply, the single syllable just

enough to make Zee's face crumple up. "Oh, honey, not you!" Asia was up immediately, reaching for her baby. "I wasn't mad at you."

"Just me," her mother said dryly, putting her hand over the latch to the bouncy seat. "Don't take him out, Asia. I just got him settled."

"Please, please, *please* quit telling me what to do."

"Well, someone should have," Roz muttered, pushing up from the table. "If I'd have been with you when you were seeing that man, I would have—"

"Mother." She ground out the word, getting right in Roz's face so she could whisper instead of yell and scare the baby. "That is ancient history, completely done, and you gave me your word you wouldn't tell Dad or anyone else."

"That's asking a lot."

"Your word," she insisted. "Doesn't that mean anything?"

"It obviously means everything, since I haven't told him, and never will."

"Good," Asia said. "Now drop it. How many times do I have to tell you I want to forget my bad, bad choices? I'd like to say it was the biggest mistake of my life, but..." She slid a glance to Zee. "But that mistake gave me the greatest thing that ever happened."

Roz stared at her, her shoulders sinking just enough for Asia to know she could take the win on this fight.

"He is the best," her mother agreed. "Just look at his fine little self."

"So fine," Asia whispered, a smile pulling like it always did when she looked at her sweet boy.

"And you said Dane is very good with him. That bodes well, don't you think?"

"Because he'll be a wonderful roommate." Asia narrowed her eyes. "And that is all."

With a classic Roz harrumph, her mother headed to the sink to rinse her cup. "What did you and your *friend* do last night?" she asked with fake coyness.

"We had a drink and played a piano in a bar," she said, leaning against the counter to sip her bitter brew. "And we wrote a song together."

Roz made an impressed face. "And now you have another day of running around Sanibel together."

"Running around?" she snorted. "Trudging from apartment to townhouse and back to an apartment. We only have one to see today."

"Are you taking Zane?"

"Of course."

"Because your father can cover the store for me or I can just keep him—"

"He's coming with me," she said. "After we look at this townhouse, I need to come back and get some work done."

Her mother nodded and returned to the table, leaning over to fuss with Zee and make him smile.

"What happens when Zane does DNA testing some-day?" she asked.

Asia froze in the act of pouring the dregs of coffee

down the drain. "I'll cross that bridge when I come to it. Anything could happen between now and then."

"Zane could...find out."

"Find out what? That his father has Type O blood, brown eyes, and...whatever else you find out when you do DNA? So what? That's who I picked from the sperm bank."

"He could find out his father's name," Roz murmured.

Asia practically shuddered. She loathed this conversation. She'd told the lie about Zee being a sperm bank baby so many times, and so effectively, that she'd really started to believe it.

It *could* be true. His biological father certainly had all the physical traits she might have looked for in a donor — tall, handsome, intelligent, even successful. Had he been Zee's donor, she would never know he was also a liar and a cheat with a mean streak a mile wide.

"Mama, please. Just stop talking about it?"

"But what if Zane wants to know? He will, you know he will."

She knew no such thing, and didn't even want to think about it now, years before she had to.

"He has no claim on Zee. He lied to me and he has..." She couldn't say the words. Still. After what? After more than a year from the day she found out how horribly she'd been deceived.

"He has a claim on Zee, whether you like it or not."

Fury made her whip around to look at her mother. "I gave you this gift," Asia said through gritted teeth. "I gave you my secret and in return, you promised that you wouldn't tell anyone, even Dad. And you promised to let it go, forget about it, and just love Zee."

"I simply couldn't love Zane any more, no matter who his—"

"Mother!"

Roz clamped her mouth closed and turned, busying herself at the sink again. But she couldn't stay silent for long. After a deep sigh, she murmured, "I guess that's why you don't want a man in your life."

"Because the one I had was a filthy liar with a short fuse?" Asia guessed.

"Because if you ever *do* fall in love, you'd have to tell that man what really happened. And you're so busy holding onto what you like to call 'your truth' that you don't want to ever be honest. And love means being honest."

Man, she hated it when Roz Turner was right.

But her mother *wasn't* going to win this. Asia took a few steps closer and looked down the few inches that separated her from her mother.

"I'm not going to fall in love, because love means giving control to another person and I have done that my whole life. I gave it to you, and I gave it to…him." She'd never say his name. "I did that because, for some reason I'll never understand but have a shrink to thank for telling me, being controlled is where I'm comfortable."

"That's such a load of—"

"And I'm breaking that cycle, Rosalind Turner. Starting now. So, yes, I'm going to look at a rental unit.

Yes, I'm taking my son with me. And yes, I'm going to solve my future problems all by myself without a man lording his power over me or a mother who thinks she knows best. *I* am the queen of my life and *I* know best. Is that clear?"

Her mother swallowed and nodded, defeat softening her usually proud jaw. "Take a few bottles in a cooler in case he gets hungry. It's hard to find a place to nurse him."

She sighed and let her shoulders fall. "Good idea, Mama. Thank you."

SHE TRIED to shake off the argument, but Asia was still vibrating when she picked up Dane. Enough that he asked if she was okay, and she tried to joke about her smother. He commiserated with a few funny lines about how he felt like he was sleeping on a Disney World ride, and by the time they reached the Tortoise Way Town-houses, she'd put the morning frustrations to the side.

But then they were hit with a new frustration when they walked into the two-story unit in the back corner of a quiet, well-appointed complex.

The furnished townhouse was...perfect. *Almost*. For Asia, it was a dream. Clean, bright, with a huge bedroom and ensuite on the second floor, along with a small laundry room up there for blissful convenience. The bedroom was big enough for a crib and a desk so she could work up there, with a small balcony that overlooked miles of green toward the Ding Darling sanctuary and the bay beyond. The stairs were compact and could easily be gated for safety when Zee started toddling around.

Dane's downstairs bedroom was smaller, off the living room, but also had its own bathroom, plus there was a small powder room for guests.

And since it was a bit dated and off the beaten path, the rent wasn't astronomical.

She pushed Zee's stroller through the very small living room and eat-in area—it couldn't be legitimately called a dining room—and wanted to whimper for how much she loved the vibe of this place.

But even with the first-floor location, there was simply no room for a piano. No matter how you cut it, even if they took out the dining table and ate at the simple Formica kitchen counter, the townhouse wasn't big enough for a grand piano. The second bedroom couldn't possibly accommodate the instrument. The last option was the living room, which would require they give up the sofa, tables, and TV. They might fit two chairs in there with a piano, but that would never work.

She could see the disappointment on Dane's face as they walked through the unit, which was otherwise exactly what the doctor ordered.

He sighed as he opened the sliding glass door to a small, enclosed yard with a magnolia tree and a patch of grass, plus an undersized patio bathed in sunlight to grow herbs and flowers.

Perfect.

"Let's just take a pass," she said, gesturing for him to come back in.

"Instead of standing out here imagining Zee taking his first steps in that grass while I grilled up some burgers and dogs?" He put his hand on the back of a rocking sofa with faded cushions. "And speaking of dogs, we could get one. Zee would love that."

Her heart folded in half with how sweet he was. She honestly had forgotten men like Dane Whitney existed. "Zee's first steps in the grass are not a weighted pro," she reminded him. "And, yes, a dog would be fun."

"But the perfect place is a major pro, and this unit?" He gave her a look. "You can see that it's perfect."

"Except for one major problem, Dane." She rocked the stroller to and fro to keep Zee asleep. "It's *not* perfect for your most beloved belonging."

He curled a lip, but didn't say anything, taking another walk into the kitchen, which was light, bright and had tons of cabinets. Darn it.

The unit manager, Sally, who'd been outside on the phone, walked in, smiling at them. "Well?" she asked, brushing back some blond strays that had escaped a clip. "Will this work?"

"No," Asia said.

"We're thinking about it," Dane said at the same time.

Asia threw him a look. "Not seriously, since we need a little more space on the first floor for a piano."

"You could put it in the second bedroom," Sally said, then crinkled her nose. "I guess you couldn't get it through the doorway. It would have to come in through the sliding glass doors."

"And we need the bedroom for sleeping," Dane said.

She nodded. "Oh, of course, for the little guy. He's so quiet, I forgot you two had a baby."

They shared a quick glance, so used to the mistake that they didn't bother to correct people anymore.

"We have to be able to get a grand piano in the living area," Asia told her. "And that's just not feasible with this layout."

"Unless...we didn't get the piano," Dane said.

"What are you talking about?" Asia asked him.

On an awkward laugh, the manager held up both hands. "Tell you what. You guys stay here and iron things out, and I'll head back to the office. Stop by with the key and a verdict when you are done. If you want to put in an application, we can. If not, I understand."

They thanked her and when she left, they stood in the living room with a beat of silence.

"Dane, you're not thinking of giving up the piano, are you?"

His look said he was.

"Why?"

"Because we met Jimmy Thanos, and he said I could come to his bar as often as I want to play. I can get my piano needs met—on a Steinway, no less—and you can get your smother problem fixed."

"Dane, it's okay. She's not that bad."

"You were still humming from whatever transpired

this morning when you got to Shellseeker Beach," he said matter of factly. "I think it is that bad."

She angled her head, studying him. Was he really that sensitive? Or was it a ploy to get her guard down? Final question—would she ever trust a man again?

"It wasn't pleasant," she finally admitted. "I'm hitting the wall with Roz, but—"

"Then let's take this place."

"But Dane, I don't get it. The piano was so important."

"Tell you what. Let's negotiate a six-month lease," he suggested. "Six months will fly by, and we'll know better where we want to be or what we want to do."

She wasn't sure she followed, since she'd want to be here and wanted to do exactly what she was doing now. That wasn't the case for him, of course. He'd need six months just to get his sea legs in his new life, and then...

Something was bothering her about this. What was it? She rooted around for the real reason for her threads of discontent, like her therapist had taught her, but nothing was tying up in a bow of self-awareness.

Meanwhile, Dane had pushed the sliders wide open, and the magnolia-scented air floated in and made her just love the place even more.

"We could get some decent patio furniture out here and it's like another living room." He glanced in at her. "Until it rains."

She smiled, ready to make a joke about putting the piano out there when her phone rang and she pulled it from her bag, wincing at the name. "Oh, dang it."

"Problem?" he asked.

"It's Toni, my boss. I was supposed to call her this morning about a situation with a client, but I got so wrapped up fighting with my mother that I forgot."

"See? You need to get out of there, Asia, or you're going to lose your job."

He actually wasn't that far from the truth. She held up the phone and inched the stroller in his direction. "Mind if I run into that bedroom real quick and talk to her? Zee is fine."

"Of course. I got him."

"Thank you." She tapped the phone and headed inside, putting her head in the work game. "Hey, Toni. Sorry I missed our chat this morning. Have you heard from the client yet?"

She headed into the downstairs bedroom, closing the door for privacy while Toni filled her in on a new account. She perched on the edge of a cheap dresser, closing her eyes to concentrate, but she could barely process what Toni said.

Something powerful wound up her chest, a familiar anxiety that had to have been the result of the upsetting discussion with her mother.

What would Nancy, the world's greatest therapist, tell her to do?

"Inch out of your comfort zone, Asia, one baby step at a time."

Was it the fact that her mother's fears and opinions were controlling her again? Was she falling back into old habits of letting much stronger people make her decisions?

Maybe...but not quite. It was deeper than that. It was...Dane.

But Dane wasn't a controlling man. On the contrary, he was downright flexible and compliant, kind and considerate. Why would she worry about—

"You got that, Asia?"

She swallowed a curse, clueless as to what Toni had just said. "I think so," she replied vaguely.

"This is a great solution. You run the numbers on that offer, we might have placed Jack Wilkerson and made Ergo Data Processing one happy client."

Oh, okay. Relief washed through her. "I can do that this afternoon, Toni. No problem."

"Asia, is everything okay?" Toni asked. "You seem distracted."

"I'm just closing the deal on a new apartment, Toni. I've got this with Wilkerson and Ergo. No worries."

"Great. Talk soon."

Her boss signed off, but Asia didn't move. She stayed frozen in the same spot, digging some more, trying to use all the tools her therapist had given her to identify the source of her stress and manage it. To be the controller instead of the person being controlled. To...

Dane. *Yes*, she thought with a nod. This had to do with him. What was it? Could her mother be right? Was she attracted to him, and fighting that with everything she had?

On one level, she *was* attracted. How could she not

be? He was good-looking and smart, wildly mature for his younger age, but beyond that, he was just so fundamentally good. And, try as he might, he couldn't hide his low-key crush on her, which was sweet and endearing, too.

Until it wasn't.

She closed her eyes and bit her lip, thinking about his offer to take this place even though it meant sacrificing his biggest need. Why? Could his crush be that bad? Maybe, but more important...what did that do to the balance of power in their fledgling friendship?

It gave the power to him. She would owe him something. And that...*that* was at the very core of her unease. She'd be controllable again, and she didn't want that. Nancy said Asia should stay far away from relationships like that.

But Nancy also urged Asia to trust again.

With a soft grunt, she pushed off the dresser that was bracing her, and headed for the living room, intending to put her foot down and say no, this unit wasn't perfect. Dane was still on the patio, but she stopped dead in her tracks at what she saw.

He was seated on the rocking sofa, holding Zee in his arms, gently gliding him back and forth.

"Oh, no, no, Mr. Zee. There's no crying. Your mama will be back soon."

Zee answered with a small protest, nothing serious, but enough to make Asia take another step closer to relieve Dane of the duty. But when he started talking again, she stopped.

"Oh, is that so?" he asked in the kindest, most interested voice. "Do you want to tell me more?"

Another cry, this one a little louder.

"Really? That's amazing. Is that all to your story?"

He paused a beat and Zee opened up and let out a good squawk.

"Oh, you like when I talk, do you? That makes you quiet, doesn't it?"

She couldn't see Zee from this angle, only Dane's face as he gazed down at the bundle of baby in his arms. He stared at Zee with wonder and amusement and so much *goodness*.

How could she ever doubt a man like that? How could she worry about him trying to control her?

"Okay, okay, little guy. I'll talk," he murmured. "I don't do much of that, you know. Talking's not really in my wheelhouse, as they say. I prefer to listen, but if it's what you need right now, let me, uh...think of something to say." He laughed softly, as if he knew he sounded a little ridiculous but didn't care.

"Um, let's see. We can talk about your mother. She's nice." Another soft laugh. "Now there's an understatement. She's just about the closest thing to a ten that I've ever known on a personal level. Not that we're personal," he added quickly, with so much seriousness it almost made her laugh.. "Oh, no, Zee-zee. Don't make that assumption like every other idiot we meet."

Zee-zee? She might have just died.

"Because they're idiots if they think Asia Turner would notice I'm alive."

And there he was, she thought with a wry smile, the man she could trust. The very one that her therapist told her she needed to find and keep. The one she didn't think existed. But he was right here, offering to make a sacrifice, and she had to trust that he wouldn't use that to exercise control over her.

She wouldn't be obligated to him, just grateful. And that was what she wanted after a lifetime of being stuck in her comfort zone of letting others make her decisions.

This was one decision she should make, and for the right reasons.

He hesitated in his soliloquy long enough for Zee to give a furious holler, prompting her to hustle outside to the patio.

"What's all the ruckus?" she joked, reaching down to take the baby.

"We're just talking." Dane looked up at her, his some-times-green, sometimes-brown eyes as warm and kind and unflustered as they could be. "He's got a nice set of pipes." He winked at her. "Maybe there's a place for him in the band."

She laughed, hating that her eyes filled a little as she finally got her hands on Zee's tiny body and lifted him. "Come here, you little screamer."

He quieted almost immediately, nestling into her. As he did, she looked down at Dane, a well of emotion she wasn't expecting bubbling up and choking her.

If she trusted him enough to take this townhouse and let him have that little bit of power over her, would she be tempted to trust him with...the truth? Because she couldn't do that. She could never do that.

"Everything okay with work?" he asked, searching her face and proving that he really was the most sensitive man she'd ever met.

"I made a decision," she said.

He lifted his brows, waiting.

"Let's take it."

A broad smile spread over his face. "I knew you'd see it my way."

"No, no, it's not *your* way," she said quickly, but she shook that off and reached for his hand. "*Our* way. We're in this together, Dane."

He held her fingers lightly, glancing at their joined hands, then up to her face. "Perfect."

And right then, it was. Her therapist would be so proud. Or not. It all remained to be seen.

Chapter Nine

Eliza

E liza stepped out of her bedroom, drawn to the rare smell of coffee in the kitchen. Teddy was a tea elitist through-and-through, so Eliza had learned to live without her beloved coffee. But this morning, the scent was a siren call that she followed, pleasantly surprised to find her son in the kitchen, humming and tapping the counter to the beat of one of many melodies that play in his head.

"Good morning, Dane," she said brightly.

He greeted her with a smile, as he had since the day before when he and Asia found a townhouse and applied to rent it. He hadn't told her much about the place and had joked about jinxing it, but she could tell this turn of events had put him in a good mood.

Was it because he was leaving the *Frozen* nest? Moving in with Asia, however platonic? Or maybe he was falling under the magical spell of Shellseeker Beach, as she'd hoped.

Whatever the reason, a happy kid was a happy mom.

"Ooh, that smells good," she said, sidling up the old-school percolator that had probably been in this house nearly as long as Teddy. "And this beast so rarely makes an appearance."

"It's great coffee." He lifted his cup in a mock toast. "And I had to bribe Teddy in order for her to get out that beast."

"What did she want?" Eliza asked, amused by the idea of him bribing her dear friend. "Oh, wait, let me guess. She needs you to move some furniture out of the cottage where we're putting Mia Watson from *The Last Resort*."

He gave her a confused look. "Not following."

"We're being included on the website and in the magazine called *The Last Resort*, which goes to every travel agency in the known world. They're doing a huge feature on the best 'hidden-gems' of family-owned Florida resorts, and Shellseeker Cottages was selected."

"Cool," he said, getting a cup out for her and putting it on the counter. "But no, that wasn't the bribe. She wants me to write a song for her."

"Oh, sweet. Will you?"

"Sure. What should I call it? *Hibiscus and Crystal*?"

She laughed, liking that he already knew the amazing woman that Eliza loved. "You should call it *Theo*. That's what your grandfather called her. Did you know that?"

"No, I didn't. But I'll file that away. And do you think she wanted some furniture moved? 'Cause I can do that today."

"Oh, that would be great. I'll take you down to the cottage when we finish the coffee. We just want to open up the rooms a little to give it an airy feeling for the reviewer, who also requested a writing desk."

"You give guests the furniture they want?"

"We give this one whatever she wants," Eliza said on a laugh. "This is a huge marketing opportunity for us."

"Sounds like it. Did you make it happen?" he asked.

"It was a team effort, believe me. But I drove the process, yeah."

He leaned against the cabinet, studying her for a moment. "Who knew you could add 'inn proprietor' to your resume at such a late date, Mom."

She snorted. "Such a late date? Honey, I'm fifty-four, not ninety-four."

"But it's a big change of career. Honestly, when I think about it, it's impressive."

"Thank you." She let the compliment sink in, as warm and tasty as the coffee when she took her first sip. "Mmm. This is fabulous. Well done, barista."

He didn't laugh, though, because he was studying her, thinking. "You've had three careers, Mom," he mused. "Broadway singer and dancer, talent agent, and now this."

"Oh, please, Dane. I was a wanna-be on Broadway, so calling it a career is a stretch. I was a talent agent, but never loved it all that much. And I'm still learning the hospitality ropes." She smiled up at him. "My best career was being a mom. Those, my dear son, were my glory days."

He smiled back at her, seeming more relaxed than he'd been since he arrived.

"News on the townhouse?" she guessed.

"We should know if we got it this morning." He shifted a little and sipped his coffee, the body language indicating that there might be more to say.

"You're not worried about getting approved, are you?"

He laughed softly. "Well, I am pretty solidly unemployed, but my credit rating is perfect and I have enough in savings to ease their worries. Asia's job is great, so we should be getting good news."

"You still think it's the perfect place?" she asked, sensing there might be more.

"Oh, yeah, it's just..." Another sip, then he said, "I can't fit the piano."

She blinked, surprised. "You can't? I thought that was the whole reason for moving."

"It was...and it wasn't. The place is primo, as I told you, and Asia really likes it and..."

And he really likes Asia, she thought, but covered that with a drink of coffee.

"And I found a place to play piano. You know, that dive that Miles knew about."

"Little...something?" She lifted her brows, definitely not expecting this.

"Little Blue's."

"Ah." She nodded, taking in this new turn of events. "So you can play as often as you like? I know you can spend hours on that piano."

"Days," he said on a laugh. "Jimmy, the owner, told me I can play all afternoon, any day of the week. The place is practically empty, and all he asks is that I pour a drink or two now and again, or fill in when he has to leave."

Ohhh. "So you're going to be a bartender."

"Not exactly," he said, bristling with a touch of defensiveness. "Just filling in for the guy, who, by the way, is one of the premier keyboardists who ever lived. I can learn a lot from Jimmy Thanos. He's—"

Eliza literally spit her coffee in shock.

"Mom!" Dane jumped back from the spray. "What the—"

"Jimmy Thanos?" Her voice rose just saying a name she hadn't thought about for so many years. "Jimmy...the piano player?"

"Do you know him? I didn't know you followed jazz and blues."

"Do I..." Dang it, she could feel the flush deepen on her face, the curse of a redhead. "Yes," she managed, pulling off a paper towel to wipe her hand, cup, and poor Dane's arm. "We did a play off-Broadway together. The longest run I ever had, and he was in the orchestra. He is very talented."

And there went the blush again, just thinking about how talented he was at flirting, teasing, and doing his very best at getting Eliza into bed. Never succeeded, but yeah. Jimmy got an A for effort.

"How well did you know him?" Dane asked, a note of wariness in his voice.

"We were friends. Good friends," she added, not wanting to lie.

"Did you date him?"

She nodded. "Before Dad, and back then, dating isn't what it is now," she added quickly. "We just went out a lot, did the clubs and stuff, you know?"

He looked like he didn't know, and didn't want to.

She had to nip this in the bud. "Dane, you have to let go of the fact that I'm some kind of...of goddess on a pedestal. I had a life before your dad, and..." This was hard to say but she had to. "I'll have one after."

He stared at her, clearly trying not to react to that statement. "But you know him, really? Have you stayed in touch or followed his career?"

"No, no. I met Dad, and I know Jimmy went on to be in Square None. I assumed he lived the life of a musician on the road and such, but, honestly? I kind of forgot he existed until you said his name."

"But Sanibel is small. You've never heard he lives here or saw him?"

She shrugged. "I've never been to that bar, and I've never run into him when I'm out with Miles."

His eyes shuttered at the mention of the name, but she ignored it.

"Unless Jimmy gets to Shellseeker Beach or comes to one of our pop-up pizza events, it's quite possible we could live here ten years and never run into each other. Anyway, if I saw him in the grocery store? I'm not sure I'd recognize him."

He didn't look convinced. "But Miles knows him. He never mentioned a famous musician owns that bar?"

"Does Jimmy want people to know that?" she asked.

"It's quite possible Miles is respecting his privacy, which is second nature to a private investigator. He doesn't break a trust, which is why people..." She lifted a brow to say the obvious. "Trust him."

Dane shook his head, letting out a soft whistle. "You really went out with Jimmy Thanos. Wow."

"Yep." She gave him a playful jab. "Yet another career—party girl with musicians of note, back in the day."

"You should come and see him," he said. "Maybe we'll go in and I'll play some night. I can uh, *re*introduce you to him."

"Sure." She was just about to open her mouth and ask if she could bring Miles, but thought better of it. "I'd love that. You know, it's been about..." She did some mental math. "Thirty-four years since I saw him. I actually turned twenty-one when I was in that play."

His eyes flickered. "Wow. That's something, Mom."

"Something from the past," she said, remembering Jimmy's dark good looks and cocky humor. "How's he look?"

"Not as good as you. Maybe lived a little harder on the road, though."

She laughed at that as she rinsed out her coffee cup and added it to the dishwasher. "He's a few years older than I am, but thanks. Want to go do that furniture now?"

"Sure, hang on a sec." He reached into his pocket and glanced at his phone, letting out a soft hoot. "We got it!" He turned to her, his eyes bright again. "We got the townhouse for six months."

"Congratulations!" She gave him a hug, so thrilled to see her son this happy. She wasn't exactly sure why, but sometimes, a mother doesn't question, she accepts. And that's exactly what Eliza decided to do.

"You LOOK AMAZING," Eliza said, eyeing Camille's freshly made-up face and always silky-smooth skin as they settled under a huge umbrella in the garden, the boardwalk and beach in plain view. But all eyes were on Camille, who did look remarkable for a woman a month out of open-heart surgery. "How do you do it?"

She gestured toward her long sheer sleeves and ankle-length cotton palazzo pants. "Cover everything on the bottom." Then she patted her cheek. "Paint the top."

As they laughed at that, Camille reached for Claire's hand. "And I'm well cared for by my daughter."

"And your fiancé," Claire added, lifting a brow. "It seems Buck is hanging out with you more than I am."

Camille sipped the iced tea that Teddy had made and set up on the table, the spark in her eyes unmistakable. "I can't seem to get rid of that man."

"Would you want to?" Olivia asked, sounding a little worried. As she should be—the "surprise wedding" technically fell on her shoulders, since Buck had gone to her first.

"No." Camille set down the glass and held out her left hand, her gorgeous solitaire glinting in the sun. "He's quite wonderful, that big Southern fisherman....guy." She laughed. "Not sure what to call him."

"Multimillionaire works," Teddy joked. "I've known the man most of my life and had no idea he was Daddy Warbucks himself."

"I'm surprised you didn't sense his aura," Olivia said to Teddy, the empath. "Green for money."

As they laughed, Camille looked skyward. "Money's not important. And before you all scoff at that, I'm telling you, he could be broke and homeless, and I'd still love the man."

Olivia sighed with a mix of relief and romantic awe. "So you're ready to say 'I do' then, Camille? No second thoughts about accepting his proposal moments before your surgery?"

"Livvie." Camille frowned at her. "Do you know something I don't? Is he cheating on me? About to back out?"

"Oh, no, no!" Olivia drew back, looking shocked that Camille would ask, but Eliza knew that she just wanted to be sure before going ahead and planning this event. "I love that you're so happy and in love...Cami." She winked as she used the nickname that only Buck seemed to get away with.

"I am and I am," Camille assured her. "Although Buck says there's something called 'pump head' or 'pump brain.' I don't know, but apparently people are in a fog after open-heart surgery."

"It's been over a month," Teddy said. "I can feel

you're thinking clearly just by being around you. Your fog has lifted and left you with an aura of sunshine yellow."

"Is that love?" Camille asked. "Because I'm in a happy haze of that."

Eliza and Olivia shared a quick look, no doubt both thinking the same thing: *let's get them married!*

"But I feel like I've missed so much," Camille continued, sitting forward. "Life in Shellseeker Beach has gone on without me. Fill me in on all the happenings. What's this I hear about Dane and...Asia living together?"

"Not in the romantic sense," Eliza told her. "They're moving in to get their independence and space, and they found a great two-bedroom townhouse near Ding Darling. In fact, they just got word that their application cleared, so I think they're moving in very soon."

"I see. And are we certain this is...*amour platonique*?"

"It is," Eliza confirmed.

"Ehhh, maybe," Olivia added. "My brother's got a crush for days, but I don't think Asia's in the market for a man."

"Interesting," Camille said on a nod. "And how are you and Deeley doing? No word from the distant relatives coming to rock your boat?"

"Not yet, but it's only been a few days." Olivia rolled her eyes. "I swear, every time Deeley and I get ready to sink in and live our life, something happens."

"Well, what's your game plan?" Camille asked.

"Game plan?" She drew back. "Should I have one?"

Camille looked at the others as if she expected support. "You're not just going to let them run roughshod over you and Deeley and do some legal maneuvering and take your son away."

"My son." Olivia sighed on a smile. "He's not, yet. But I honestly just hope that they see he is well cared for, deeply loved, and a solid little almost-three-year-old." She glanced at Eliza and Teddy, looking uncertain. "Not enough of a game plan?"

Camille swiped her hand. "You need to marry him, as soon as possible."

Olivia inched back at the order. "We've only been dating a few months, Camille. And he was gone for one of them."

"I was seeing Buck for a few weeks before he proposed. And I'm more than ready to say 'I do.'"

Which was good news—the very news they'd come here today to establish—but lost on Olivia as she looked out into the distance, thinking.

"My game plan," she finally said, "is the village concept." At their confused looks, she gestured toward all of them. "This village. My mother, my de facto grand-mother,"—she nodded to Teddy, who beamed—"my Aunt Claire, my French *grandmère*, and those not at this table. They say it takes a village to raise a child, and Deeley and I have a whole beach full of family."

Eliza reached her hand out to Olivia. "I think that's a wise game plan."

"Well, I think you should marry him," Camille said. "You'd have better standing in court."

"Do you think that's true, Claire?" Eliza asked her sister. "You're the lawyer."

Claire looked just uncertain enough to make Olivia groan.

"I haven't done a lot of family law," Claire started. "I'm a corporate attorney, but of course, if you are in a legal battle for custody or guardianship, the length and stability of your relationship is a factor. But only one factor, Liv," she added quickly.

"And the village? Will that help?"

"If we are all willing to testify, which I know we are."

Olivia nodded. "Good to know, but I hope it doesn't come to that."

"You should marry him," Camille said again, undeterred. "What are you waiting for?"

"What are *you* waiting for?" Olivia countered with a quick laugh.

"For my doctor to say I'm strong enough for a wild night of..." Camille's eyes flickered. "Dancing on the beach at sunset."

They cracked up, but Olivia leaned closer, looking like she was determined to get one last commitment from Camille.

"Is that what you want, Camille?" Olivia asked. "A sunset wedding on the beach?"

"Don't change the subject, *cherie*," Camille replied. "When a man loves a woman and a woman loves a man and nothing is in the way of their nuptials, they should walk down the aisle in front of their friends and family and vow to be together forever."

"That's sweet, *Maman*," Claire said.

"Very romantic," Teddy agreed, refilling their teas.

"And not very practical," Olivia replied. "It takes time to plan a wedding."

Camille gave her signature French shrug. "Not if that's all you want in the world."

"Good to hear you say that." Olivia clapped her hands like the subject was closed. "I think you and Buck should get married very soon, don't you?"

"As soon as humanly possible," Camille replied, taking a sip of tea while the others shared a quick, secret look. Guess they were having a surprise wedding on the beach.

They all glanced up as a small family came down the path toward the beach, pulling Eliza's attention. No new guests were expected today, but this group was definitely looking around with interest.

A lot of tourists cruised up and down the three boardwalks that were technically part of the Shellseeker Cottages property, but also the only easy way to get to the public beach.

"They might be wondering if we have vacancies," Eliza mused, gazing at the couple and the three kids scampering around, obviously dying to get to the beach but, for some reason, not walking toward it.

Teddy started to push up. "I'll go tell them the bad news."

But it was Olivia's reaction that froze everyone.

She stared at them, the blood draining from her face, and Eliza instantly knew who they were and what they were looking for.

"Livvie," she whispered, taking her hand. "Deep breath, baby. You don't know what they want."

Before she could answer, the father of the group waved at them. "'Scuze me," he called. "Does anyone know where I can find a man named Connor Deeley? He says he works here."

Olivia went bone white as she stared at Eliza, speechless.

"Do you want to talk to them?" Eliza asked on a whisper.

But Olivia was squirming in her seat instead of running to greet them. "The *one* day I put Bash in daycare in the morning. You know I always have him with me until I have to go into the store. I'm sitting here like a lady who lunches and he's in daycare!"

"I'll talk to them and buy some time," Teddy said, pushing up.

"And I'll give Deeley a heads up." Claire pulled out her phone. "Noah's at the cabana with him today."

"And I'll get Bash from daycare," Eliza said. "When you talk to them, tell them he's off with his...Grandma 'Liza. Then I'll bring him here and we'll...be your village, Liv. Don't worry."

But she could tell by the look on Olivia's face that the advice was falling on deaf ears.

Camille extended her left hand, flashing her diamond. "Would you like to borrow this?"

Olivia managed a smile, shaking her head. Eliza took off to get Bash, praying that the arrival of this family didn't spell trouble for her daughter.

Chapter Ten

Olivia

"Livvie!" Teddy called from where she'd just held a lively conversation with the Brennans and their three kids. The two boys looked at the Gulf like they'd love to be in it and not having adult conversations, and the bored little girl was using the boardwalk rail as her own personal monkey bars. The parents were doing the talking, though, and Olivia just knew they were asking about Bash. "Can you come here a moment, dear? I think you'll want to meet these people!"

Reminding herself that she shouldn't know anything about this family except that they'd called Deeley and said they might be coming—without mentioning that it would be the same week—she stood with the speed of a woman being called to her sentencing.

"I don't need your ring, Camille," she whispered. "I'm not starting a relationship with these people on a lie."

With that, she walked across the stones and sand to meet them at the top of the boardwalk.

"Hello," she called in her brightest voice.

"Olivia Whitney," Teddy said as she reached them,

"this is Jennifer and Will Brennan, and their children, Riley, Caleb, and Bella."

As much as she wanted to pretend not to know who they were, it would be a lie not to recognize their names, so she let her face light up with just a little more enthusiasm than she felt.

"The Brennan family!" She extended her hand. "Connor and I have been looking forward to meeting you since you called."

"Oh, you're his wife?" Will asked, taking her hand. "So good to meet you."

"Not..." She swallowed a grunt and almost kicked herself for not taking that ring. "I'm his girlfriend." Strike one, she thought as she shook the woman's hand as well. "Welcome to Shellseeker Beach, Jennifer."

"Just Jenny. Is Sebastian here?" she asked, glancing around. "We're so anxious to meet him we didn't even check into our hotel."

"Sebastian!" The little girl, Bella, called out as she did an impressive chin-up on the boardwalk railing. "I can't wait!"

So the kids were all in on it.

"He's with my mother," Olivia said brightly. "But I'll call her and have her bring him here. Would you like me to take you down to meet Deeley? Er, Connor? We call him Deeley," she added quickly, low-grade nervousness building.

"Oh, sure." Jennifer glanced at her husband, then back at Olivia. "We thought they'd be together."

"And they often are," Olivia said. "If only we had

known when you were coming, we could have been sure to all be together."

"Sorry for the surprise," Will said quickly. "We thought..."

"We didn't want to intrude," Jennifer explained.

Well, you did, Olivia thought, but covered with a smile. "Not a problem! Let's go talk to Connor, and my... oh." She looked past the couple toward the beach, where Deeley jogged in their direction. Shirtless. What was he thinking?

He was thinking he was at the beach and never, ever wore a shirt.

"Here he comes."

Jennifer turned and spotted him, adjusting her sunglasses as if the sight of Deeley's muscular and tattooed physique was just too much for her.

"I'll go meet him," Will said, walking down the boardwalk as if he had to head off this long-haired, bare-chested beach bum before he reached the womenfolk.

Strike two.

"It's truly a shame we didn't know you were coming," Teddy said, pulling Jennifer's attention. "We might have been able to get you into one of our cottages."

Olivia knew that wasn't true—they were booked and had a short waiting list in case of a cancellation—but she loved Teddy for saying so.

"Can I give you a tour?" Teddy added. "Maybe some iced tea? I have cookies in the tea hut for the kids."

Jenny just gave her a tight smile and shook her head. "We're really just here to meet Sebastian."

"Bash," Olivia corrected. "He goes by Bash."

"Bash?" She bit back a laugh. "The poor thing can't be called Bash."

Annoyance straightened Olivia's spine as she tried—and failed—to like this woman. "Well, that's what he answers to," she said with false warmth. "And, trust me, it fits."

Deeley and Will came up the boardwalk, talking to each other, and slowing their step as they approached.

"This is my wife, Jenny. Jenn, this is Connor Deeley, Sebastian's guardian."

"Jenny." He shook her hand and looked like he suddenly realized that he'd left so fast, he'd never bothered with a shirt. "You, uh, caught us off guard."

She gave a quick smile, which Olivia interpreted as, "That's what we intended," but then Jenny said, "We're sorry for that. We made a very spontaneous decision, and the kids were dying to see the beach."

"Yeah, can we go down?" The oldest, Riley, asked, sounding impatient.

"How about a paddleboard ride?" Deeley suggested. "I've got a couple of boards that would be perfect for you two."

"And me?" the little girl asked, flipping herself over the railing with grace of a gymnast.

"We're here to meet Sebastian," Jenny reminded them, then looked at Deeley. "When can we do that?"

"Uh..." He glanced at Olivia. "Don't you have him?"

Shoot! Deeley had left early for a sunrise kayak tour and didn't know that she'd changed her plans and put

Bash into the daycare center an hour early so she could have that conversation with Camille.

"No, he's uh, with my mother."

He looked surprised at that, and uncomfortable, since it was pretty obvious his guardian didn't know where he was or who he was with.

"She's bringing him here to meet you," Olivia said.

Jenny turned and frowned, obviously unsure how Olivia's mother could possibly know they were here. "You just said you'd contact her," she remarked with a little too much accusation.

"That's what I mean, she's coming. After I call her. And I will," Olivia replied, hating that this woman had her flustered, and lying. "Right now."

She took out her phone to fake text her mother as Deeley tried the paddleboard possibility again.

"Please, Mom?" the younger boy whined.

Jenny put a hand on her oldest son's shoulder and didn't say a word, but he just nodded as if she had.

"We'll wait, thank you, sir," he said.

Wow. Discipline. What a concept. Just wait until this lady saw Bash when he had candy and no nap.

Will stepped forward, and said, "Why don't we go check into our hotel, Jenn? The kids can change into bathing suits and we'll come back when it's a more convenient time."

"That'd be great," Olivia said, relieved. "It'll be a bit before she's here with Bash."

"You don't have to work?" Deeley asked her.

Of course she did, and Ileana had specifically asked for this afternoon off. "I'll, uh, figure something out."

"Do you work full-time, Olivia?" Jenny asked.

"I own a clothing store," she said, discomfort crawling all over her for no reason except she didn't want to be judged harshly.

"Well, then, if you have to work, why don't we just see you tonight?" Will asked. "We can come to your house, Connor. Would that work?"

"Of course," he said. "Livvie and I can make you dinner."

But...the village. They were all looking at her expectantly, leaving her with no out, and no village. "Yes," Olivia said brightly. "That would be great."

"Oh?" Jenny angled her head. "So you live together?"

And there it was. Strike three. Or four. Or nine. Whatever it was, she could see the judgment on Umpire Jenny's face.

"Yes," Olivia said with resignation in her voice. "We do."

THE VILLAGE CAME THROUGH AFTER ALL.

As soon as they heard what had happened—and Deeley abjectly apologized for the spontaneous dinner invitation—they all jumped into action, so that Olivia was able to work and close the store early.

While she did, Claire and Teddy did a run to Bailey's and bought a feast of a dinner, brought it to Olivia and

Deeley's house, and got a gorgeous family style meal set up so all she had to do was heat the dishes. Eliza kept Bash all day and got him to take a three-hour nap, so he was in great spirits when she dropped him off.

Deeley cleaned the house like royalty was on the way, giving Olivia time to freshen up—and sneak a glass of wine—and by the time the Brennans knocked on the door, they felt ready for anything.

"Welcome," Deeley said as he opened the door, with Olivia standing behind him, holding Bash in her arms.

"Ohh!" Jenny sailed past Deeley, arms out. "Is this our little boy?"

Olivia squeezed him a little tighter. "This is Bash. Say hello to Miss Jenny, honey."

In response, he dropped his head on Olivia's shoulder and couldn't get his thumb in his mouth fast enough.

"He gets shy sometimes," Olivia said, knowing she sounded like a typical mom, and not caring. He *did* get shy around strangers. He was two.

"Oooh, no thumbie," Jenny said, reaching to ease it out of his mouth.

He flipped his head and faced the other way.

"Ohh, Sebastian," she said, undaunted. "I'm your Auntie Jenny."

"Is this him?" Bella came waltzing in, circling Olivia to look up at Bash's turned face. "Hi, Sebastian! That's the name of a lobster, did you know that?"

Olivia could feel his little legs clench as he held on like a scared kitten.

The two boys and their father came in next, far less

intrusive than the ladies in the Brennan family, all saying a gentle hello to Bash.

Caleb, the younger son, caught Bash's attention, and brought him out of his shyness.

"Play cars?" Bash asked, as if he instinctively knew a seven-year-old boy would play cars.

"Sure. You have any?"

Olivia slowly lowered him to the floor and he was off, dragging Caleb with him to the toybox in the living room. The other kids followed, and Deeley stood next to Olivia, putting an arm around her in solidarity.

"Can we offer you something to drink?" he asked. "Wine or non-alcoholic? Some sparkling water or soda?"

"The water sounds good," Jenny replied, her gaze past them into the living room to watch the kids.

"I'll take the wine," Will said. "I'm on vacation."

Deeley went to get them drinks while Olivia drew them into the undersized living room which...wasn't quite as neat as two minutes ago. The toy bin was already open, the cars and Legos were coming out, and Bella had found a stash of *Frozen* paraphernalia that Harper had left here not so long ago.

"Sebastian, can we talk?" Jenny said, perching on the edge of the sofa.

Seriously? The woman had three kids. Didn't she know that toddlers don't converse? Well, maybe hers did. Olivia started to walk closer, but Will held up a hand, stopping her.

"Can you show me around?" he asked, not giving her a chance to supervise this conversation.

Sanibel Sunsets 149

"Sure. There's not much, but I'll show you our backyard."

In the kitchen, Deeley uncorked wine, smiling when they walked in. "Red okay?" he asked. "We have white, too."

"Red is fine, largest glass." He laughed. "Don't tell my flock."

"Oh, you're a minister." Olivia purposely didn't make it a question, since she knew that, but opened the door for him to say more.

"I am. Small Presbyterian church about a half hour outside of Minneapolis. I've had the church for about fifteen years now."

"That sounds wonderful," Olivia said. "And does Jenny work with you?"

"Well, she's a pastor's wife, which comes with a whole long list of things to do, but, no. Jenn wants to be with the kids full-time. She homeschools two days a week, and they're in the church school the other three. She's there a lot, too, volunteering for everything."

Deeley handed him the glass of wine and offered one to Olivia, but this whole thing had her too queasy. "I'll take a Pellegrino, and one for Jenny."

After he got those from the fridge, Deeley tipped his head toward the living room. "Should we..."

"Uh, yeah, but..." Will glanced to the doorway, clearly wanting some privacy. "I just want to say something to you two, because I'm sure you're uncertain why we're here."

They shared a look and both nodded.

"But you're more than welcome to be here," Deeley added. "Our plan is for Bash to know whatever family he can when he gets older. We will share his past and the loss of his parents, and I hope he'll want you in his life."

Will looked down at the wine, as if he didn't know what to say to that.

"Unless you want more than that," Deeley said, the words drawing the other man's attention.

"We just don't know yet," he said simply. "That's why we're here. My wife..." He swallowed uncomfortably. "She seems to feel God's hand is in this—we both do, to be fair—and Jenny thinks that her...distant cousin, Sebastian, should..."

"Should what?" Olivia prodded.

"Should be with family."

The queasiness threatened to rise up and make her gag.

"He is with family," Deeley said, strong and confident. "We are the only family he knows."

Will nodded, clearly uncomfortable. He rubbed his beard, looking from one to the other. "I know that, but she...feels strongly. And to appease her, I've agreed that we should come and see your living situation."

So it was a big, fat test and the prize? Bash.

They heard a soft shriek and children's laughter, Bash's familiar giggle louder than them all.

"Then come and research," Olivia said, gesturing him out. "I think you'll see a very well-adjusted, healthy, happy little boy who is loved beyond measure."

She didn't wait for a response but walked out, feeling sick from her head to her toes.

The kids were a welcome distraction from small talk, all three of them lively and personable, especially the little girl, Bella. She took to Olivia, nattering on about their dog, their toys, and her best friends, and the boys played Legos and cars and endlessly amused Bash.

For his part, Bash had totally risen to the occasion, without one single outburst or tantrum. He didn't even suck his thumb, the little angel. And he'd gone to both Deeley and "Wibbie" to show them cars, giving them a chance to hug and kiss him and demonstrate how they felt about him.

Jenny observed, for the most part, while Deeley and Will talked sports and fishing. Jenny also gave a string of maternal advice, guidance, and corrections to her already-perfect children, sounding a lot like Roz telling Asia how to walk, sit, and breathe.

After a bit, Olivia put out dinner, and, of course, the pastor led them in a prayer. Bash squawked during it, pounding his highchair, but they chuckled over the interruption.

As the food was passed and eaten, the conversation stayed moving as they discussed the kids' sports—at least five different teams between the three of them—and life in Minneapolis, and Deeley and Olivia shared all the wonders of living on Sanibel Island.

Through it all, Bash stayed on astoundingly good behavior, eliciting lots of praise from Olivia and an extra cookie for dessert, despite the fact that Jenny limited her children to one.

As the meal came to an end, Olivia felt normal for the first time all night. Not sick to her stomach, not shaky. Will was very cool, and clearly wrapped up in a busy life as a man with a big family, a thriving church, and a fine sense of humor and balance. Jenny? Wound a little tighter and highly unpredictable.

She talked endlessly about her grandmother, who she reminded Bash four times was his great-great-aunt, who'd died recently. Grandma Evie was apparently beloved by all, and could do no wrong.

"And, oh, how thrilled she'd be to learn about you, little Sebastian," she cooed at him. "It breaks my heart that you didn't meet."

It didn't break Olivia's. She counted her blessings that old Evie wasn't here to add to the fight for Bash.

After dessert, the kids asked for permission to leave the table—now that was a trick she hoped to teach Bash—and asked if they could take him to play in the backyard. The minute they left the table, Jenny leaned forward, her gaze direct.

"How long have you and Connor been dating?" she asked.

Ah, the inquisition has begun, Olivia thought. "Oh, basically since I got to Sanibel, right, Deeley?" She purposely didn't say "less than six months" because it seemed so brief and unstable.

Deeley nodded, silently communicating that he understood that. "I went to fix a sink in her mother's cottage and from the minute I saw her, I knew she was special."

"Ah, that's sweet," Jenny said. "And when are you getting married?" At the beat of awkward silence, she added a laugh. "I guess I'm not supposed to ask that, but... under the circumstances, I'd like to know."

"Under what circumstances?" Deeley countered. "Do you mean Bash?"

The other woman shifted in her seat, visibly uncomfortable. "Well, yes." She looked at her husband, having that same kind of silent spousal communication Deeley and Olivia had just shared. "Since he's part of our family now, we wanted to be sure he's in the right place."

Not sure what that had to do with marriage, but Olivia knew what talking point to use as a counter.

"I hope you'll stay long enough to meet my mother, and the extended family we have here on Sanibel," Olivia said. "Bash is surrounded by people who love him, in addition to the two of us."

"But he's in daycare," she said, as if Olivia and Deeley put him in jail every morning.

"He's with a special babysitter for the few hours that we have to work," Olivia replied.

"It's fine," Will assured her. "All Jenny's trying to do is—"

"Take my child." Deeley's words, even though he'd ground them out through his teeth, brought everything else to a halt.

The other three turned to him, no one more surprised than Olivia at the determination in his golden eyes.

"No one has said—"

Deeley wiped away the pastor's excuse with a sharp hand, his gaze locked on Jenny. "You don't have to say anything. You're here to decide if he's in good hands and if you should add him to your family."

They both stared at him, then Jenny shrugged. "We don't mean to upset you, Connor, but I won't lie. You're right. We do want to know that he's in the right place."

"He's *home*," Deeley said, emphasizing the word. "And this child has not had it easy, I might add. For the first time in a long time, he has true stability and if you don't think that's changed him, then you should have seen him a few months ago. He wouldn't have made it through the prayer."

"And speaking of prayer," Jenny said. "Are you raising him in faith?"

"We don't know yet," Deeley said. "We're raising him in love, though. And plenty of it."

"So much!" Olivia interjected. "He has everything our own child would have and…"

"And we plan to legally adopt him when the time's right," Deeley said. "And we don't expect any reason why we shouldn't."

Will and Jenny exchanged another look, one that made Olivia's blood run cold.

"Well," the pastor said. "My wife might have a reason."

"What?" Deeley and Olivia asked in unison.

"My grandmother," Jenny said. "When she was ill and passing on to the next life, she asked that I do what I can to end this age-old feud between the two sides of her family. Most of the people involved are gone, but I believe that bringing Evie's nephew from the Royce side —however many generations removed—into *our* family will mend all fences."

Olivia felt her whole expression change to one of disgust. "For that reason, you'd try to take our child?"

"We aren't there yet," Will said softly. "We simply wanted to—"

"Please don't do that," Olivia whispered, looking from one to the other. "Please don't try to take him."

"I'm not pleading with you," Deeley said. "You *cannot* have him, and if you try, we will make that family feud look like a sitcom."

Jenny met his gaze, not backing down. "I believe in my heart that considering the possibility is the proper thing to do. We're blood relatives."

"You're total strangers," he fired back.

"Please, please." Will held out his hands in a peace-making gesture. "We want to the do the best thing for the child, and what the Lord would direct me to do."

Deeley leaned forward. "I don't know about the Lord—"

Jenny's eyes flickered.

"But the *court* directed this decision months ago. Bash's father named me guardian—"

"In a text before he committed suicide on a mission with you." Jenny's eyebrows shot up as she made the statement. "I'm so sorry to be the voice of truth and reason, but we've done a deep dive and all our homework,

Connor. And, yes, you have a lovely little home here and Bash seems happy, but you two aren't stable. You could break up as quickly as you got together, then where would that leave Bash?"

"With me," Deeley insisted. "And we're not going to break up. Everything you say is true, on paper, but we don't live *on paper*. Bash was left an orphan, and since that day—before, even—I've been financially and emotionally and physically responsible for that boy." He nodded toward Olivia. "Olivia and I are, for all intents and purposes, his parents. And we do not intend for that to change, no matter what it takes."

"But we need to know that," Jenny said softly. "Try to see this from our standpoint."

"You don't get a standpoint," Deeley murmured.

"I'm sorry," Will said. "But the fact is, as his blood relatives, we do."

They all sat quiet for two pounding heartbeats when the sliding door in the kitchen screeched open.

"Mom! Mom! Sebastian got hurt!"

All four of them shot up so fast, the table shook, heading out to the back with Deeley in the lead. Before they got there, Olivia heard a power squeal of pain, misery, and fury from Bash that she recognized all too well.

Deeley went straight to the crying child on the grass.

"What happened?" Will asked Riley.

"He was running around like a crazy thing, and I tried to stop him and he went flying."

"He's fine, he's fine." Deeley scooped him up and turned to Olivia. "Standard first aid, Liv."

She checked out the bleeding knee, cooing softly as Deeley carried him into the hall bathroom that they affectionately called ICU. On the way, she snagged a tissue to wipe his teary, snotty face.

Deeley put him on the toilet seat while Olivia crouched down to examine the boo-boo. Deeley soaked a clean washcloth, handing it over like, well, like they'd done it a dozen times.

Bash wailed when the cold rag hit his knee, but Olivia knew to stroke his hair and hum, whispering calming words when he gasped for his next howl.

Then came the gauze to dry it, the Neosporin, and lastly, Deeley spread out an array of colorful Band-Aids from tractors to dinosaurs, and Bash, finally calm, picked one with tiny dog faces.

"There you go," Olivia said as she smoothed the bandage into place.

Deeley crouched down next to her. "All better, little man?"

He managed a teary nod. "Hurts, Wibbie."

"I know, babycakes." She reached for him. "And this is an unfair end to a perfect day. You were so, so good today."

"A-plus day, Basho," Deeley agreed. "I'm so proud of you, buddy."

He crawled into Olivia's arms and found her shoulder, while Deeley rubbed his little back.

"He's a sleepy man, aren't you, honey?" she whispered.

Bash nodded, already sucking his thumb.

"Then let's get you washed, brushed, and PJ'd for bed." Olivia pushed up, and Deeley helped her to her feet.

"I'll take care of our company, Liv."

"We're fine," Will said.

They both turned to see the couple standing just outside the bathroom door, arm-in-arm as they took in the scene.

For a second, no one spoke, including Bash, who just nestled deeper into Olivia's arms.

"I'm sorry, I..." Olivia's voice trailed off as Jenny came closer, smiling at Bash.

"There's no need to apologize," Jenny said softly, putting a hand on Bash's leg, but looking at Olivia. "If anyone should, it's me. I don't want to blow in here and wreck your lives."

Olivia just looked at her, biting her tongue not to say the obvious: *But that's exactly what you're doing.*

"We really, really want what's best for him, long term." Jenny rubbed his back.

Olivia nodded. "I know that," she said, kindly letting the other woman off the hook.

"We do," her husband said. "And it's clear what that is."

"Thank you," Olivia whispered.

"Thank you," Jenny said. "For an eye-opening evening."

Deeley gestured toward the hall. "Why don't I get you on your way so Livvie can take care of Bash?"

"Of course, but..." Jenny bit her lip and glanced at the sink. "Don't take this the wrong way, but I'd like to get a sample of..." She shifted from one foot to the other. "DNA. For a test. Just to, you know, be sure."

"You're not touching this child," she said.

"Just..." Jenny looked past her and pointed at the Sponge Bob SquarePants toothbrush hanging in the holder. "If I might."

Olivia shrugged and walked out, completely over this night. Carrying Bash into his room, she closed the door behind them and let out a breath she felt like she'd been holding since that afternoon. She took two steps to the rocking chair and collapsed, pressing Bash to her chest.

"Wibbie," he murmured, finding his spot with his legs wrapped around her. "I sleepy."

Exhaustion pressed so hard she could barely breathe. "Me, too, precious," she whispered as she rocked him slowly. "I sleepy, too."

Chapter Eleven

Dane

As Dane parked and walked up to the front door of Little Blue's, he thought about how he'd bring up the subject of the past. Did he just say to the guy, "Oh, hey, funny thing. You dated my mother..."

He almost laughed just thinking about it, but then, it wasn't funny. It was weird. Thinking of Mom with any guy who wasn't Dad was weird, but Jimmy might not even remember her. It was more than a lifetime ago—Dane's lifetime, plus more—and it didn't sound like they'd been that serious, more like friends. He hoped.

Guess he'd find out.

He doubted anyone would be hanging in the bar this early, but Jimmy said to come anytime at all. The door was open, and with daylight pouring in and the over-heads on, the darkened bar looked barren, empty, and maybe not as clean as he'd hoped.

Not a soul was in sight, so Dane stood for a moment, taking it in, his gaze naturally drawn to the Steinway.

Now *that* was clean. Polished to a shine, as a matter of fact, and clearly well-loved.

"Well, there's my young protégé."

Dane turned at the sound, spotting Jimmy coming

out from behind the bar carrying a bottle of 409 and a rag. A protégé? He took that as a compliment as he nodded hello. "Hey, Jimmy."

"You're in time to wipe things down," he said, playfully waving the rag. "Nah, just kidding."

"I'm happy to help," he said. "Half an hour of cleaning for every hour of playing?" He was only partially joking. Helping out would make him feel less like a "user" of the beloved instrument.

"Play me a tune while I work," Jimmy said.

"Deal." He started walking toward the piano, then slowed down, his heart rate kicking up at what he was about to say. "So, Jimmy, I think we have a mutual acquaintance."

"In this town?" He spritzed some cleaner on a table. "It's possible, but not a lot of people know my past."

"Well, this one does."

He looked up from the table as he started to wipe. "Ruh-roh. What's her name?"

"You a player, Jimmy? I mean, not the piano kind."

"I did okay in my day, but..." His eyes flickered. "Now you got me worried. Who is she?"

Dane rubbed his chin, his fingers still not completely used to the whiskers he didn't shave seven days a week. "Uh, my mother."

He looked up, eyes wide. "Oh, snap. I'm sure I didn't...what's her name?"

"Eliza Whitney, but you knew her as Eliza Vanderveen. In New York. In a—"

"Are you kidding me?" He dropped the rag and

straightened. "Eliza?" He practically whispered the name. "Eliza from New York? The redhead with..." He caught himself, and closed his eyes. "An angel's voice."

Dane smiled at the description, vaguely aware that Miles Anderson had said essentially the same thing and he hadn't smiled. "So you do remember her."

"Not a woman you forget," he said, then held up a hand. "Don't worry. I never..." He shook his head. "But not for lack of trying."

Dane took a step backwards.

"Sorry, TMI," Jimmy said on a laugh. "So, Eliza's your mother? Whatever happened to her? I landed a recording gig with a tour tacked on, and next time I was in New York, I heard she'd moved out west. And, man, I was sad to hear that."

"She met and married my dad, and they went to L.A. He, um, passed away about a year ago."

"Oh, kid, I'm sorry." He looked down at the table as if he just remembered he was cleaning it. "What brought her to Sanibel?"

"Her dad lived here, and owned the Shellseeker Cottages."

"Dutch? He was Eliza's dad?" He choked. "Holy... heck. I never knew that—never knew his last name, in fact —but he popped in now and again when he was mad at the world. Never talked about his family, just the war and being a Pan Am pilot. Dutch was your granddaddy?" He tapped his head and flicked his fingers. "Mind blown, son."

Dane laughed. "Small world."

"Ain't it, though." He shook his head again. "Dutch was a good guy. Man, you've had a rough year or so. Grandfather and dad."

"I didn't know Dutch that well, but yeah. My dad was a great guy, too. The year's had its ups and downs. I quit my job to play music, so there was that."

Jimmy shifted from one foot to the other, eyeing Dane as he seemed to process all this new information. "What kind of job?"

"I was a computer engineer for a tech firm out in Silicon Valley."

"What?" He blew out a whistle. "Dang, boy, that takes nerve. What brought you here?"

"My mom and my sister like it, and I needed a place to live and write music."

"And what are you doing for work?"

Dane shrugged. "Living off savings, and hoping to sell some songs."

"Yeah? I got an idea." Jimmy flipped the rag, sending it arcing toward Dane fast enough that he almost didn't grab it. But he snagged the damp cloth. "Work for me," Jimmy said.

Dane blinked at him. "Excuse me?"

"You too good for manual labor, techie?"

Laughing, he twirled the rag, suddenly seeing where this was going and liking it very much. "Not me," he said. "I can clean. Never poured."

"There's nothing to it. I'll pay minimum plus you keep all your tips and can put your heart and soul into that piano seven days a week, twenty-four hours a day. I'll give you a key. Just...work for me."

The offer came so fast, Dane almost took a step backwards. "Seriously?" But even as he asked, he knew Jimmy Thanos was dead serious. "No interview? No training?"

"With your pedigree? That talented mother and a hoot of a grandfather? And whatever fancy education you have, and a big old pair of, uh, steel nerves to leave a decent paycheck to play music? I know all I need to know about you, kid. When can you start?"

"How about...now?"

He looked skyward. "Thank you, thank you, thank you."

"What do you need me to do?"

Jimmy gestured toward the rag. "Clean. Then I'll give you a lesson in bartending. Rule number one: listen. Rule number two: be generous with the shots. Rule number three: wear comfortable sneakers, because a hard day's work is...hard. Got it?"

He grinned. "Yes."

"Oh, and I'll want you to do one other thing."

"What's that?"

He nodded to the piano. "Entertain the customers when you're not behind the bar. Think you could do all that?"

"I know I can." He stepped forward and extended his hand toward Jimmy. "Boss."

Jimmy gave a soft hoot and they shook hands, both beaming with satisfaction.

Jimmy sent Dane home at five, after that honest day's work, with an invitation to come back later just to play. Eliza was welcome, of course, and the pretty girl he'd been with the other night.

Just as he was walking to his mother's car, which he'd borrowed for the day, Dane got a text from that pretty girl and that just made the smile on his face grow bigger.

Asia Turner: *I got the keys! I'm at the townhouse now getting some stuff put away. Come on over and see! When can you move in?*

"Right this minute," he muttered as he got into the car. Moving wouldn't take him much time, since all he had was the clothes he'd packed. He'd planned to move in tomorrow, but now he just wanted to see the place and tell Asia that he was gainfully employed.

Not sure why her opinion mattered, but it did.

When he knocked, she swung open the door and just about took his breath away with her hair up in some wild hairdo, a tank top, and shorts that barely covered her long legs.

"Oh, you look surprised," she said.

"No baby in your arms," he replied, covering for his reaction. "I'm not used to that."

"He's asleep upstairs in the Pack 'n' Play, already in love with his new room. Come in, I'm unpacking kitchen stuff. Well..." She leaned in to whisper. "I'm being told *how* to unpack."

He held up his hands. "Don't get too close unless you want a whiff of beer."

"Beer?" Roz Turner walked out into the entry hall from the small kitchen, her hair wild and curly instead of tucked into a turban. "Are you a day-drinker, Dane?"

"No, ma'am," he said, coming closer. "I'm a gainfully employed bartender-slash-busboy-slash-piano player. Jimmy hired me to work at Little Blue's."

"Dane!" Asia shocked him with a spontaneous hug. "That's fantastic. You can play and make money! Exactly what you wanted."

Roz beckoned him in and added her own congratulations hug.

"You'll love it there," she said. "Little Blue's is a Sanibel institution, known mostly to the locals. And Asia just told me the owner is some famous guy. No one knew that."

"He keeps it on the DL, but he's really open with me," Dane told them. "And super weird coincidence? He knew my mother thirty-some years ago in New York."

"Get outta town!" Asia exclaimed.

"Not a coincidence," Roz said. "I don't believe in them. It happened for a reason. How did he know her?"

"He knew her *well*, apparently," he said dryly. "They were in a play together—I guess when my mom was a singer and dancer and he was in the orchestra, before he made it big in a band. I get the impression they might have been more than friends."

"Hmmm." Roz lifted a brow. "Some competition for Miles?"

"Mother." Asia elbowed her. "Stop making drama where there is none." Then she looked at Dane. "There *is* none, right?"

"None that I know of. If Miles has competition, then..."'

"Then you'd be happy," Asia said.

"Really?" Roz frowned. "Why? You don't like him? Miles is good people, Dane."

"I don't *not* like him," he said, feeling like he was in a typical two-on-one battle of his mother and sister disagreeing with him. "And no, I wouldn't be happy. I just don't think she should be serious with anyone yet," he added. "Not Miles, not Jimmy, not anyone. My dad hasn't been gone a year, you know."

"What I know is"—Roz pivoted back to the kitchen— "what you think doesn't matter. Eliza Whitney is a grown woman, beautiful and vibrant, and if she wants a man, it's not your call."

Asia shot him a look and whispered, "Says the woman who thinks *everything* is her call."

He laughed at that. "I'm painfully aware of that, Roz," he said, then followed Asia into the kitchen, blinking at the open boxes, dishes, pots and pans, and all manner of utensils. "Wow, did you own all this?"

"My brother shipped some stuff I had in storage up north when I moved here and it's been in my parents' garage for months," she said.

"The rest is my duplicates," Roz told him, lifting a spatula. "I can spare lots of stuff. When are you moving in, Dane?"

"Not sure, but it'll only take about one easy trip, since everything I own fits in a suitcase and a backpack. I thought this place was furnished."

"Not to *my* standards," Roz quipped. "You'll need sheets and towels and...things."

"My standards are pretty low," he joked, "but I can hit the Walmart on the mainland and get what I need. I'm not worried. And hey..." He grinned at Asia. "I have a job."

"That's so cool!" She tapped his arm and hooted.

"Asia, hush," her mother said. "Or you will have that baby back in your arms. And he's had such a fussy day."

"He's had a normal baby day," she said to Dane. "Which means he fusses at times. Hope you can deal."

"I can deal," he assured her.

"He wouldn't fuss if you didn't pick him up every time he so much as whimpers." Roz yanked open a drawer and tsked noisily. "Asia, this shouldn't be silverware. Not this close to the stove. This is for cooking utensils. I'll redo it."

Asia let out a sigh. "So tell me more about Jimmy and the bar."

"Find out for yourself," he said. "He wants me to come and play tonight, no busing tables or pouring drinks. And he specifically invited you back."

"Sweet. But I can't—"

"Yes, you can," her mother interjected. "I am quite capable of babysitting my grandson, here or at my house. Whatever you like, Asia. Please, since I'm never going to see him again."

Asia rolled her eyes. "Never? I'm literally ten minutes away."

"You'll want a little fun after a long day of moving," Roz insisted, waving a wooden spoon in her direction. "You should go, Asia."

She angled her head and looked up at Dane, holding his gaze for a moment. "I kind of want to say no. I'd like to stay here and nest..."

"Whatever you like," he said, even though he really wanted her to go.

"But I did write a few more lines of our song and want to play it."

Dane drew back, stunned. "You did?"

"I did, in a notebook like a real songwriter," she said, so enthused he wasn't sure if she was joking or not.

"So it wasn't just...the rum and Coke."

"Stop it," she hit his arm again. "I had half a drink, and I won't have any tonight. But I'd love to hear if I remembered the music right."

He couldn't quite wrap his head around this, just stared at her as he processed the fact that she actually was writing a song with him. This beautiful creature who was also his roommate.

How had this even happened?

"You are staring like you just want me to stop talking about the song," she said.

"No, no, I'm staring...because I was trying to remember the melody." Liar, liar.

Over her shoulder, he saw Roz observing the whole

exchange with a look he couldn't quite interpret. Smug? Amused? Curious?

Whatever, he had to stop drooling over Asia or someone was going to call him on it. Knowing these two women, it could be both of them.

But he was saved by a soft cry coming from a baby monitor on the counter.

"Duty calls," he teased, pushing away from the countertop. "I'll let you go. Tonight, Asia?"

She took less than a second to nod. "I'll drop the baby off with you, Mom, and pick you up, Dane. Around eight?"

"Perfect."

And it was. Everything was so perfect right then, he couldn't quite believe it.

Dane was still smiling when he got home and found his mother at the kitchen table, making an enormous flower arrangement.

"You were gone a long time."

"Oh, man." He made a face, realizing he'd had her car the entire day. "I hope you didn't need the car, Mom."

"No, we have extra cars. My father's is still here. How was your day?" she asked.

"Spectacular." He plucked an apple from a bowl of fruit and sat at the table, fighting a frisson of déjà vu, taken back to childhood when he'd come home from school and talk to her.

"Spectacular? Like this guest welcome arrangement?"

"Almost. Let me guess—another specialty for whosi-whatsit, the magazine reviewer?"

She chuckled, turning to the vase to admire her work. "Her name is Mia Watson, and she'll be here tomorrow. Why was your day spectacular, Dane?"

"Well, I got a job."

She inched around the flowers, eyes wide. "Really?"

"Your, uh, ex. Jimmy. Made me an offer I couldn't refuse, and I spent the day learning how to bartend. Sorry if that's a disappointment, since I have that hard-earned Caltech engineering degree."

"Dane!" She abandoned the flowers and came around to hug him, reminding him that no matter what he threw at Eliza Whitney, she was supportive. Just that thought made him hug her back.

"And he's going to let me play that amazing Steinway to my heart's content. Good guy, that Jimmy."

"He is, but..." She drew back and narrowed her eyes. "He's not really my ex, you know. I mean, we only went out a few times. Well, more than a few, but it wasn't serious."

"It was serious enough for him to remember you right down to the color of your hair."

"Oh." She flicked off the comment. "People remember red hair."

"He also described your 'angelic' voice."

A soft flush covered her cheeks. "That was nice of him."

"And did you know Dutch was a regular at that bar?" he asked before taking a bite of the apple.

She stared at him, absorbing that. "No. So he and my father talked and..." Her eyes flickered. "Well, my dad didn't talk much about me, so my name wouldn't have come up. Anyway, it continues to be a small world, but you have things happening. Wonderful things! What kind of hours are you going to work?"

"As many as I want. That dude is itching to get out, go fishing, live life, and leave the bar, but he's had a hard time finding people to work. So, most every day, I suppose. I'm going tonight just to play, and Asia's coming, too." He pointed the apple at her. "He told me to invite you."

She studied him for a minute, considering the invitation before she shook her head. "I don't know, honey. We have a very big week ahead, with Mia coming and Olivia planning Camille's surprise wedding and..."

"You're scared to see him, aren't you?"

"No, no. Why would I be?"

"I don't know. Maybe you might...realize you're jumping into a new relationship too soon."

She angled her head. "Dane, you've met Miles. You know he's a great guy."

"He is. So's Jimmy. Not that I think you should be with anyone, I just worry that you're being, you know, impulsive. Lonely, maybe. Falling too fast."

She stared at him and sighed. "I'm not being any of those things, but thank you for caring."

"Sarcasm?" he asked, truly not sure.

"Not really, but..." She shook her head again and picked up an orange lily to slide into her bouquet. "I'll definitely get to Little Blue's and see Jimmy. I'd love that. But not tonight. If you're working there, we'll have plenty of opportunities."

He finished the apple, tossed the core, and when he passed his mother, gave her a light kiss on the head. "Thanks for being so supportive, Mom. You're really the best."

She smiled up at him. "I think that's the first time you've given me a kiss since you got here, you know that?"

"Must be my new job. Oh." He gave her a look. "Any chance you have extra sheets or towels? Asia's moved in and I'm hoping to do the same this weekend."

"Dane. This is a resort. We have nothing *but* sheets and towels." She gave him a smile. "And tea, crystals, and seashells. We'll give you enough to get started."

"Thanks, Mom." He headed into his Disney palace for one of the last times, smiling at the rug. *Destiny awaits!*

Right now, he believed it.

Chapter Twelve

Asia

"You have fun on your date now, Asia," Roz whispered, whisking Zee from her arms.

"Really?" Asia almost choked. "You're going right there, now? You want to have a little argument before I leave on what we both know, without a shadow of a doubt, is *not* a date."

"We don't know that, shadow or not." Her mother looked smug as all get out, turning away and holding Zee possessively. "Now, off with you, child. Leave me with my bundle of joy."

Dad stepped out from the living area and shot Roz a look, giving his bald head a rub. "Something tells me she isn't talking about me."

Asia laughed, so grateful for her down-to-earth, wry-humored father. "Just get her off the date kick, Dad. Dane is a friend, a friendly roommate, and now my co-songwriter. Isn't that enough for a guy I just met?"

But even his eyebrow flicked up as he glanced at the white cotton dress she wore, like she'd put on a stinking wedding gown. "Maybe, but you do look real pretty, Aje."

She rolled her eyes. "You're both too much. Take care

of my baby and I'll see you at ten, latest." She blew them a kiss and dumped the diaper bag, heading out before they could engage in more nonsense.

It wasn't a date, and she sure hoped Dane knew that.

When she pulled into the lot behind Shellseeker Cottages, she spotted him immediately, hanging out on a bench in the garden. He stood and walked to the car, dipping down to get in and give her a smile.

"I had to wait down there to save you the indignity of picking me up."

"No indignity at all," she assured him. "Unless your mother and Teddy are going to grill me on my intentions tonight."

He laughed. "No. Did Roz?"

Her look, she hoped, answered the question.

"They'll get used to it," he said. "It's all new and the whole roommate thing, you know?"

"Yes." She grinned at him. "I'm glad you understand. And, honestly, I don't mind picking you up."

"I don't like borrowing cars or getting rides, so my first order of business is to buy a car. I sold my Beamer before I left, but now that I'm gainfully employed, I can't freeload."

"A Beamer, huh?" Exactly the car that someone else she knew used to drive. But the two men couldn't be more different. "Is that what you're buying again?"

"Not on a bartender's salary." He got comfortable under the seatbelt and locked his hands behind his head, letting out a happy sigh. "I still can't believe Jimmy

Thanos offered me a job. And he's so interested in my music. It's like I walked into a dream mentor."

"Did he offer the job and the mentoring before or after you mentioned your mother?"

He let his arms clunk down. "Do you think that's why?"

"Oh, no, no," she assured him.

"Heck yeah, you do."

"No, Dane. I was just curious if that intrigued him or...what?"

"He was definitely intrigued, but..." He screwed up his face. "He's too cool to be that underhanded and he hasn't seen her in more than three decades. For all he knows, she might not have aged that well."

"But she did," Asia said, pulling out into traffic. "You know she's gorgeous, right?"

"Stop," he groaned. "I had no idea my mother's love life would be a factor when I moved here. She shouldn't even *have* one, for crying out loud."

The little bit of humor had left his voice and Asia could tell the subject deeply troubled him.

"You gotta let go, Dane," she said softly. "Her life—love and otherwise—isn't your concern. You should just want her to be happy."

"Yeah, you're right, but..."

"No buts."

"There's a but."

She glowered at him, making him laugh. "Not your concern."

She expected him to laugh, but he gave her a serious look. "You're not the first person to say that to me."

"I know. I heard my mother chiding you this afternoon. This time, this one and only time, Roz Turner is right."

He turned, looking out the window, quiet for a long time. Then he said, "I feel like my dad would have wanted me to keep an eye on her," he said quietly. "So I feel like I'm really letting him down."

Her heart dropped at the admission, the first time she really understood why he was so opposed to his mother's relationship. "But Miles is such a good man."

"No arguing that, but it's very soon. Too soon, in my opinion, which I know"—he raised his hand—"is not my business, even though it feels like it is."

"Didn't your father want Eliza to find love again?" she asked. "I mean, it's my understanding that he was sick for a long time, and you all knew...well, you knew. Surely they discussed what her life would be like."

"I don't think they did, to be honest. We all knew, at some point, that he wasn't going to make it, but we coped by pretending that wasn't true." He sighed deeply. "We all pretended to hope right to the end."

"Even your dad?"

He swallowed. "He didn't talk much at the end at all."

She reached over and put a comforting hand on his arm. "Don't talk about it if it's still too hard, Dane."

"I want to," he said, raw determination in his voice. "I

really want to, because I feel like my mother and sister have somehow finished grieving, and they've healed."

"They're heal*ing*," she corrected. "But it's fair to say they're ahead of you. They've had Teddy and Shellseeker and Sanibel and this found family around them. You haven't."

He looked straight ahead, quiet for the remaining mile and even when she pulled into the gravel lot next door to Little Blue's.

She put the car in Park and took off her seatbelt, turning to him, rooting for the right words that would get him back to that satisfied and happy mood he'd left behind when she picked him up.

Without giving it too much thought, she reached in the back for her bag and pulled out the red dragon notebook.

"We need a name," she said, flipping the cover.

"A name?"

"For our song. The one we're writing. The one we're going to work on tonight if the bar..." She looked around at the practically deserted parking lot. "It's empty. We're going in to write and play."

For a long time, he just looked at her, then unlatched his seatbelt, turning a little to glance at the notebook. "What do we have so far?" he asked.

She turned the book so he could read the words.

"Something...something...is *old*?" he read, trying not to react.

"Hey, I'm a rookie! Cut me some slack."

He laughed with her, the tension in his jaw finally

relaxing as they held each other's gazes. "You're awesome, rookie. I think we're going to write an amazing song."

"Even though it's about your mother?"

He inched back. "How do you know that?"

"Because I saw pain in your expression when we were writing, and I knew you were upset about Miles. Something incited you to write, which I imagine is how lots of great songs get written."

He searched her eyes intently. "It was about my mother and what I saw that night." He looked toward the roof of the car. "Kissing Miles."

"Ew. Imagine that. Kissing," she teased. "How's that for a title? *Kissing Miles*."

"Please, no."

He looked at her again with just enough heat in his eyes for her to know...he *was* imagining kissing. And, God help her, so was she.

She swallowed and looked down. "So, is it going to be called *Mother's Song*?" she asked, going for light to cut through the tension that had suddenly grown thick.

He gave a soft laugh, taking her cue. "How about something not too original and we'll go with the first line —*Change of Heart*."

"Whoa, cliché alert," she teased, but his smile wavered. "What is it, Dane?"

"I don't know," he admitted. "I'm just not feeling it, I guess. Not feeling like writing a song about her or for her..."

"Because you're mad at her?" she guessed.

"Because..." He leaned his head back and closed his eyes, and Asia watched, waiting for him to get to whatever realization he needed. "She's not at the root of my emotions."

She almost didn't want to ask, but she had to. "Who is?" she whispered.

His eyes opened and flashed and her heart fluttered. Was he going to say...her? What would she—

"My dad."

"Oh." She wasn't sure if she was disappointed or relieved.

"Yeah, see, writing songs has been the closest thing to getting over this I have. My grief, I mean. The loss. The anger that I'm twenty-eight years old and don't have a father."

"Dane," she said, reaching a comforting hand out to him. "I can't imagine what that feels like. I'm so sorry."

He nodded, looking down at her hand, silent.

"But you still have a father," she whispered. "I mean, you have everything he was to you. You have his love, his guidance, his memory. You have every lesson he ever taught you, right?"

He didn't answer, but she saw his Adam's apple move as he swallowed and, she imagined, fought tears.

"What did he teach you that you remember most?" she asked gently.

He snorted. "No guts, no glory," he said huskily. "Ask Livvie. It was our dad's motto in life and I...I don't remember his last words to me, because whenever they were spoken, I didn't know he'd go into a coma and not come out, but it's a fair bet they were...no guts, no glory. He lived by that idea."

"And was it that philosophy that helped you quit a tech job to become a musician?"

"Of course."

Asia leaned back against the driver's door and stared at him, a little surprised he didn't already realize what she was about to say. "Dane. *That's* your song. Have you written it?"

"No guts?" He shrugged. "Also a cliché."

"Maybe not the way you're going to write it."

He stared at her, silent.

"I'll help you," she offered, adding pressure on his arm. "But this one has to come from you."

All he could do was nod, and swallow again.

With a warm smile, she closed the notebook. "*Change of Heart* can wait. Let's start this one. Write the melody and—"

"Asia." He put his hand over hers, closing his fingers tightly. "Thank you."

"It's nothing, Dane, I..." Her voice trailed off as he lifted her hand to his lips and gave her knuckles a featherlight kiss.

"It's not nothing," he said softly. "It's...I don't know what it is, but it's really...nice."

She knew what it was. Attraction. Strong, real, and terrifying.

She managed a smile, slipped her hand free, and tipped her head toward Little Blue's. "Well, you gotta do better than 'nice' if we're going to blow in there like

Lennon and McCartney and write a song that wins us open mic night."

The joke worked, breaking the tension as they got out of the car. But her knuckles were still tingling from that kiss.

DANE WAS different inside Little Blue's, Asia noticed. He seemed so much more relaxed, but maybe it was because he worked there now. He joked with Jimmy, moved a table for some customers, went right into the kitchen to get them both some burgers and fries, and wasted no time getting on that piano after they'd eaten and had something to drink.

"You don't have to come up there and sit with me," he said, pushing up. "Let me go mess around with some melodies."

"Okay. I'll sit at the bar. Better view of the piano and I can pretend there's something more than ice in this Coke."

"If you want to drink, Asia, I'm sure you can take some of the backup bottles at your mom's house. No judgment from me."

"But plenty from her," she said on a laugh, making her way to one of several empty seats at the bar. "It's fine. Play for me, Music Man. That's intoxicating enough."

That was all he needed to stride over to the small stage, take a seat at the piano, and stare at it with reverence.

"He's got it, you know."

At the comment, Asia turned to see Jimmy behind the bar, a rueful smile on his face as he looked at Dane.

"Talent?" she guessed.

"Oh, yeah, but there's plenty of that to go around in this world." He leaned down on one elbow to talk privately, not taking his eyes off the stage. "I don't know whether I should take him under my wing and teach him the industry and all I know, or if I should kick him out of here and never listen to another note he plays."

Her jaw loosened. "Why would you do that?"

"Because he's got it. The thing. The burn. The passion. The *soul*." He dragged out the last word and stood up straight, letting his shoulders sag. "And I'm so jealous of his youth and potential that I could punch him in the face."

She laughed, although she wasn't sure if that was the right response. "Well, don't."

"I won't, but..." He narrowed his eyes. "Oh, to have a whole life ahead of me. Man, I'd do things different."

"What would you do?" she asked, vaguely aware that Dane had started plucking out some chords, but the heart-to-heart conversation with a musical legend was just as intriguing.

"For one, I wouldn't be alone."

She inched back, surprised by that. "Alone...in life?"

"Exactly. I had a lot of women in my life, more than I'm proud of, but no one who was that soft place to fall at the end of a hard day."

She sighed. "That's sad and sweet and..." She lifted her brows. "Never too late, Jimmy."

"Yeah. Why do you think I keep asking my boy to bring his mother in here? Did he tell you we used to be a thing?"

"He did. Not sure he used those words, though." Now this was beyond interesting, and also a little concerning. Did Jimmy know Eliza was seeing someone? "How much of a thing?"

"Not as much as I'd have liked, but, man. Perfect example. I went off on an extended tour and when I got back, she was gone to L.A. with Mr. Right."

"And that's why we have him." She pointed to the stage.

"Yeah, yeah. But it's a new day, huh?"

Asia got a little closer, leaning in. "She's not an entirely free woman, Jimmy. Didn't Dane tell you? She's dating Miles Anderson."

He blinked and she could have sworn a little color drained from his ruddy cheeks. "Is it serious?" he asked after a moment.

"Well, she's a fairly new widow, as you know. So I don't think it's that serious, but they are compatible and happy and..." She thought of how many times she'd seen Eliza glowing with Miles—and Miles looking like he'd personally won the lottery every time they were together. "It's solid, so I wouldn't rock that boat."

He made a face. "She got a sister?"

Laughing as she took a sip from her straw, she nodded. "As a matter of fact, yes. And she lives here on

Sanibel, but, alas, there's a man in her life, too. Father of her son, though they're not married."

He grunted and picked up a rag, playfully pointing it at her. "And you're too young, beautiful, and nuts about Dane, I suppose," he said, his smile just silly enough for her to know he was joking and not hitting on her.

Then she realized what he'd said. "Nuts about..." She glanced at Dane, not sure how to respond. "We're just, you know, friends. We both needed to share a place and I have a child and we don't really..."

Jimmy chuckled, nodding at a couple who sat at the other end of the bar. "Like I said, nuts. 'Scuze me, Asia."

She lifted her Coke and nodded, then turned back to Dane, who had his eyes closed as his fingers moved, a plaintive, soft, emotional tune magically taking shape under his touch. He was talented and she didn't care what Jimmy said, that kind of skill was rare. Plus, he had the passion and...guts.

She smiled, thinking of the theme of the song he was working on, wishing she'd met this amazing Ben Whitney who'd won the heart of such a desirable woman.

Just then, Dane turned, looking right at her, holding her gaze, making her whole body...do stupid things. Stupid, stupid things.

What was she thinking? Unlike Jimmy, she *did* want to be alone...with Zee. He was the only man she needed in her life, wasn't he? And if she let Dane in, wouldn't they live a lie unless she told him the truth about her son?

The corner of Dane's mouth kicked up and he tipped his head in a silent invitation to join him.

But she stayed still, looking at him, feeling things she had no right or desire to feel, knowing what a tangled web she was getting into.

"No guts, no glory," he mouthed, lifting one finger to beckon her up there.

No guts, no glory.

But she didn't need glory. She needed...she needed... she...stood up and slowly walked to the stage, never taking her eyes off him.

Dane's smile grew and he inched over on the bench, making room for her.

"I can't do this alone," he said softly.

The truth was, neither could she. Maybe she was like Jimmy, after all. Maybe she would regret living her life without a man. Maybe this one—this kind, good-hearted, deeply passionate and wildly brilliant man could be the very glory she needed the guts to get.

"Play it from the top, Music Man."

He turned back to the keys and hit a sweet-sounding note, then played a melody with his right hand, high and sweet, and then launched into what she knew was the first verse.

He leaned closer to her and sang in her ear, "Living on an island of fear and uncertainty...looking for the answer to where I gotta be."

She lifted her brows. "I like it."

"You floated in on the morning tide and took me by surprise, and now I have to make a choice that..."

"Might not be so wise," she finished, wanting to laugh, but they were looking at each other too intently to laugh at anything right then. "We can do better, Dane," she added on a whisper.

"Can we? I'm starting to doubt that."

She sighed, smiled, and leaned into him. "Take it from the top and we'll see what happens."

Chapter Thirteen

Eliza

"Morning walk time!" Claire tapped on the open sliding glass doors of the beach house and called inside cheerily.

"I'm tying up my sneakers," Eliza replied from the living room. "Come on in!"

She looked up to see the always welcome and beautiful face of Claire Sutherland, sister, best friend, and walking buddy.

"I feel like it's been ages since I've seen you," Claire said. "Oh, pretty!" She gestured toward the massive bouquet on the table. "From Miles?"

"From me, to Mia Watson. Can we walk it down to Slipper Snail? I want to check out that cottage one last time and make sure it's perfectly ready for our guest of honor."

"Sure. I forgot the reviewer is getting here today. How long is she staying?"

"I've cleared Slipper Snail for two weeks, but could do some fancy maneuvering if she wants more."

"You think she will? That seems like a long stay just to write a review."

Eliza shrugged as she stood up and closed her hands

around the vase. "She mentioned she might make a vacation out of it, and that's just fine with me. We've kept one cottage open and can juggle guests when they arrive."

"You got that?" Claire asked, letting her go ahead to the sliding glass doors.

"I sure do." Eliza gave her sister a quick kiss on the cheek. "God, I missed these mornings. What is happening in your life?"

"What isn't happening would be a better question," Claire said as they made their way down to the path and headed toward the beachfront cottages. "I have an offer on the apartment in Manhattan, and a good realtor friend who's handling everything. I started studying for the Florida bar, and DJ found a darling little office space on the mainland that I may rent."

Eliza slowed her step and let her jaw drop. "No wonder you've bagged our morning walks. Girl, you are busy. I thought you were going to work from home until you passed the bar."

"I can't. Sophia is...loud."

Eliza lifted a brow. "How goes it with DJ's daughter?"

"Loud." Claire laughed. "I mean, she talks a lot, she plays a lot of music, she's in the pool, she wants to hang out, she's...a teenager. I've never had one of those before, remember?"

"They can be a challenge," Eliza agreed. "Although Dane was only loud on the piano and Liv..."

"Could do no wrong."

"Not that much. I was lucky."

"I doubt luck had much to do with it," Claire said. "You can tell by the relationship you have with Olivia that there's a special connection there. It's amazing and I'm jealous."

"You have a wonderful relationship with Noah," Eliza reminded her. "And I think it would take years and maybe a miracle to have with Sophia what I have with Olivia. Isn't she spending a lot of time with DJ? Wasn't that the whole idea of her living these months on Sanibel and not in California with her mother?"

"Yes, but he's busy, too." She leaned in. "He's back in discussions with Luigi to buy the pizza restaurant at the close of this tourist season."

"What? Seriously? Way to bury the real news." Eliza managed to give her sister a nudge, clinging to the heavy vase. "You guys are downright settled. Starting businesses, being a family. I'd dance with joy, but I might drop this whole arrangement."

"You might drop it when I tell you what you can't see over those flowers."

"What?"

"The doors to Slipper Snail are open," Claire said. "Are you sure Mia didn't check in last night? Or maybe someone else is in there?"

"I sure as heck hope not." Frowning, they stepped up to the patio of the cottage, and instantly got a whiff of lemon cleaning solution, and heard humming. "Is that Katie?"

"Yes, I'm here in the bathroom!" Katie stepped out in

her Shellseeker Cottages polo shirt and shorts, a cleaning brush in hand.

"You've done this place already, Katie," Eliza said, surprised to see her.

"I know, but...perfection, Eliza. We need perfection. And that bouquet has nailed it! Put it right here, I think." She gestured toward the small eat-in table, her long blond ponytail swinging like a pendulum. "Hi, Claire. You both look so surprised to see me here. I want to blow Mia's socks off with every aspect of this resort as much as everyone else, so I thought I'd go over everything one last time. And it's crazy busy today with check-ins."

"You're such a good kid," Claire said, giving Katie a hug. The two of them had hit it off when Claire first came to Sanibel but now, with Katie and Noah dating and looking more and more serious?

Katie was the daughter Claire longed for—she just didn't realize it yet.

"Thank you!" Katie exclaimed and swept a hand around. "How's it look?"

"Like a dream, Katie," Eliza said. "You've outdone yourself and earned your title as the world's greatest housekeeper."

She took an elaborate bow, deep enough to make that ponytail flop over her head, and with a flourish that made them laugh.

"Then you'll forgive me when I run off to go clean Junonia and Sunray Venus, and please tell me there's at least one early check-out, because the only other person I have working today just called in sick."

"You need help?" Eliza asked, eyes wide. "I didn't know Becky called in. What can I do?"

"Nothing, boss. You just worry about *The Last Resort* review. That's going to change the game around here. Although..." She made a face. "I don't have high hopes for Becky all this week. She's got a bad flu."

"Oof," Eliza said. "Not a week to be down a staff member."

"I'll figure it out," she said on a sigh. And Eliza knew what that sigh was for—all that time away from Harper, her five-year-old daughter.

"Maybe we can get a temporary housekeeper—"

"Sophia!" Claire exclaimed, getting them both to turn in surprise. "She could work until school starts in the fall. Would that help you, Katie?"

"Like winning the lottery," she said. "Does Sophia want to work? She's kind of big on...the pool and shopping."

"She's bored out of her mind and loves hanging with you," Claire said. "If you asked her, she might. If I asked her, it would probably go over like the proverbial lead balloon."

"I won't ask, I'll beg," Katie said, then turned to Eliza. "Is this in the budget?"

"For the time when the most important reviewer ever is staying on-site at the property? I'll find the budget."

Katie looked like she wanted to hug Eliza. "I have been so worried about this week, Eliza. Thank you!"

"You should have asked."

"I thought Becky would be here. Is it too early to call Sophia?"

Claire wrinkled her nose. "She's probably still asleep, but feel free. And don't expect totally smooth sailing," she warned. "You know Sophia."

"The drama mama, as Noah calls her?" She flipped her hand. "I can handle it as long as she can make a bed, clean a shower, and take out trash."

Claire's whole face kind of softened as she looked at Katie, then reached for her. "You are truly one of my favorite humans on Earth, Katie Bettencourt."

Smiling, she hugged back and looked over Claire's shoulder at Eliza, a tad confused. "Why am I getting loved on so hard, you two?"

"Because you two deserve each other in the most wonderful way," Eliza said, feeling a broad smile stretch as the two of them separated.

Claire turned and looked at her, understanding in her eyes. "I guess I do have what you have, Eliza," she said.

"Totally confused," Katie joked. "What are you two talking about?"

"Mothers and daughters," Eliza said. "And daughters...in-law."

Color deepened in Katie's cheeks. "Oh, stop it now, ladies. Noah and I are...still new and finding our way."

Claire took her hand and gave it a squeeze. "No pressure from us, Katie. Just love, I promise."

"Aw. I love you guys right back. Now I gotta call Sophia. And thank you for coming in here and solving all my problems."

"You solved mine," Claire said, stepping away. "Let's walk, Eliza."

After they said goodbye and headed down the boardwalk to the sand, Eliza leaned closer to whisper, "You know what I was thinking up there, right?"

"That I have my very own Olivia and her name is Katie Bettencourt, maybe Hutchins, if I'm lucky?"

"Well, duh, yes, I was thinking that. But also..." Eliza put her arm around Claire. "This is a good season, isn't it?"

"Tourist season? The best."

"No, *our* season. This season. This time in our lives as sisters with families and businesses and...each other."

"The best season of all," Claire agreed, wrapping Eliza in a hug as warm as the sun rising overhead.

ELIZA's amazing mood didn't evaporate all morning, and only got better when she spotted Mia Watson in the parking lot opening an SUV with two sunhats on her head.

"I couldn't pack them!" She tapped the straw hats with one hand and waved to Eliza with the other. "So don't judge."

"Judge-free zone," Eliza assured her as she reached Mia. "Well, for us. You're the resort reviewer. I guess it's your job to judge."

They exchanged a warm hug, the connection between them real and palpable.

"How's Camille?" Mia asked. "The last time I saw you she was in the hospital."

"She's amazing. Healing, very much in love and..." Eliza leaned in. "Has no idea her fiancé is planning a surprise wedding very soon."

"What?"

"Right here at sunset a week from Saturday."

"What amazing pictures we'll get!" she exclaimed. "I have a killer camera to get magazine-quality shots, so please tell me I'm invited."

"Are you kidding? Front row for sure!"

"Love it." Mia flipped back some of her long butterscotch curls as she lifted the SUV's hatchback to reveal her baggage—and plenty of it. "Brace yourself, I definitely overpacked. I think I brought ten bathing suits."

"You'll want them all. A few sundresses, shorts, and sneakers. But..." Eliza lifted her brows. "Yeah. You should be covered."

Mia let out a giddy laugh. "There's a lot of work stuff packed, too. Remember, I have to set up an office in... which cottage am I in again?"

"Slipper Snail, which is a one-bedroom but has a little den and since you said you wanted an office, we moved the sleeper sofa out and replaced it with a desk and comfy chair."

"Oh, Eliza. Thank you. So appreciated, because..." She tugged her to the backseat and opened the door, showing a very large monitor wrapped in beach towels. "I brought my iMac. I still have to do page layouts for my department."

"Yikes, this really is a working vacation for you, isn't it?"

"Yes, but I might have a little fun." She smiled with a gleam in her blue eyes.

"I hope so!" Eliza turned and looked up at the beach house, searching for any sign of Dane. "If my son is available, he can carry this stuff down to Slipper Snail. You want to come with me while I find him, and get the keys?"

"Yes. Is the car safe here?"

"Absolutely. But you might want to, I don't know, leave one hat behind."

Laughing, she took off the extra hat, closed the hatch, and followed Eliza with a bounce in her step.

"For a working vacay, you seem excited," Eliza said. "And that means a lot, because I know you had nine other properties to choose from."

"This was always my favorite, plus..." She gave Eliza an elbow nudge. "There was a surprise incentive, so if I'm distracted during this visit, you only have yourself to blame."

Eliza frowned. "What...wait. The Dornenbergs?"

"Yes!" She threw her head back with a laugh, curls bouncing. "Jeff and Valerie were so kind to come down here last month to give a testimony for Shellseeker Cottages. It really was what put me over the edge when we had to make our final selections for this feature."

Eliza gave a fist pump. "I'm so glad you took that gesture in the spirit it was meant," she said. "I didn't want you to think we were bribing you, but the family aspect of the resort was so important to us. And you knew them from when you were a child on vacation here, so it made sense."

"We've stayed in touch," she said. "We've exchanged some texts, since they wanted to be sure my time here overlapped with their annual vacation."

"And it does," Eliza said. "In fact, they're in Junonia, our two-bedroom cottage, and it's spitting distance from yours, so you'll be nice and cozy."

"Oh, well..." She gave a sly smile. "That'll be...interesting."

Eliza eyed her, trying to guess what she meant. "Awkward or fun or..."

Mia bit her lip and crinkled her nose. "Their son, Alec? The boy I kissed on vacation when I was a teenager? He's going to come down for a week."

"Yes!" Eliza gave a playful fist pump as they walked under the beach house and headed toward the stairs. "How awesome that you'll get to see him again."

"That's what Valerie Dornenberg thinks. Between us, she's gone full-blown matchmaker and is on a mission to get her divorced son remarried. She says she thinks our reunion is kismet."

Eliza drew back, eyes wide. "Does he know about this?"

"He does. In fact, we started following each other on Facebook, then exchanged messages and emails." She let out a happy sigh. "He's just as sweet as he was, what? Twenty-seven years ago? He's forty-one, has one son, went through a pretty nasty split that he really never saw coming. Anyway..." She gave a little shudder. "I'm kind of excited to see him."

Chills danced up Eliza's arms despite the heat. "Well, that is spectacular news."

"We'll see how it goes. I promise you, I'm here to write an amazing feature story on Shellseeker Cottages, not to, you know..."

"Recreate the kiss in the gazebo," Eliza teased, making Mia's musical laugh ring out again.

"Would that be so bad?" Mia asked. "I mean, it could make a very cute sidebar story in the feature."

"Is that Mia?"

They turned at the sound of Teddy's voice, seeing her come down the steps of the main house, arms outstretched, silver curls fluttering in the breeze. "Welcome back to Shellseeker Beach, my dear!"

Mia took the hug that Teddy offered. "I'm so happy to be here, Teddy!"

After they exchanged pleasantries, Eliza said, "I was hoping Dane could help us get bags and some heavier things to Slipper Snail."

"He's taken a run to his new place," Teddy said. "But Noah is around, I believe, at the tea hut. I'll text him to help us out. And you..." She put an arm around Mia. "Oh my," she said. "Someone is very excited and a little nervous."

Mia gave her a surprised look. "Is it that obvious?"

"Only to Teddy," Eliza assured her. "She is our resident empath and is rarely wrong."

"Never wrong," Teddy corrected with a light laugh.

"And, my girl, you feel blissfully pink, which is the color of hope and an open heart."

Mia turned and shared a secret smile with Eliza. "I have both."

And Eliza had no doubt that Shellseeker Cottages would get a wonderful writeup in *The Last Resort.* Unless things tanked with Alec and Mia, but she had a feeling that wouldn't happen.

Chapter Fourteen

Olivia

Teddy called an impromptu girls' night at the beach house for some desperately needed wedding planning. *Surprise* wedding planning.

Teddy and Eliza had opened the doors to the beach house for Olivia, Claire, Katie, her sister, Jadyn, and Sophia, which meant a lot of chatter and catching up before they got down to the business of planning the final details of a wedding the bride didn't know about.

"You look worried," Katie said, sidling up next to Olivia. "Problems at the store without Camille?"

"Sanibel Sisters is the smoothest thing in my life right now," Olivia assured her. "I have a great salesperson and, my goodness, tourists like to shop. I honestly had no idea that people shopped quite this much on vacation."

"They shop and they eat and make messes out of their cottages," Katie said with a rueful laugh. "But, like you, I have a new assistant." She pointed to the lovely teenager, Sophia, currently telling a story and punctuating everything with hand gestures so wild, Teddy kept moving wine glasses away.

"How's that working out?" Olivia asked.

"She talks more than she works, but it's fine. How's Ileana?"

"A godsend now that we have to pull off this wedding. Can we start talking about that? Deeley's home with Bash and is terrible at the concept of bedtimes."

Katie laughed. "Like Noah and Harper. He's teaching her to play video games now. If I hear the sound of *Mario Kart* one more time, I might cry." She made a face. "Should I say no to video games for a five-year-old?"

"You're asking me?" Olivia scoffed. "I think *Mario Kart* is harmless. If Noah wants to dive into *Fortnite*? I might put my foot down."

Katie smiled at her. "You're going to be an amazing mother to Bash."

Olivia just let her eyes grow wide, silent, the slightest lightheadedness washing over her, as it seemed to every time she thought about how much she wanted to be Bash's mother and how tentative her hold was on that right now.

Teddy came over and put a hand on Olivia's back. "I know you want to start."

"Can you taste my nerves, Teddy?" she asked with a smile, the question coming at a time when there was a rare lull in Sophia's chatter, so the others all heard.

"What are you nervous about, Liv?" her mother asked, coming closer.

"A surprise wedding," she told them all.

"You are not in this alone," Claire assured her. "I know Buck asked you to pull this off, but she's my mother and I'm one hundred percent here to help do anything that needs to be done."

"We all are," Teddy added.

"Good because I made the mistake of going on one of those wedding planning websites and I nearly threw up at the first checklist, and this is from a person who uses a checklist to get through her morning bathroom routine. Why is there so much to a wedding?"

"Not this one," Claire said.

"This is just one of my regular parties," Teddy assured her. "With a few 'I do's' and music. And a surprise bride."

"All right," Olivia agreed. "Let's start making lists and assignments."

Teddy ushered them all toward the living room. "I was going to wait for Roz and Asia," she said, "but Roz said Zee was having a little meltdown and they were running late. So let's start."

A few minutes later, Olivia felt a tiny bit better, because apparently everyone knew more about weddings than she did.

"Wait. What's a sweetheart table?" she asked, peering over Jadyn's shoulder as she sketched out the layout for a reception.

"Where the bride and groom sit."

"They weren't popular when I got married," Eliza said. "It's a new thing."

"Then maybe Camille won't want that." Olivia shrugged and wrinkled her nose.

"Oh, I think she'd love that," Claire assured her.

"And she'll love having Miles officiate and Dane play a keyboard when she walks down the aisle."

"But how do we know?" Olivia asked with just a little whine in her voice. "She may not want an aisle or a surprise wedding or...what is she going to wear and how can I get her there without giving it away? Why does he want this?"

"Because he loves her," Claire said. "And, knowing her, she won't hate the idea of being the center of attention without having to lift a finger to make it happen. Have you met my mother?"

While they laughed about that, Eliza put her hand on Olivia's arm. "You're way too tense about this, honey."

"I'm tense about..." She felt her throat thicken, the third or fourth time that day she'd been overcome with emotion. "Everything."

The group cooed with sympathy which, oddly enough, did nothing to make her feel less like crying.

"It has nothing to do with the wedding," her mother said gently. "You are under stress."

"Until this whole thing with Bash is finalized and done, and we've adopted him, gotten married—with a sweetheart table, because that's so cute—then I'm not going to feel great."

"I have an idea!" Jadyn said, looking up at her. "Why don't you two just follow Camille and Buck and have a double ring ceremony."

"That's so awesome!" Sophia exclaimed, waving her hand within inches of a delicate amethyst crystal that Teddy snagged before it hit the floor.

After the reaction to the idea died down, her mother leaned in closer. "Would you feel better if we were planning *your* wedding, Liv?"

"First of all, he hasn't asked."

"But he's going to," Katie chimed in. "I have no doubt."

"Probably," Olivia agreed. "But, no, that's not what's bothering me. I don't like things up in the air, and, as you all know, I don't like not having a plan. And this wedding is icing on the unplanned cake."

"That's not on the list!" Katie lifted her paper and pen. "Wedding cake! Or do we want a dessert buffet? We'll order from Bailey's. All the food, too."

And they were off and running and wedding planning while Olivia mostly listened and felt vaguely sick and unable to concentrate. Why hadn't they heard anything from the Brennans? Did that mean—

"Okay, you wanted to know how to get her to the beach in the perfect dress?" Teddy clapped her hands to get everyone's attention. "I have an idea."

"Hit me." Olivia blinked and forced herself to concentrate.

"Do you have something in mind from the store? Something she loved? It doesn't have to be white."

Olivia frowned, thinking about that. "We got a delivery from one of my favorite designers of a selection of cocktail dresses that would be beautiful. There was a cream-colored lace dress that Camille flipped over when I ordered it. Also a blue silk shift that I loved, and a pink gauzy thing I think you'd look gorgeous in, Mom, or you, Claire."

"Let's take 'em all," her mother joked.

"And tell Camille you need her to try on the lace dress and wear it to the beach," Teddy said.

Olivia tilted her head and considered that. "And she's just going to say yes? I'd need a reason for that."

"A photo shoot!" Katie suggested. "For an ad you're doing?"

"She'd think I'd lost my marketing mind."

"I know!" Mom said. "Tell her that we're doing some shots for *The Last Resort* review and we want that to double as a way to get Sanibel Sisters some publicity, so we're all wearing clothes you carry at the store."

"Brilliant!" Olivia said, pointing at her.

"Yes!" Claire agreed. "We can all get dressed here together and do our makeup and she'll think it's for a photo shoot. Which will also explain the tent on the beach she'll see from up on the deck."

"It could work," Olivia said.

"It *will* work," her mother assured her, patting her back again. "The first thing we're going to do is assign jobs to every person in this room."

"Including us!" Roz's voice boomed from outside the sliding glass doors, followed by her smiling face, and Asia behind her.

"Did we miss all the planning?" Asia asked. "It's totally Zee's fault."

"Where is he?" At least three of them asked the question at the same time.

"With Dane," she said on a sigh so dreamy that Olivia and her mother had to share a surprised look. "Little Zee had the worst teething, miserable, diarrhea-filled, cranky, miserable, pain in the backside—did I say *miserable*—day a child could have."

"No, but you said diarrhea," Sophia joked. "Sounds...delightful."

"It can be delightful, except for that." Asia plopped on the sofa and pushed back her long braids. "But not today."

"And my brother can handle all this misery and diarrhea?" Olivia asked, making them laugh.

"The hard part is over. Zee is crashed, and I didn't want to bring him. Dane's not working tonight and offered to sit." Asia beamed at Eliza. "Your son is a gem and a half."

The genuine warmth and affection in her voice surprised Olivia more than the words. Yes, Dane could be a gem, she supposed. But to have a woman of Asia's caliber—someone so beautiful and independent and brilliant and capable—need Dane Whitney?

Once again, Olivia exchanged a look with her mother. *What was happening here*, they silently, secretly asked each other.

"Did we miss everything?" Roz said, coming into the room after pouring herself some wine. "I'm an excellent wedding planner, you know. There will be seashells, and plenty of them!"

When they agreed and Jadyn wrote "seashells along

the aisle" on her paper, Roz leaned forward and looked hard at Olivia.

"You'll be happy to know I gave you a glowing report today."

She frowned. "Some old customers from when I ran Sanibel Treasures for you?"

"No, no. Those people from Minneapolis. Bash's kin. They came in and did what felt like a forty-minute interview, but they did buy a few things."

Olivia felt the blood drain from her face. "Wait...what?"

"I thought you knew they were going all over town talking to people about you and Deeley," Roz said. "A little intrusive, if you ask me, but I gave you an A-plus on everything, and even told them you ran my store at an excellent profit last summer."

Her words ran together, and Olivia's last sip of hibiscus tea turned to a metallic taste in her mouth. She was vaguely aware that her mother's hand was on her back again, soothing.

"Why are they doing that?" she managed to ask, even though she knew the answer. "Are they trying to find dirt on us?" She looked at Claire. "Is that legal?"

She made an uncertain face. "It's not against the law, but the bigger question is what are they going to do with that information?"

"What information?" her mother asked. "You don't have anything to hide."

"We don't, but...it's so..." She shuddered. "I feel violated. And terrified." Back came the sickening sensation as she stood. "I have to tell Deeley. I have to..." Woozy, she dropped back down.

"Honey, honey, relax," Mom said, wrapping her arms around her. "They're doing due diligence, right, Claire? Just making sure Bash is in good hands, which, of course, he is."

Everyone turned to Claire again, who already had her phone out, clicking away. "I've done a search on Florida law regarding kinship guardians, and I'll forward some case law for you."

Olivia's heart slipped in gratitude for her aunt, a quietly brilliant attorney. "What's it say? Can you net it out for me?"

"They don't have a powerful legal position, Liv," she said, the words as reassuring as her mother's touch. "The state has named Deeley as Bash's legal guardian until he is eighteen. They won't yank that away from him without a very good reason."

"Like the fact that blood relatives want to take Bash?"

"Hard to say, and it would take a ruthless attorney or a very weak judge. Most likely, both." Claire shook her head. "If Deeley wasn't in the picture, then, yes, they could take him with a court order based on something called 'kinship guardianship' and a blood test to prove they're relatives."

"They took his toothbrush," she said glumly. "So I suppose they're doing that."

"But the courts have determined that Deeley is the right guardian, so they'd have to find some real problems in your home life to make the compelling argument to take him away."

"What would be a compelling argument?"

"That you two are somehow unstable—financially, emotionally, spiritually, something that would seriously impact Bash's well-being," Claire said. "And, of course, if there's any issues regarding his safety or security."

Olivia just stared at her. What happened to the whole "you've opened our eyes" thing that Jenny said when she left the house?

"Oh, safety is what they're focused on," Roz said. "Those are the questions they asked. Does he wear a lot of Band-Aids? Does he ever have bruises? Is he unnaturally hungry? Oh, does he cry a lot? I had to laugh, since Bash is...well, not exactly a well-behaved child."

Olivia had to bite back a howl. "Bash? Does he ever *not* have a Band-Aid on would be a better question. Deeley literally calls him 'Bruiser.' And hungry? The kid is bottomless, but not because I don't feed him constantly. And, yes, he cries! Shocker. He's a toddler!"

She threw herself back on the sofa to a chorus of sympathy, giving in to the tears.

"Liv, listen to me," Claire said, bringing them all to silence. "They have the burden of proving that he is their blood kin, and that you are somehow unfit, unstable, or unable to care for Bash. Nothing, absolutely nothing, indicates that is true."

"Is there anything we can do to sort of seal that deal?" Olivia asked.

Claire considered it with a shrug. "It would probably

help your case to be Mr. and Mrs., just for stability. That's no reason to rush into a wedding, though."

Olivia nodded. "Who thought I'd be a shotgun bride with a child that isn't mine..." Her voice caught as she put her hands to her mouth. "Who else have they talked to?" she asked. "Well, that's rhetorical. None of you would know."

"They talked to Noah and me," Katie said, making Olivia jerk her head up in surprise. "But they didn't tell us they were interviewing us. We were having pizza at Luigi's, and they walked by and saw the Shellseeker Cottages logo on my shirt. They told us who they were, and it was all so friendly, but now that I think about it, they asked a lot of questions about Bash." She smiled. "Harper answered most of them, assuring them that she was with him in daycare and he was her favorite."

"In daycare," she said glumly.

"Not any daycare," Jadyn said, waving her hand. "Mine! And now I know why they stopped in the other day."

"They did?" Olivia gasped.

"They just said they wanted to bring Bash a gift, which they did."

"What was it?"

"A coloring book about..." she swallowed. "Adoption."

Olivia stared at her, ice forming in her veins. "What?"

"Actually, he was so not interested in it that when

they left, I stuck it on a bookshelf and completely forgot about it. He never opened it, Liv, I promise."

Olivia searched her face, so confused by these people. "Anyone else?" she asked, looking around.

"No, but I saw them on the beach a few days ago," Teddy said. "I think they were talking to people who'd rented from Deeley."

"Great. Now they probably heard that Deeley had Bash on a paddleboard in shark-infested waters."

"Hardly shark-infested," Katie said. "And he was fine. Deeley saved him."

"I wonder why they haven't talked to me," Eliza said. "I think I know you better than anyone."

"Because they know you won't say one bad thing about Bash, Deeley, or me," Olivia replied, the words tight in her throat. "They're looking for dirt and anyone who looks hard enough can find it. I mean, how hard would it be to discover that I was in Sanibel Treasures when a fire started?"

"Through no fault of your own!" her mother insisted.

"But they did know about that," Roz said, making Olivia—and several others—groan.

"What can I do?" she asked, throwing up her hands.

"Just carry on," her mother said.

"Don't let them rattle you," Teddy added.

"And, for heaven's sake, keep an eye on Bash," Claire added. "His safety and security is the only real stance they have. If they so much as get a picture of him running alone on the beach, you could be in trouble."

"So leash him up? That sounds like my only option."

"Liv, come on," Mom said. "You're being too hard on yourself."

She looked at her mother and sighed. "It's really simple, Mom. If we lose Bash, we'll be crushed. We are a family, no matter what."

"Then you'll fight for him, Liv. I know you will."

She reached over and hugged her mother. "To the death," she whispered.

Chapter Fifteen

Dane

I t didn't take long for Dane to have a routine that he really liked. He arrived at midday, usually after helping his mother and Teddy around the resort, which he promised to continue to do even though he'd moved into the townhouse.

He'd gone onto the mainland and bought an old Honda to get him around, so he wouldn't mind zipping down to the beach in the morning, then doing what needed to be done at Shellseeker Cottages. After that, he'd eat and head into the bar, where Jimmy might have a variety of stuff waiting for him.

Sometimes, he tended bar, cleaned the place, and helped with inventory. Or he did a little backup work in the kitchen with the line cook, Steve, who made the super-simple menu items. One day, he helped Jimmy through a thorny computer issue, and another he ran some errands.

And every spare minute, he got his hands on that Steinway.

Like this spare minute, when he closed his eyes and dug deeper into the bridge of *Guts and Glory*, which some days seemed like a masterpiece, but today—

"Sounds good, kid."

He looked up, surprised to see Jimmy, who hadn't been here when he'd arrived. "Oh, hey. The bar was empty—and spotless—and Steve has the kitchen—"

Jimmy held up a hand as he jogged over to the stage and jumped up with surprising agility for a man of about sixty.

"No guilt, my man. You come for the piano, not that fat paycheck." He grinned and came closer. "Mind if I pop a squat?"

Dane tipped his head in invitation. "Sure. But no fake compliments. I'm up to my eyeballs in a rough spot on the bridge."

"Ah, the tricky transition. That's why I played what other guys wrote." He put his hand on the keyboard and instantly Dane backed off, not even sure what to say. "But you know what I liked?" He played the bridge, and took it up to the minor chord. "Does that work?"

Dane closed his eyes again, listening to the play-through. "Yeah, yeah. And that diminished B? Whoa, that's nice." Without even thinking, he put his hand on the piano keys, two octaves down, and copied the rich, melodic notes.

Jimmy hummed, moving his fingers like they were liquid mercury poured over black and white keys. Dane worked to keep up with him, missed a note, found a better one, then laughed when they slid into the very last chorus.

"It's a good song," Jimmy said. "What's it called?"

"Working title? *Guts and Glory*."

He nodded. "You need one to have the other, eh?"

"Something like that."

Jimmy lifted his hands, plucked a few single keys, then stopped. "Your girlfriend writes the lyrics, I take it. That can be amazing...or a disaster."

So many things wrong with that, from the terminology to the tense. "Well, Asia—who's my friend and roommate, not girlfriend—dabbles in poetry and she's taken a pass at a few lines. We're not exactly Stevie Nicks and Mick Fleetwood."

"Good, 'cause those two were an inferno, then a cinder, if you get my drift." He tipped his head, thinking. "Roommate, as in...there's *really* no romance between you and that gorgeous woman? She tried to tell me the same thing, but I didn't buy it."

He opened his mouth to say, "None at all," but that didn't feel entirely right. "Maybe a spark, but no inferno or cinder."

"Yet."

Dane laughed and elbowed the other man. "I like the way you think, man."

"What's stopping you?"

Oof, the list was long. "We just met a few weeks ago, and both needed a place to live."

"And she has a kid, right? I seem to recall her saying something when she turns down free drinks."

"Yes, she has a baby, about six months old."

"That explains a lot. Where's the baby daddy?"

"There isn't one."

Jimmy snorted. "*Riiiiight.* Immaculate conception?"

"Sperm bank."

"Seriously?" Jimmy's brows shot up. "Now that's a new one on me. You sure? 'Cause why not have one the old-fashioned way?"

He thought about that, and realized that Asia had never really told him. In fact, she never talked about that at all. Livvie was the one who'd told him Zee was conceived through medicine by Asia's choice, and he'd never asked, because it was none of his business. And he figured she didn't want to talk about it.

"Thinking of adding a line to that song?" Jimmy teased, leaning in. "Here, let me write it for you. 'There's no glory at the sperm bank, but it takes some guts to rob...'" He closed his eyes and bellowed. "It sounds a whole lot better than that clown whose name was Bob."

Dane snorted and punctuated the joke with a slamming G minor.

Jimmy's smile faded as he looked at Dane. "You really believe her?"

"I have no reason not to."

The other man nodded, and pushed off the bench. "Hey, listen, kid. I have some news."

Dane turned, curious.

"I got a friend in A&R at Palm Valley Records, down in Miami. You know them?"

"I've heard of them. They do a lot of rap and Latin music, right?"

He nodded. "They do, but they're branching out into pop and soft rock, and my buddy Paul Margolis is looking for songs for some new artists they just signed. He's coming to Sanibel for a while, like he does every year, and I can get him here for the open mic. You want to play for him?"

Dane blinked in response, not able to wrap his head around auditioning for the artists and repertoire executive at a legit label. "Are you kidding?"

"I told you I never kid about music. I'll make it happen."

"That's amazing, Jimmy, thanks." He pushed up and closed the key cover. "And I should restock some of the inventory before tonight's rush."

Jimmy smiled and gestured toward the piano "Work on your song, kid. That's where your future is, not a bar. I like listening to it."

He turned and popped off the stage, humming the song they'd just played together.

Dane finished the bridge, polished the last chorus, and spent the rest of the day looking forward to telling Asia the news about Palm Valley Records.

Funny, she was his first thought. Not his mother, not Liv. But Asia. He wasn't sure when that happened, but it had.

WHEN DANE WALKED into the townhouse around six, Asia turned from the stove with a grin a mile wide. "I hope you like chicken parmesan."

What he liked was...*her*. Blinding smile, espresso eyes, warmth from top to bottom.

Wow, he had it bad.

"Like it? I love it." He put his backpack on the counter and inhaled, smiling at the aroma and their casually domestic conversation. "Asia! It smells like an Italian restaurant."

"Garlic knots. Supposedly good for the milk production, but can cause colic." She wrinkled her nose. "Hope I don't have to pay the price after the midnight feeding."

Domestic? Forget that. This was downright...marital conversation. And Dane tried to be bothered, but couldn't.

Instead, he glanced around the first floor of the townhouse, which she was not-so-slowly transforming into a home. A few too many "shell art" items on the wall, but he knew that was Roz, not Asia.

"Looks clean, huh?" she asked, following his gaze.

"It looks great."

"My baby was an absolute angel today, Dane. I mean, I don't think he cried at all. Just hung out in his bouncy seat, slept for hours at a time, kept an actual schedule so I could do work—I placed someone in a management position at a new client today, thank you very much—and then I had time to clean and make an amazing dinner." She pointed a white plastic spatula at him. "I am the queen."

He beamed at her, sliding onto a stool to stare at her, very happy to be on the other side of a bar for a change. Very happy to be alive right at that moment and in her presence. "All hail Queen Asia."

She waved the spatula as if it were her scepter. "Can the queen pour you a drink?"

"No, thank you." He pushed off the stool. "Just water, and I'll get it. You've done enough for one insanely productive day. But I'll make it a bubbly water, because..." He pulled a bottle of sparkling water out of the fridge. "We are celebrating."

"My wonderful day?"

"And mine." He twisted off the top and held it up in a mock toast. "An A&R exec from a Miami label who is looking to buy songs for new artists is coming to Little Blue's for the open mic night."

She drew back. "And...wait, wait. I know this. Artists and repertoire? Right?"

"Yes, ma'am. And this would be the guy who selects songs—that's the repertoire part—for those artists to record."

Her eyes grew wide and even more beautiful. "Dane Whitney! That's amazing!" She threw her arms around him and squeezed.

"It is." He backed away before he did something stupid, like press a kiss on her hair...or lips. "But, Queen Asia, we need a song. An original, knock your socks off, can't be anything but Grammy-winning song with lyrics and melody and a chorus and bridge and...and...and..."

"All the song parts," she joked, maybe a little bit aware that when he looked into her eyes for too long, he literally forgot everything, including his train of thought.

"Yeah, those," he agreed. "I don't have a piano here,

though. And I know you don't want to go back to Little Blue's tonight to work on it, so—"

"Let's buy one."

"A piano?" His brows shot up.

"One of those little keyboard thingies. Can you use that?"

"For writing purposes? I sure could."

"Well, there's a Walmart in Fort Myers. Let's go after dinner."

"But...Zee?"

"Is portable." She practically sang the words, turning back to the stove. "And, oh my gosh, the garlic knots are done. Perfection! Hope you're hungry!"

As much as he didn't think his day could improve one iota, it continued to chug uphill. Dinner was a ten, Zee never cried all the way across the bridge, into Fort Myers, through Walmart, and back home. And by eleven o'clock that night, they had a pretty darn good song.

He played through the melody for the sixtieth time at least, then turned to say something to Asia, only to see her conked out on the sofa, head back, jaw slack. And even like that she looked like a queen.

Lifting his fingers from the cheap keyboard that he already kind of loved, he took a moment to just drink her in, something he rarely got to do. She was, without a doubt, the most beautiful woman he'd ever seen.

Oh, sure, there were specimens of perfection running around California but they...they were nothing compared to this woman. Asia had fire on the inside, along with a sense of humor, a sharply-honed purpose, and a poet's soul that could really turn a beautiful phrase. Her voice, her laugh, her touch, her essence—all beautiful.

She was the quintessential mother, and friend, and, oh, *man*. This was bad. This was really, really *bad*.

He'd fallen for her. Hard.

Her eyes fluttered and he knew he should look away and not get caught staring like an eighth grader but...he couldn't.

"Am I drooling?" she asked, sitting up and wiping her lips self-consciously.

"No. I am. Sorry." He pushed up and tapped the Off button on the electric keyboard on his way up. "Song-writing party is over, and you have to get on up to your room and join Zee for sleep. Thanks for—"

"Dane."

He picked up her notebook from the coffee table and flipped it closed, handing the dragon-covered pad to her. "Yeah?" he asked, trying to sound casual.

"What does that mean?"

"What does 'the songwriting party is over' mean?"

She angled her head and narrowed her eyes. "When a genius plays dumb, it's not attractive. And one thing you are, Music Man, is attractive."

His whole gut tightened so intensely, he couldn't even respond to the compliment. "What does what mean?" he asked again.

"When you said you were drooling."

He almost smiled. "Now who's playing dumb?"

For a long, long time, she just stared at him, smoking

him with those impossibly dark eyes, searing him though her thick lashes.

"What are we going to do?" She barely whispered the words.

"What are...we're going to..." He knew what she meant. She felt it, too. Maybe she didn't have it quite as bad, or maybe she did. Was that even possible? "We're going to..."

A smile tipped her lips. "I can't wait to hear this."

"You will, as soon as I figure out what to say."

Still holding his gaze, not even blinking, she pushed up from the sofa and rounded the coffee table. Even in bare feet, she wasn't much shorter than he was, maybe two inches.

And when she came to stand right in front of him, their faces were almost perfectly aligned. Eyes to eyes. Nose to nose. Mouth to mouth.

And heart to heart, which, at the moment, was slamming his ribs.

"Then I'll say it for you," she said softly. "We're going to figure it out, stay in our lanes, respect each other, and... and...not let it be too awkward."

"That might be difficult," he said, his hand aching to stroke her cheek and just feel if her skin was as incredibly smooth as it looked. "And complicated. And I'm going to take a wild guess and say you hate complicated."

Her eyes shuttered. "What makes you say that?"

"A woman who chooses to..." He rooted around for the right words without making a crass sperm bank joke like Jimmy had. "A route of such independence that you don't want a man in order to have a baby—"

"Stop." She put a finger to his lips. "Don't go there."

He knew it. But why? He nodded and took a tiny step backwards, as a way to show he totally respected that request. "But you don't like complicated, am I right?"

"I guess it depends. What I do like is...you. And that, like it or not, is going to be complicated."

He took one more step back to give her space. "Can't be any harder than writing a song, huh?" he asked, wanting to break the tension, because he could see it was straining her.

She managed a smile. "Maybe a little."

With that, she blew him an air kiss and slipped up the stairs to her room.

Dane didn't sleep for hours, but then, why would he want that perfect day to ever end?

Chapter Sixteen

Eliza

T he morning they were going to put Ben's ashes in the Gulf was a rare rainy day, so the look on Miles's face when he opened the door didn't surprise Eliza at all.

"Weather mirrors mood," she said, reaching down to pet Tinkerbell, who knew nothing about bad moods, only wagging tails.

"How's yours?" Miles asked, crouching down to get face to face with the two of them.

"I'm okay," she said. "Not...excited, but ready to have this over with. And very grateful we aren't renting kayaks."

"Then you're probably not going to love what I have to say."

They stood at the same time, slowly. "You don't want to go out in this?"

"I can, and I've checked the weather closely. It won't be smooth out there today. I don't trust someone who isn't seasoned, however, so I'm going to have to say no to Dane —or anyone else—driving the boat. More severe storms can come up fast in the Gulf and someone skilled has to be at the helm."

She winced, then nodded. "I get that. Safety first."

"I'm more than happy to take you, Eliza," he said as he ushered her into his house. "We have rain slickers, and I have no issues with a little whitewater." He tipped his head toward the large boat at the dock in the back. "She's seaworthy. But—"

"I get it," she said, holding up a hand. "I'm not going to argue with the captain."

"If you want to try another day, I think we'll be back to typical Sanibel winter weather tomorrow or later this week."

She sighed, thinking about those options. "I wanted to get this...done." She pressed a hand on her heart as guilt rose up. "Not like it's a chore, but this is the anniversary of..." And that guilt slid right up to her throat, turned into grief, and darn near choked her. "Sorry."

"Hey, hey." He wrapped his arms around her, both of them easing into an embrace that was warm and safe and familiar. "I have some happy news," he whispered into her ear. "I'm going to be a grandfather."

She gasped softly, pulling back. "Janie's pregnant?"

He nodded, a huge smile pulling. "I just got off the phone with her. And Matt, of course. They are over the moon."

"I know she's been trying for a long time. That's really wonderful, Miles. Congratulations!"

"Thank you, not that I had a thing to do with it," he said on a laugh. "She's so nervous after trying for so long, though, that they're not going to make their annual trip down here this winter, so I'm not thrilled about that."

"You should go to see her."

"Charlottesville in February?" He glanced out at the boat. "And leave..." Then he looked at her. "My favorite things?"

She laughed softly and leaned into him. "So, what do we do about today?"

"I think you should let me take you, Eliza. Unless that makes you very uncomfortable, or your kids. Consider me a taxi driver, not part of the ceremony."

She sighed, not sure at all how that would go over.

"If I'm at the helm, and you guys are in the fishing chairs, I can't even hear what you're saying," he added.

She turned at the sound of a car pulling in, recognizing Olivia's Mazda. "Let's see what Liv says."

"Go ask her. I'll wait with Tink."

She headed back outside, grateful the rain had stopped on her way over.

"Hey, Elizabeth Mary," Olivia said as she climbed out of the car, dressed in jeans and a soft cotton sweater exactly the color of the gunmetal sky.

"Hey, Livvie Bug." She was about to announce their problem when Olivia added a second squeeze and a little moan that didn't sound good at all. "What's wrong, honey?"

"Nothing. Everything. This day. This event. This... worry on my heart." Her voice cracked, making Eliza hug her again. "This is like the fourth time I've cried this morning," she said.

"Honey, it's hard, I know. We knew this day wasn't

going to be easy, but Dad wouldn't want us to be miserable."

"I'm not, just weepy." She searched Eliza's face. "Are you okay?"

"Well, we do have a bit of a dilemma."

"You forgot the ashes?" Olivia guessed.

"No, they're in my car, in a special box placed in a cushioned bag surrounded by a few crystals and a sprinkling of periwinkle and hibiscus petals."

That made Olivia smile. "How much do I love Teddy? What's the problem?"

Eliza pointed to the sky. "Weather. Miles won't let Dane drive the boat in this, even if it's not raining. There could be whitecaps and some rough winds, so it's him at the helm or we reschedule."

"I'm okay with him at the helm, but Dane might have a fit."

"That's what I'm worried about," Eliza said, glancing past her as a little black Honda motored up. "Guess we're about to find out."

He pulled in behind Olivia and bounded out of the car with a surprising bounce in his step.

"Someone put the fun in funeral," Olivia joked under her breath.

Hoping that meant he'd go with the plan and not make even more whitewater, Eliza walked to the car to greet him, but let Olivia break the news.

"Sorry, skipper," she said when he got out. "Captain Miles has to drive the boat today due to a weather alert.

Are you okay with that or do we need to reschedule to keep the Whitney family event private?"

Eliza braced for his negative reaction, but he didn't say a word, looking from one to the other, then to the sky.

"Yeah, I guess it is a crappy day. I didn't notice."

On the anniversary of his father's death? Eliza searched his face, trying to guess if he was covering his disappointment or resentment or...nope. This was Happy Dane. Well, Content Dane. The boy she remembered from long ago, in fact.

"So you're cool with him taking us?" Olivia pressed. "Because I want to do this today. It's been hanging over our heads and we're ready, so—"

"It's fine," he said. "We've all said our goodbyes. This is a formality for Mom, right?"

Eliza let out a breath and nodded. It was for all of them, but if that made him feel better, and accept Miles on the boat? Then, yes, let it be a formality for her.

"Why don't you two go inside and talk to Miles. I'll get the..." She glanced at her car.

"No, Mom," Dane said. "You go in. Is your car unlocked? I'll bring the ashes up."

"Yes, it is. Thank you, honey." On impulse, she reached out and hugged him, so grateful that he was being a team player and not pouting about Miles.

As she and Olivia walked toward the house, they exchanged a look.

"Wasn't expecting that reaction," Eliza whispered. "Were you?"

"He's changing, Mom. Right before our eyes."

"Do you think it's Sanibel? The magic of the island is working on him."

She smiled as they reached the door. "The magic that's working on him starts with an *A*, ends with an *a*, and has a 'jah' in the middle. Our boy is smitten."

"I guess he is," Eliza agreed. "Well, okay, but why would that make him amenable to Miles driving the boat today? To...anything about Miles?"

"His heart's changing, Mom. That's all it'll take. You'll see."

Really? Eliza glanced over her shoulder, looking at Dane as he gingerly pulled out the gift bag Teddy had given her to carry the cremation container. "Huh. Well... that's wonderful."

Holding on to that lovely thought, and Olivia's hand, she took a deep breath and prepared to bury her husband.

THE WEATHER LET UP ENOUGH for Miles to agree they could head out of his canal, and into the Gulf.

"Not too far," he said to Eliza as he fired up the engine and she stood next to him at the helm. "I don't want to get caught out there and have trouble getting back. It's happened to me before."

She nodded, turning to look at Dane and Olivia, sitting on the swivel chairs in the stern, leaning toward each other, talking. Miles was right about them having privacy. Whatever they said to each other was impossible to hear from the helm, but if they were stopped?

Knowing Miles, he'd go below, because he was just that classy.

She looked up at him, smiling. "Thanks for doing this, Miles. Above and beyond."

"Not at all." He glanced over his shoulder and stole a look at the kids. "Dane was downright warm."

"Livvie thinks Asia is working some kind of magic and changing his heart."

He cocked a brow. "Whatever it takes, right?"

"Right."

They rumbled at a low speed with no wake down the canal, and Eliza slipped into the other seat next to Miles, inhaling the salty air. A few pelicans were perched on a weathered dock they passed, their mighty wings tucked in as they rested. Boats bobbed behind houses and one lone manatee lumbered into a small mangrove cove.

The gray, overcast day gave this normally jewel-toned environment a sad and washed-out palette, and the sunless sky made Eliza glad she'd grabbed a light windbreaker on the way out the door.

"Do you have a speech or something?" Miles asked gently.

"Should I?" She thought about it for a second, then shook her head. "I just thought we'd all say what we loved most about Ben, and flutter those ashes into the sea." Her gaze shifted to the bag that Dane had brought, where the box was tucked away, held securely on his lap. She tried to remember that wasn't Ben, not anymore.

"What was it?" he asked.

She gave him a questioning look.

"What you loved most about Ben," he clarified. "What was it?"

She sighed and smiled, knowing full well that this wasn't Miles being intrusive—he was the furthest thing from that—but caring, and giving her a chance to think about it before she was on the spot.

"He made me laugh," she said simply. "Every day, every morning, every night. He had a very funny way of seeing the world with irony and honesty."

"Good quality to have."

"It was. And...he loved with things other than words."

"How so?"

"He didn't say he loved me that often, but I never once left the house, even if it was to walk down the street and see my neighbor friend, that he didn't say, 'Be careful.' He ended so many conversations like that. At first, I was sad because he didn't say, 'I love you.' But then I realized that was how he said it." She gave a wistful smile. "You're sweet to care about it."

He glanced down from the steering wheel he stood behind, guiding them through the last inlet to the open water.

"I care about you, E," he said. "Your marriage to Ben is a huge part of you, and one that I admire, respect, and..." He lifted a shoulder. "Yeah, I'm jealous, but not because you loved another man. Because you've had such a great love in your life. It's amazing."

She pointed at him. "You just stop being so perfect, Miles Anderson. Stop it right now."

He laughed, and so did she, at the very moment that Dane and Olivia turned and caught that. A shadow crossed Dane's expression, but not Olivia's. She looked happy for Eliza, just like Miles was.

"Gonna kick it up a bit," Miles called out. "Grab a seat and hang on to your hats."

Eliza stayed in the seat next to him, and Dane and Olivia settled deeper into the swivel chairs. As Miles pushed the throttle and the bow of the boat lifted, Eliza closed her eyes and let the wind whip her hair back and gravity pull her toward the back of the seat.

Was it wrong to be talking so intimately with another man on the anniversary of the very day Ben died? Wrong to feel this connection during the throwing of his ashes, whatever that was called? Did her feelings have a whiff of infidelity?

If Ben was watching, would he be hurt? Or maybe he would just say...

Be careful.

She opened her eyes, caught sight of her kids next to each other. Dane had both arms wrapped around the bag, cradling his father's ashes, his eyes closed tight. Olivia was...not okay.

She frowned—every cell in Eliza's body wanted to leap out of the seat and go to her daughter, who was bent forward with both hands over her mouth.

"Liv!" she called over the engine. "Everything okay?"

Without sitting up, Olivia raised a hand to communicate…it was? It wasn't?

Dane instantly leaned over and put one hand on her back, saying something Eliza couldn't hear. Miles turned and looked over his shoulder.

"She's seasick," he called.

"Can we anchor?" Eliza asked Miles.

"Your call," Miles said, lowering the throttle, slowing the boat, and quieting the engine.

"This is good," Eliza said, barely looking around at how far they had or hadn't made it offshore. Instead, she got up and went to Olivia, crouching next to her.

"What's wrong?"

She lifted her head, bone white. "I'm gonna hurl."

"Go below." Eliza helped her up. "Want me to come?"

She shook her head and clung to the walls of the companionway as she made her way to the small cabin below deck.

"Does this always happen to her?" Dane asked.

"Never, but these are rougher seas than we've ever been on before."

Mother Nature punctuated that with enough of a wave to nearly make Eliza lose her balance. With a soft shriek, she slammed her hand on the back of the chair to keep from falling.

"Be careful, Mom."

She smiled at him, knowing he couldn't realize he was echoing his father, but taking that as a sign that this was the spot.

"Let's have our little ceremony when she gets back," she said. "If she feels up to it."

Dane nodded. "You want to go check on her?"

"I'll give her a second, then go down. Would you..." She gestured toward the bag. "Handle that?"

"Sure." He stood and placed the bag on the seat, then reached for her. "It's going to be okay, Mom." He added a hug that nearly broke her heart.

"I know." She kissed him on the cheek then headed below deck, just as Olivia came out of the head, wiping her mouth with a damp cloth. "You okay, Livvie Bug?"

"Pukey." She shrugged. "I feel better, but geez. Who knew I was such a lightweight?"

"You've never been out here when there were white-caps," Eliza said, reaching for her. "It's a rough ride."

"No, I don't think that's it. I woke up this way."

"Well, you knew it was going to be a tough and emotional day."

"I guess." She patted her mouth again. "But I've had these dizzy spells lately, too. Maybe I need to get checked."

"Really?" Eliza came closer. "That's weird. What kind of dizzy? Like you have a virus or did you eat some-thing bad?"

She shook her head, her eyes closing. "Maybe I'm fighting something. I've been exhausted. I literally fell asleep in the back office at Sanibel Sisters the other day and didn't wake up until I heard a customer asking for... What? Why are you looking at me that way?"

"Exhausted? Dizzy? Throwing up?" Her voice rose

with each symptom, the possibility so obvious, she couldn't believe Olivia didn't see it.

"Yeah, I..." Then she saw it. The very little bit of blood left in her cheeks slipped away and Olivia put her hand on her stomach. "Oh my God."

"Is it possible?"

"It's..." She sighed. "Anything's possible, Mom."

"Livvie."

She took a step back as the boat rose and fell on a wave. "Mommy," she whispered, barely breathing the word.

"Yeah. Exactly. You might be one."

Her jaw slowly dropped and her eyes widened. "I can't believe it. I can't—"

"Mom? Liv?" Dane poked his head through the doorway. "Miles says there's a storm brewing. Let's do this, okay?"

"There's a storm brewing all right," Olivia muttered, her hand still on her stomach. "Holy...cow, Mom."

They exchanged a look, silently agreeing not to say a word, then turned to Dane and followed him back up.

There, Miles had opened up the table where they normally ate lovely cold dinners and watched the sunset. Dane had taken Teddy's crystals and laid them out in a circle around the carved wooden box with Ben's initials on the top. A plastic bag held the brightly colored flower petals.

Miles had stopped the boat and dropped the anchor, and very sweetly secured a small bottle of sherry and three glasses on the table.

"You okay, Liv?" he asked.

Her eyes were glistening as she offered a tentative smile. "I'm good, Miles. I'm ready."

"Well, just a few things to note," he said to them all. "The wind is headed east, so you'll want to turn to the starboard side to be safe. This is completely legal, by the way, but the only thing you can put in the water besides the ashes are the flower petals."

"Teddy told me that," Eliza said.

"I'm going to wait downstairs. Let me know when you're ready to head back."

"Thank you," Eliza whispered.

"Yeah, thanks, Miles," Olivia added.

Dane took a step closer, clearly emotional as he put a hand on Miles's shoulder. "Appreciate you, man."

Miles gave a tight smile and a nod, then headed below deck, leaving them alone.

For a long moment, nobody spoke, but when they held hands in a circle, she could feel that Dane's were damp and Olivia's were trembling. The salt spray tickled Eliza's face and did a fine job of covering her tears.

Tears of joy, if she had to be one hundred percent honest. But wasn't that just like Ben, who'd always had exquisite timing. Maybe he had a hand in this. Maybe he slipped over to God and said, "Hey, my girl needs a baby."

Biting back a smile at that thought, Eliza took the lead, said a prayer, then thanked Ben for the best years a woman could ask for.

Dane could barely speak, but he hung his head and

gruffly told his father that he would never be forgotten, and that he was a better man for having had Ben Whitney as his father.

So, so true.

Olivia was a hot mess of pouring tears and out-of-control emotions, stopping after a few attempts and ending with, "I'll love you forever, Daddy."

"Now?" Dane asked, reaching for the box.

Eliza gave him a nod. "Not all of them," she said. "I'd like to save a little."

He lifted the bag from inside and stepped starboard, giving Olivia a look. "You want a turn?"

She shook her head. "I'll just do flower petals, if you don't mind."

"Mom?"

"Flowers for me. You send him off to heaven, Dane."

He did, opening the bag, letting the ashes fall. They didn't flutter in the breeze, but fell straight to the water, swirling in a beautiful circle, like God Himself had used them for a finger painting. Olivia scooped up a bunch of flower petals and stepped next to her brother and opened her hands, watching the lavender periwinkles and pink hibiscus petals fly and float over the circle of Ben's ashes.

Eliza took a handful of petals, too, and stepped between them, tossing them toward the others and whispering the only thing she could think to say. "Be careful, my love. Be careful."

She glanced at Olivia, who was smiling and crying at the same time. "I remember, Mom," she whispered. "That's how Dad said, 'I love you.'"

The fact that she knew that nearly folded her in half. "I'm glad you remember, honey."

Olivia put her head on Eliza's shoulder as Dane closed the bag and stepped back to the table to store the rest.

"If it's a boy," Olivia whispered, "I'm going to name him Ben."

Eliza turned and hugged her, both of them sobbing with sadness and joy. Dane joined them and wrapped them in a big hug as the first fat drops of rain splattered on their faces and washed away the tears.

Chapter Seventeen

Olivia

She had to take a test. That was all that mattered to Olivia—making sure this wasn't some virus or reaction to saying that final goodbye to Dad.

The rain had started in earnest just as they pulled into Miles's canal, giving them all a good soak. She hadn't lingered long at Miles's, not even bothering to dry her hair. She barely whispered much to her mother when they were alone, other than to promise she'd call after she took a test.

Dane was headed to work at Little Blue's and Mom stayed at Miles's to help him put away the boat. But Olivia was a woman on a mission to find the nearest and most accurate pregnancy test she could get her hands on.

The timing made sense, even if nothing else did. She was late, but had chalked it up to the stress of Bash and the Brennans' arrival, planning the insane surprise wedding, and knowing the anniversary of Dad's death had been right around the corner. And she'd been tired and out of sorts lately, but did that mean—

Her phone hummed and the dashboard screen lit up with a call, flashing Deeley's name and number.

Oh, boy. Oh, boy. Oh, *boy or girl.* How was he going to take this?

She sucked in a breath and had to accept the answer: he wasn't going to take this well. Since they'd started dating, Deeley had been crystal clear where he stood on kids—there weren't going to be any but Bash.

Granted, they hadn't discussed it for a long, long time. They had their hands full of toddler at the moment, but what was he going to say? She almost didn't want to know. She wanted to cling to the possibility of a pregnancy without sharing it, or having her possible joy shot down.

"Hey," she said, infusing her voice with calm and light.

"Babe. How'd it go? I can't stop thinking about you."

Her heart turned over and filled with love. "Thanks. It was fine. Not too bad."

"I wish I'd have been there for you. You know I wanted to."

He'd all but begged that morning, but she and Mom and Dane had decided they wanted to do this all alone as a tight unit. They wanted to share the grief and goodbye to the fourth member of their team. And now she was glad they'd made that decision.

If he'd been on the boat when she and Mom...yeah, she'd have told him in a heartbeat.

"It's fine," she promised him, even though deep in her heart she didn't know if anything was fine. "There was some laughter, and really crappy weather, so Miles drove the boat."

"Yeah, he texted me and told me that. Dane was cool? And it was okay to have someone else there?"

"Dane was perfect, in fact." She'd forgotten all about Dane's change of heart. "Miles stayed below deck during our little impromptu ceremony."

"And Eliza?" he asked. "She's okay? Does she need anything to cheer her up?"

Oh, she's cheered, Olivia thought. The idea of a grandchild took a lot of the sting away. "She's with Miles," Olivia said instead. "You know, it wasn't easy, but it was really nice. White caps, though. I, um, got a little nauseated."

"Really?" Genuine concern came through in his voice. "Was it the stress, you think? You said you didn't even want breakfast this morning."

Because it would have come right back up, she knew. "Yeah, the stress. Emotion. All kinds of things." *Like the fact that I might be pregnant.* She squinted through the rain for a place to buy a test. Gas station? No. Welcome Center?

Just what she needed—Penny Conway to find out. She might as well head straight to the local newspaper.

"Are you totally rained out today?" she asked.

He grunted. "Had a few diehards rent boards, but yeah, I'm probably going to get Bash and take him home for the afternoon. Let him get a good nap in his own bed, and Noah can open up here if it clears."

She barely heard what he said, with her entire being focused on the stores along the main road. Bake shop.

Wine and beer. Fish market. Would they sell pregnancy tests at a fish market?

"And still no word from...the you-know-who's," he added, forcing her to pay attention.

The you know...oh. The Brennans. "How long can they hang around here interviewing people?" she asked, increasing the speed of the wipers. As she did, her gaze landed on a familiar sign. "Oh, Bailey's!"

"Bailey's? Why are you going there? Don't you work until seven?"

Work? She couldn't even think about it.

"Um, no. I wanted to stop in and get..." She swallowed. "Some samples for Camille's wedding." And now she was officially lying to the man she loved.

"Ah, yes, the surprise wedding." He chuckled. "Would you want one of those, Liv?"

A wave of dizziness washed over her as she turned into the parking lot. "Oh, I don't know." She couldn't help mentally adding: *Would you want a surprise baby?*

Except she knew the answer would be a resounding no and...she'd have that discussion when she had to.

First, a test.

"Hey, I better go," she said. "I'll see you tonight?"

"No, no, one second, Liv. Don't buy dinner at Bailey's, okay?"

Dinner was the last thing she wanted. "Okay."

"I have something special planned."

"You do?"

She turned into the lot, praying for a parking spot

close to the entrance, because she was not waiting for the rain to let up.

"This was rough on you today, and I don't want... well, I want to ease the pain. When I dropped Bash off, Jadyn said she could babysit tonight, if your mom and Teddy aren't available."

"My mom is, but..." Olivia might have to break some pretty huge news tonight. "What did you have in mind?"

"It's a surprise. Only if it stops raining. If not, Plan B."

Plan B for Baby.

"Okay." She snagged a parking spot. "I'll text my mom and make sure she and Teddy can watch him, and you can drop him off there."

"Maybe now that Dane's moved out, Bash can spend the night there." The invitation in his voice was unmistakable. "That might be nice, huh?"

"That would be awesome," she said. Especially if she had to break news this big and...unwelcome. She tamped down the thought, refusing to go there. "Call me later."

"You bet. I love you, Liv. So much. Be careful, babe."

Be careful. She clung to the words. "I love you, too, Connor."

"Oh, Connor, huh?" He gave a low laugh. "You're serious."

"You have no idea."

He laughed again, blissfully clueless about what she really meant. After she hung up, she sat in the car for a moment, figuring out her game plan. Buy the test, drive home, take the test, and...and...and cross that bridge or jump off it.

Swearing under her breath, she embraced the fact that life had just *changed*. From top to bottom. Beginning to end. Would Deeley be so furious, he'd...what? Leave her? Not a chance. Never in a million years. They'd figure this out. They always did.

Or was this...yet another landmine in their always-exploding relationship?

Taking a deep, calming breath, she pushed open the door and cursed herself for leaving the umbrella she always had in the car in the back office of Sanibel Sisters. Not that it mattered. She already looked like a drowned rat who'd been weeping on a boat not an hour ago.

She didn't even want to think about what the rain and tears had done to her mascara. It was bad enough to feel her locks of long hair hanging like wet snakes down to her soaked shoulders.

What*ever*. She was on a mission.

Inside, the air conditioning gave her wet body a chill, but she cruised back to the small pharmacy section, skimmed the shelves, found the feminine products and... there were the tests.

Instant results. She wanted instant results.

They had three kinds, the brand names blurring in her eyes as she flipped them over one after the other trying to figure out which would be the fastest, and most accurate.

She took all three and hustled toward the shortest

line, looking down at her selection as she placed them on the conveyer belt and put a yellow bar behind them.

Clear Blue, First Response, and Preg Mate? What the heck was—

"Olivia? Is that you?"

She turned to the voice and let out a gasp at the sight of Jenny Brennan clutching a six-pack of Coke, a bag of Lays potato chips, and a Godiva chocolate bar.

"Jenny." Time kind of stood still as she stared at the other woman, processing this chance encounter, thinking about how she looked and...oh, no.

Jenny glanced down at the conveyor belt, then up at Olivia, a question in her eyes.

A million answers danced around her head, ranging from, "Oh, those! For my, um, friend..." to, "Bugger off, woman. What I'm buying is none of your business."

But she said nothing, nothing at all.

"I'll tell you," Jenny said brightly, lifting the Lays. "Being stuck in a hotel room with three kids on a rainy day is not for the faint of heart."

"I...bet."

"Wish I could tell you these are for the kids, but..." She wiggled the chocolate bar. "Mommy needs a break."

Normally, she would have laughed at that, and let the confession take down a whole world of awkward, but... nothing about this was normal. Nothing.

"Well," Olivia said on a sigh. "Wish *I* could tell *you* that these are for someone else." She gestured toward the pink and blue elephants in the room. "But that would be a lie. And you might think a lot of things about me, but I'm not a liar."

Jenny's eyes grew wide.

"Did you find everything you needed?" the cashier asked as she swiped the First Response box.

"Everything. Thank you." Olivia took a breath and looked at the other woman, the woman who might think she had a snowball's chance of taking Bash away from Olivia and Deeley. "Are you done interviewing everyone who's ever met Connor or me?" she asked.

Paling a little, Jenny looked down, quiet.

"Well, when you are," Olivia said, "please stop by and let us know when you're leaving, okay?"

Swallowing, she met Olivia's gaze. "This isn't easy for anyone. We want to do the right thing, and..."

"That's fifty-two dollars and six cents," the cashier said.

"Dang," Olivia muttered, reaching into her bag for her wallet.

"Kids are expensive," Jenny whispered, which got her a sharp look from Olivia right before she shoved her credit card into the reader.

"Like I said, let us know when you're done...threatening our lives." Olivia yanked out the card, slid it in her wallet, and grabbed the bag the cashier offered. "Because if you want to do the right thing? It would be to leave us alone and let us raise our child."

Jenny dropped her gaze to the bag. "Looks like you're going to have a...*nother* child."

"That remains to be seen. All that matters to you is

that we have one, and his name is Sebastian…Deeley. Or it will be, as soon as we adopt him."

With that, she pivoted out of the store, walked through the drizzling rain to her car, and sat in the front seat, shocked that she still had tears left to shed.

But she did, and for ten minutes, she let them stream down her face.

Olivia wasn't sure how long she sat in Bailey's parking lot, but by the time she pulled it together, the rain had let up. Now she had to take that test, and fast. But…didn't Deeley say he was going to get Bash and go home? Then she couldn't go there. Or maybe he said he was going to her Mom's or…what *did* he say?

Something about tonight, something special.

She forced herself to breathe and think, considering where she was. Asia and Dane's townhouse wasn't far at all, and she knew Dane had gone to Little Blue's. Asia would be home and she had the ideal understanding arms to fall into.

Traffic was blissfully light, since most of the tourists were inside, waiting for the sun to shine, so Olivia arrived at the Tortoise Way Townhouses in just a few minutes. She grabbed the Bailey's bag and her purse, hustling toward their unit to knock on the door lightly, knowing the bell might wake Zee.

"Liv?" she heard Asia say in surprise from the other

side of the door as she unlatched it. "I didn't know you were coming over."

"Neither did I. I need to use your bathroom."

She drew back, her dark eyes flickering in surprise. "Okay, sure, come on in. Oh, honey, that must have been a bad event for you."

"At Bailey's? You can't imagine..." She shook her head, realizing she still looked like a dumpster after the rain, and her friend had no idea why. "You mean the ashes. Yeah, it was...something."

Asia's beautifully shaped brows drew together as she took in Olivia's appearance, obviously seeing past the runny mascara and wet hair. "Honey, are you okay? Sick or..."

She lifted the bag. "Or. Go ahead, look inside."

Asia inched the bag open and sucked in a breath. "Whoa. Whoa. Triple whoa. Three of them? You really want to be sure."

"Of course I do, so...bathroom? Do I need to do anything special?" she asked as Asia led her into the tiny townhouse.

"Just pee on the stick, girl, and I'll be right here waiting for you."

"I knew this was the right place to go."

"As opposed to, uh, the house you live in about seven minutes from here?" Asia asked.

"Deeley might be there."

One brow headed north. "And you don't want him to know?"

"Not...yet." She huffed out a breath. "Gimme a second. I'll be right back."

She slipped into the powder room and released one more agonizing sigh before opening the bag.

"Go with First Response," Asia said from the other side of the door. "It was the fastest for me."

Smiling at the advice, and the fact that her friend was so close, she followed the directions, placed the stick on a tissue on the counter, and washed her hands. Only then did she look up and into the mirror, almost laughing out loud at what Jenny Brennan had seen.

Only it wasn't funny, not at all. Her nemesis had seen a woman who looked unstable buying three pregnancy tests. Jenny probably looked at Olivia the way Olivia had looked at Bash's mother. With pity and that smug sense that...she was better than that poor pathetic creature who didn't have her life together.

Tamping that thought down, she opened the door, not surprised to find Asia right there, inches away.

"Well?"

"I haven't looked yet."

Asia gave her a smile and put her hands on Olivia's shoulders. "Girl, you and your man have been through some stuff. Serious stuff. You're stronger than ever. You're going to be great parents."

"He doesn't want kids."

"Tell Bash. What about you? What will you do?"

"Dance with joy. Deeley, I just don't know." She leaned against the doorjamb and grunted. "It's been one hurdle after another with us. When is it going to get easy?"

"Eh, easy is overrated. How are you feeling?" Asia put a loving, maternal hand on Olivia's cheek. "Other than wiped out and like breakfast could come up every day."

"Breakfast, lunch, and dinner. Dizzy on and off. So stinkin'—"

"Tired," Asia finished, nodding. "Aunt Asia. Has a pretty ring to it, doesn't it?"

Olivia nodded and added a meaningful look. "Goes well with Uncle Dane."

"Look at you, making stupid jokes when your fate is sitting on that counter behind you, possibly turning double-lined pink."

"They are stupid," she agreed. "Dane was surprisingly happy today. I mean, for a man who was burying his father on a boat driven by a man wooing his mother? He was...not broken." She frowned and leaned closer to Asia. "Did you do something to fix my brother?"

"If I weren't a beautiful black woman, I'd be blushing, and you'd notice."

Olivia laughed. "Well, well. Surprises in front of me and surprise..." She glanced over her shoulder. "Think it's cooked?"

Asia nodded.

"Here goes nothin'."

As she turned, Asia took her hand. "Hey, listen to me, sister," she whispered. "Every baby is a gift, whether you want it more than your next breath or think it's going to ruin your life. A child is a gift and I'm here for you. I'm always here for you."

Olivia's eyes filled, affection for this amazing woman welling up in her. Then she turned, picked up the stick and stared at the two pink lines.

Asia leaned over her shoulder and looked, too.

Then they both turned and hugged each other, silent for a long, long time.

"Aunt Asia," Olivia whispered. "That *is* pretty."

"So's 'Mommy.'" Asia kissed her cheek. "Congrats, Liv. Welcome to the club."

"Thanks. Don't tell Dane."

She zipped her lips. "Deeley needs to know first. I'm just an innocent bystander here."

This time, Olivia put her hand on Asia's smooth, sweet cheek.

"Did you feel like this?" Olivia asked. "Like...like you were standing at the precipice of a thousand-foot cliff and you had to jump, hoping to fly but knowing you might crash and burn and...and...oh, my goodness, a *baby*."

Asia laughed softly. "No," she whispered. "I didn't feel anything like that."

Olivia squeezed her eyes shut, never imagining this moment would happen, one year after Dad died. She never dreamed that Asia Turner would be the first person to know, or that she would be absolutely terrified to tell the man she loved that he was going to be a father.

This was nothing like she expected, and yet, here she was...expecting.

Chapter Eighteen

Asia

After Olivia left—but not before she dried her hair and borrowed some much-needed makeup—Asia tried to get back to work, but couldn't concentrate. Then Dane called, excited to tell her about a musical breakthrough, his happiness coming through the phone she held to her ear.

But with each word, her heart was heavier. Olivia's news was...too much. Asia wasn't sure why, only that staring at the pregnancy test and holding a trembling friend who just realized how much her life was about to change brought home a thousand memories and realizations.

Livvie and Deeley would marry, no doubt, have their baby and grow their family, and live...happily ever after.

But she would never have that.

"Could you, Aje? Now or maybe in an hour or so?"

Could she what? "I'm sorry, Dane, I—"

"Oh, yeah, I know. Zee. I thought maybe your mother could watch him while we worked on the song. You know, before the bar gets busy. It'll be dead in here until seven."

"You want me to come..."

"And sing," he finished. "Never mind. Dumb idea. I really just wanted to share the chorus with you. I think it's really good and I...wanted your opinion."

The lump in her throat grew to a painful size. "I can't," she managed. "It's just not a good time."

"Sure, sure. I'll tell you about it later. Play it on the Walmart special. Hey, I gotta go, Asia. See you."

He clicked off a little too quickly, as if her rejection had hurt him. But how could she let herself keep getting closer to him?

Every time she thought about that, Asia crumpled with another sob. She needed help. She needed advice.

Dang it all, she needed her mother.

Roz might be a know-it-all, but she was the woman who literally knew it all. The only person on the Earth who knew the truth, and Asia desperately needed advice.

She had Zee up and packed and both of them out the door in ten minutes, heading straight to her parents' house. Roz whipped the door open when Asia knocked, her brows shooting up to her flame-colored turban.

"Is he sick?" she demanded, clearly surprised by the unexpected visit.

"No. But I am."

"What's wrong?" Roz's hand flew to Asia's forehead, in full mother-mode.

"Nothing. Everything. I'm so glad you're here, Mama. I need you." Her voice cracked and she held out the baby.

"Asia baby!" She took Zee and cradled him, but her attention was on Asia. "Of course I'm here. Well, I was at work, but your father had a hankering for my lemon chicken and we made a deal. If he covered the store for me, I'd make him— Why are you crying, Asia?"

"Because you were right."

Her mother managed a sharp laugh and looked down at Zee as she swept them all into the living room. "Did you hear that, baby Zane? Your mother just spoke my favorite words: *You were right.* How often do we get to hear that?"

Asia swallowed her retort, and slumped onto the sofa with a sigh.

"What was I right about?" Roz asked, easing Zee into his bouncy seat, which was next to the sofa, along with his favorite blanket, a stuffed animal, and his teething ring.

Before she answered, Asia leaned forward and gestured toward the array of baby paraphernalia. "You're a good grandma, Roz Turner."

Roz looked up from the seatbelt she latched. "What has brought on the barrage of compliments?"

"I'm just...grateful, that's all."

"Oh, child. I'm just doing what you'll be doing for your baby. Giving *all* you got. Now..." She sat next to Asia and patted her leg. "Of all the millions of diamonds of great advice I've given you, what was I right about this time?"

She exhaled, digging around for how to start this. "Love."

"Oh my, big topic."

"You said if I want to love someone, to be with

someone and share a life, I'm going to have to be honest and tell the truth. Not my fake truth," she added with a dry laugh. "The real truth."

Her mother dropped back on the sofa, her mouth turned down as she processed this. "Dane?" she guessed.

Asia nodded. "I have...feelings."

Roz answered with nothing more than a cocked brow.

"It's obviously very early, but he's...special. He's good and kind and caring and..." Her throat grew thick. "I'm scared to tell him."

"If he's good and kind and caring—which I believe he is—then it won't send him running, if that's what you're afraid of."

"I don't know if I'm afraid of that," Asia whispered. "But I guess I am terrified he'll be profoundly disappointed in me, and never look at me the same. That my past is just too much baggage and that I'm tainted."

"Asia." She put her arm around Asia's shoulders. "Baby, you weren't tainted, just cheated and that changed who you were. You were in a relationship, albeit a very, very bad one, but surely Dane's been in bad relationships, too."

"Not that bad. Not that—"

"Shhh." She rubbed Asia's back with the same gentle touch Asia used when Zee had colic, and the movement soothed her. "He'd be a fair bit more disappointed in you if you let weeks and months go by and you don't let him know you have that baggage. Will it be too heavy for him? We don't know, but that lie could crush you, hon."

Asia closed her eyes and let the words sink in. "Yep. You're right. Man, I hate that."

Laughing, Roz pushed up to grab the teething ring that Zee had dropped. Of course, she produced a perfectly sterile new one from a plastic bag on the table. "Here you go...Zee."

"You never call him Zee," Asia said. "It's a letter, right?"

Roz settled down on the floor next to the bouncy seat, easing the teething ring into Zee's chubby little fingers. "It'll be easier this way," she said.

"Why?"

"Because...Zane and Dane? That won't do, not for two men who will be close...family."

Asia gasped softly. "I don't know about that. I just like the guy, but I don't know—"

"I do."

Asia started to argue, ready to tell her mother that it was far too soon for the word "family" to be bandied about, but then she closed her mouth.

And Roz grinned. "Go ahead, you can say it. Just one more time, right, Zee?" She bopped his nose and made him giggle. "Because a mother can never hear those words enough. So... 'You were right, Mama,'" she sang, grinning at Asia. "Dane's going to be family. I feel it in my bones, and I'm here for it. Now, go ahead and say the pretty words again, Asia."

All she could do was smile, swamped by love for her impossible, amazing, wonderful *smother*. Enough that she slid off the sofa to her knees, getting right next to Roz, and put both arms around her strong shoulders.

"I love you," Asia whispered.

Her mother patted her hand. "I love you, too, baby girl."

"I'm sorry if I disappointed you with my choices in life."

Roz leaned back to give her a look. "A person who truly loves you will never be disappointed in you. Surprised, maybe. Put off a little, sure. Wishing you'd listen to a wiser voice? Absolutely. But if someone really loves you—or is on their way to that—then they won't be disappointed or scared or unwilling to carry your baggage. The best thing you can do to know what Dane Whitney is made of is to tell him the truth. Can you do that?"

Asia pressed her cheek against Roz's shoulder. "Yes. I can now. He wanted me to go to Little Blue's and sing with him. This might be more than he bargained for."

"I've got little Zee, child. You go do what you have to do, and how he responds will tell you everything you want and need to know about this man."

Asia shuttered her eyes and nodded, knowing without a doubt that her mother was right. Dang it.

Chapter Nineteen

Dane

Nothing sounded quite right to Dane's ear.

Maybe that was because another part of his body—the thing that beat in his chest—had cracked a little from Asia's swift and solid rejection.

Yes, she couldn't pass Zee off to Roz all that frequently, but her mother was constantly asking for time with him. They'd had such a connection the other night when they played and every minute since then.

He hadn't asked her on a date, for crying out loud. Just to come and practice for the open mic night.

Or would she bag that, too?

He slammed his hands on a hard D major and tried to drag his brain back into the game.

"That sounds terrible," Jimmy said with a chuckle from the bar.

"'Cause it is." He played a few notes, then pushed away. "Utterly terrible."

"You still thinking about playing for my buddy, Paul Margolis?"

"That's all I'm thinking about, Jimmy. Well..." He gave a tight smile. It wasn't all he was thinking about, but—

"She still hasn't told you, huh?"

He turned from the piano, frowning. "Told me what? That she's going to sing that night? No, she—"

"No, about her kid, you idiot."

"I told you—"

"Yeah, yeah." Jimmy shot a wadded paper towel to the trash bin, and scored. "I think it's got you blocked."

"This song isn't even about her," he said.

"*Guts and Glory*? Who's it about?"

He let out a sigh, and knew better than to even think about lying to Jimmy. "My dad."

"Ah, yes, the stud who stole my girl."

Dane snorted, thinking of Ben Whitney as a stud. But the smile faded, thinking of Eliza Vanderveen Whitney as Jimmy's girl.

"So, did he have guts and glory?" Jimmy asked as he consolidated two nearly empty whiskey bottles.

"It was his favorite saying," Dane replied. "No guts, no glory. Kind of his philosophy of life."

Jimmy nodded, capping one whiskey bottle and tossing the empty.

Then he narrowed his eyes. "Don't make me like the dude," he joked. "I was gone for one tour and, wham! Came back, and Sweet Red had fallen hard for some producer."

Dane chuckled. "Sweet Red?"

"I called her that sometimes. For the hair, you know?"

"Yeah." He turned to the keys and played with a few notes, a line dancing around his head. *A taste of wine...a long ago time...a sip of sweet, sweet red.*

Could he fit that—

"Hello, Music Man."

He spun around at the sound of Asia's voice, yanking him from the songwriting haze. He blinked into the dim light of the bar, not sure he could trust his eyes.

"What are you..."

She climbed up on the stage, nimble and long and lovely. "Here to sing. And write. And...talk."

Something about the way she said the last word caught his attention—not just the hesitancy in her voice, but the seriousness of it.

"Okay. What do you want to start with first?" He ran his fingers over the keys and played a few notes. "*Guts and Glory*? Want to hear that new chorus?"

She swallowed and sat next to him on the piano bench, close enough that their legs were touching. Close enough that he could smell her floral scent and something else. Fear?

"Are you okay, Aje?" he asked softly.

She looked up at him, her dark eyes pinned on him. "I could be. I...I have to tell you something."

"Sure. Here, or...outside?"

She glanced to the bar where Jimmy gave a casual wave, then turned to busy himself with cutting garnishes. "Here is okay. But it's not...going to be..." She splayed her long, lean fingers over the middle octave of keys, lightly pressing for a terribly discordant note. "Easy," she finished.

"What is it?" He felt his whole body tense. "A change

in plans? You want to move? A problem with Zee? Work? What is it?"

She slid her lower lip under her teeth, still looking down. "I lied to you, and I need to tell you the truth."

"You lied about..." He glanced over her shoulder just in time to catch Jimmy give a look their way, then disappear into the back, their last conversation floating in his head. "About Zee?" he guessed.

Her shoulders sank. "You knew?"

"No, no, I just...it doesn't matter." He turned and took one of her hands in both of his, a little surprised that she was trembling. Asia. The strong, independent woman who didn't seem to be afraid of anything. "Tell me. Whatever you want to tell me, Aje. I'm here for you."

She took a deep breath and let it out slowly. "He's not a sperm bank baby," she whispered. "He's...he has a father who I know."

Dane swallowed and nodded, staying silent but still holding her hand.

"We were...involved. I met him through work. I placed him in a coveted job in London, in charge of European operations for a big company based in Ohio. Got a huge commission and he asked to take me out to celebrate before he left and...we got involved."

He knew exactly what *involved* meant, or thought he did.

"It lasted a little more than a year," she added, which made him draw back in surprise. For some reason, he thought she'd be confessing a one-night stand. "Which was much longer than it should have, but he had me... under a spell."

He managed not to react, but nodded.

"And it wasn't a good spell, Dane. He was very...controlling."

"But he lived in London?" he asked, confused.

"He did, but had to come to his company's headquarters monthly, or close to that. Every time he did, he stayed with me and..." She shrugged. "I thought he was my boyfriend. I thought he loved me. I thought I loved him. But I confused love with control, and he had plenty of that over me."

He stroked her hand. "He was upset about Zane?"

Her eyes flashed. "He doesn't know Zane exists."

He stared, speechless. He didn't know? "It doesn't seem—"

"Wait. Just wait. When I found out I was pregnant, I decided to tell him in person. I thought it would be this big dramatic moment and he'd get down on one knee and..." Her voice cracked and she took a minute to compose herself. "It wasn't like that."

"What happened?"

"I knew where his office was, of course, having been the recruiter for the position, so I flew to London, got a hotel and all prettied up, and went to his office to surprise him."

His heart tightened. "And that didn't go well," he surmised.

"Not at all, because his assistant informed me that he was *on his honeymoon* that week."

"He got married?" His whole body rose up in fury. "While seeing you?"

"He sure did. Met the daughter of a very wealthy client, had a whirlwind romance, and married her right around the time I was looking at that pregnancy test."

"Was he going to tell you?"

"I have no idea. I figured the whole thing out, searched out her social media, and honestly was beyond blindsided." She closed her eyes. "I was wrecked."

"Oh, Asia. That's horrible. What did you do?"

She whimpered. "I disappeared. I went back home, I ditched my apartment, and I quit that job. I moved in with my brother and his wife. I told them, and everyone else, that I was pregnant by my own choice with a sperm bank baby. I told my brother I didn't want to live alone while I was pregnant and they, and everyone except Rosalind Turner, bought that story as...my truth."

"But not Roz?"

"She knew about...him. Knew I had a serious boyfriend, and put it all together. I mean, not that he was married, but I told her everything. To her credit, she hasn't even told my dad. I couldn't stand for him to know."

"And the baby's father still doesn't know he has a child?"

She gave him a warning look. "He's not a nice man, Dane. He's not...calm and kind and understanding. He's controlling and forceful and has a hot, hot temper."

He squeezed her hands. "I get it."

"Maybe you do, but probably you don't," she said.

"He's also a liar who used and deceived me, and cheated on his brand-new wife. He's scum. He's worse than... trash. He doesn't deserve me or Zee or any moment of happiness."

With each word, her voice grew tighter, and so did her grip on him.

"Does he know you were in London?"

She lifted a shoulder. "I don't know if his assistant told him, or described me. I never gave my name that day. And I don't know if he ever tried to track me down, but only after this happened did I realize that we never did much outside of my apartment. He never met any of my friends, or my brother and sister-in-law. I was...a fling. And didn't even know it." Her face folded and she covered it with both her hands. "And I'm very, very embarrassed."

"So you've never seen him since then?"

She shook her head. "I ghosted him completely. Dropped all social media, changed my phone number, and...hid. After I had the baby, and my mother suggested I move, I jumped on the chance."

"Why didn't you tell him, Asia? To get financial support, if for no other reason. He owes you, on every level."

She flinched. "I'm scared of him, Dane. He'd have been furious, and he'd have been sure I didn't have that baby, one way or the other. Or he might want Zee."

The fear wafted off her now, and shame. All he could do was wrap his arms around her and pull her closer, calming the trembling that vibrated through her whole body.

"And no one knows but Roz?" he asked. "No one at all?"

She shook her head.

"Why...me?"

She let her eyes close slowly before opening them to look at him. "Because I need to know what you're made of. I need to know what the truth will do to you. I need to know if I can trust you and...and...love you someday."

For a moment, he couldn't breathe. "Asia..."

"I don't know what's going to happen, Dane. I mean, with us."

"There's an 'us'?" he asked on a soft laugh.

But she wasn't smiling. Instead, she angled her head and sighed. "There could be. I know that. Don't you?"

"Know? Hardly. Hope and dream and fantasize like a teenager with a crush? Constantly."

She did laugh at that, her whole expression softening. "Wherever this goes, I couldn't start us out on a lie. So I had to muster up the courage to tell you."

He pressed his hand on her cheek, sighing in gratitude. "Thank you," he said. "Thank you for trusting me."

She searched his eyes, looking hard at him. "Do you hate me now?"

He almost laughed. He almost threw his head back and howled at how ridiculous that was. Instead, he just pulled her closer and held her tight to his chest. "No guts, no glory, right?"

He felt her nod against him, then the pressure of her lips on his cheek.

Easing back, he held her gaze, silent for a long time. In those few seconds, he felt like the whole world shifted, repositioned, and righted itself. It felt like he was exactly where he belonged, and with the right person. He just knew.

"Asia," he whispered. "I'm always here for you and, should you want it to be, your secret is safe with me."

She closed her eyes and leaned in, their lips barely touching before he deepened the kiss, pulling her closer to—

"Hey, now!" Jimmy called. "That monkey business ain't gonna win the open mic night."

They broke apart, laughing awkwardly, then hugging again.

She just clung to him for one more heartbeat, then whispered, "Let's write our song, Dane."

"Okay, Aje. Let's write it." And he had a feeling it would be the most beautiful music he'd ever composed.

Chapter Twenty

Olivia

O livia had Buck Underwood and her Aunt Claire to thank for getting her through the afternoon she found out she was pregnant. While Ileana ran the store, Olivia sat in the back with the two of them, putting the finishing touches on his big surprise event for the next day. They finalized the menu, the tables, the music, and he even helped her pick out Camille's dress. They went with the cream lace, which was bridal and elegant and as classy as Camille.

The decisions were like a tonic that soothed her soul.

Camille had happily agreed to come to a photo shoot, and even thought it best that Olivia choose her wardrobe for the event. She'd been cleared by her doctor to be out and about, and joked about how she felt like dancing.

"Ladies," Buck said when they'd finished, "you are going to make me the happiest man alive."

"I just hope we don't give her another heart attack," Claire said. "And I'm only half-joking."

"She's ready and so am I," Buck replied with unabashed confidence. "Trust me on this."

When they'd finished, Olivia drove to Shellseeker Beach after closing the store a few minutes early, a fresh wave of stress and nausea rolling through her the closer she headed to whatever Deeley had planned for tonight.

Whatever...his plans were about to change.

She wasn't surprised to see his truck parked near the beach house, but when she went up to the main level, there was no sign of him. Bash was in the living room with her mother and Teddy, the *Let's Go Fishin'* game already set up on the coffee table.

"Wibbieeeee!" He bounded over to her, arms out, his blond curls finally starting to get long enough again to flutter when he ran.

"Baby Bash!" She scooped him up and gave him way too many kisses, which he accepted for about three seconds, then bent backwards.

"Play Fishie!" He demanded, pointing to the game.

"I can't right now," she said and braced for the first level of temper tantrum, but he just squirmed to the floor and ran back to the table. Goodness, he had changed in the months since they'd gotten guardianship.

Because they were great parents, she reminded herself, and surely Deeley would see they could do it again.

"Teddy plays!" Bash announced, flopping back to his place at the game.

"And she's winning," Teddy said in a sweet voice, swinging her toy fishing rod back and forth. "Your turn, big guy."

"It's 'Liza turn!" Bash announced, but Eliza wasn't looking at the board. Her attention was locked on Olivia, laser sharp, with a question in her eyes. Of course, she wanted to know if Olivia had taken a test. She hadn't called all afternoon, just waited patiently for the news.

Well, she couldn't tell her here and now. "Where's Deeley?" she asked, looking around.

"He told us to send you down to the cabana when you get here." Her mother pushed up and put her fishing pole in Bash's hand. "Will you fish for me, little love?"

"Yessss!" He whipped the tiny rod and string in circles with a maniacal laugh that made them all smile.

Her mother was next to her in a flash, a gentle hand on her back as she led her past the kitchen and dining area. "I have to show you something in my room," she said. "Come with me."

They turned the corner into the guest suite that was now Eliza's room. There, her mother shut the door quietly and spun around. "Well?"

"Shouldn't I tell Deeley first?" Olivia asked.

"Yes? Positive? Really?" If excitement had a face—a bright, joyous, thrilled face—then Olivia was looking at it. "Oh, Livvie!"

They threw their arms around each other and squeezed, holding onto a moment they'd both hoped would happen someday.

"Sorry I did things out of order, Mom. I'm sure you'd prefer I'd gotten married first."

"Honey, please. I'm just…" She leaned back, her eyes glistening. "But I'm going to pretend I don't know. How are you going to tell Deeley?"

"Carefully." She made a face. "You know he said he didn't want kids."

"The man who carried Bash up the steps on his shoulders half an hour ago, making horsey sounds all the way? He doesn't want kids? Sorry, but you're wrong."

Olivia smiled at the mental image. "I hope. Should I just go down to the cabana now and tell him?"

"Yes," she said without hesitation. "I don't know what he has planned, but he seemed pretty excited."

"Probably a sunset kayak ride just the two of us. He said he wanted to do something special to help me through our Dad-day. Speaking of, how are you?"

"I'm good. I'm fine, really. I stayed with Miles for a while after you and Dane left, and we just talked a lot and..." Her smile widened. "He's awesome, Liv. What a treasure he's been to get me through this first year."

"I'm happy you have him, Mom. And happy that first year is over. Now you're free to fall...you know."

Her mother smiled, a sparkle in her eye. "I know. And this next year?" She put both hands on Olivia's tummy. "Is going to be quite a ride."

They hugged again and Olivia dashed into her mother's bathroom, cleaned up and for the second time that day, borrowed makeup to brighten her skin and eyes. Then she gave Bash a kiss and headed down to the beach.

The rain had cleared up throughout the afternoon, but the storm's residue deepened the orange of the sunset tonight. And the inclement day had washed the crowds from Shellseeker Beach, leaving only a few people scattered and hunched over, looking for shells.

As Oliva got closer to Deeley's cabana, she could see he'd lowered the wooden awnings and closed the business for the day, no doubt so he didn't have to worry about customers while they took their kayak ride.

But she didn't see him, at least until she rounded the other side of the cabana, where she had to come to a stop at the sight of Deeley on his knees spreading the edges of a blanket.

"A sunset picnic?" she asked, a smile growing as she took in the basket of food, champagne on ice, and two plastic flutes.

"It's been so long since we've had one, Liv." He stood and came over to her, both arms extended. "How do you manage to look so gorgeous at the end of a day like the one you've had?"

"Because I'm ending it with you," she whispered as he pulled her closer. While they kissed, she mentally added the rest: *And because I'm pregnant.*

Just thinking that made her whole body tense.

"Oh, Liv." He gave her a gentle squeeze. "I can feel the day working on you. Come on, relax."

"This is really nice, Deeley. Thank you." Holding his hand, she walked to the blanket, which was perfectly positioned to see the sun dipping into the Gulf of Mexico with a golden glow that made everything look magical and warm.

"I can pop the bubbly, but—"

"Do you have a cold water?" she asked. "I'm parched."

"I do." He turned and flipped open a small cooler stocked with bottled water and some more food for his feast. "Here you go."

She thanked him with a smile and twisted off the top as she sat down, her pulse still thumping as she tried to find the right opening and the perfect moment to take this romantic picnic for two to another place completely.

She bought time with a long, deep pull on the bottle while he opened one of his own.

"Thank you for doing all this, Deeley," she said as she twisted the cap back on. "I'm so grateful for the privacy and adult time...because I have something to tell you."

He lifted a brow, then raised a finger. "I have something to tell you, too."

"Okay...what is it?"

He leaned closer and grinned. "You know that shack up near Tahiti Road that used to be a hot dog stand?"

"Um...I think so. Why?"

"It's for sale and...I bought it."

"What?" she blinked at him. "You bought a hot dog business?"

"I bought the property for my second rental business. This time, bikes, mopeds, scooters, and all the beach stuff." His whole face looked like Mom's when she realized Olivia was pregnant. "What do you think? I can finally open a second location. Noah's going to run this one while I get that one up and profitable, which I think I can do in six months."

"That's...amazing. Wow. Big news. Is that what we're celebrating?" Because her news might put a damper on *that* news.

"Yes, that. And...Liv..." He took her hand. "I made a decision. A big one."

"You're going to add more jet skis to this business?" she guessed, considering that's where his head was at the moment.

He laughed heartily. "Yeah, but this is bigger."

"Bigger than jet skis?" she joked.

"Bigger than...anything." He took a breath and leveled his gaze. "Liv, what are we waiting for? Let's just seal the deal."

She searched his face, unsure of what he meant. "The...deal?"

"This. Us. Let's get married, babe. Why should we wait? Let's do it fast, like Camille and Buck. Quickie on the beach." His searched her face, the light in his eyes fading as he took in her reaction. "Or we can do some kind of a big shindig if you want it. But, please, let's not wait any longer."

Her heart dropped so hard and fast, it was a wonder he didn't hear it hit the sand. This was...his proposal? *Let's seal the deal?*

"Deeley...I..."

"You don't want to?" he asked, misinterpreting her hesitation. "Livvie, I thought you—"

"I do, yes, I..." She shuddered out a sigh. "I didn't expect it...like this." Was she foolish for wanting one knee and a little speech? Was she just being a dumb girl clinging to a childish fantasy?

Or was she super emotional and pregnant?

That was the issue, not what he was saying or how he was saying it. He didn't know yet, so she couldn't possibly say yes, even to this...less-than-amazing proposal.

"I have to tell you something first," she said softly.

"Sure. Anything."

She swallowed and looked down at the water bottle in her hands, vaguely aware that she was tearing the paper by jabbing her thumbnail into the bottle grooves.

"Something happened today," she whispered. "Well, not today, but a while ago."

"Your dad?" he guessed. "I just wanted today to be about something different for you. A day you might remember."

"Oh, I will, and not because of this... *Is* this a proposal?" she asked, her voice cracking under the pressure.

A flash darkened his eyes. "Livvie, what is it? What do you want to tell me?"

"I'm, uh..." She inhaled and said the word on a sigh. "Pregnant."

"What?"

She jerked back at the word, blinking in surprise at the force of it. But then, was she really surprised? He'd said from the beginning he didn't want kids.

"Are you sure? How? When? Oh my God, Liv, that changes *everything*."

And there it was in his voice. In his eyes. In his whole body language and response. The thing she dreaded the most.

Disappointment.

And that hurt more than a dagger to her heart. Without giving any thought to it, she leaped to her feet. "Yeah, it does. And you know what? I'm not in the right frame of mind for this picnic and that...*was* that a proposal? Because, it…it didn't sound like much of one. I'm sorry. I'm…sorry."

Without waiting for an answer, she took off, running down the sand at full speed. She heard him call her name, heard the frustration and exasperation in his voice. But what she needed now was to be alone and think.

And he needed that, too.

So she ignored his calls and ran toward the beach house, aching for the arms of her mother—a person who wasn't disappointed because she was having a baby.

SHE WAS BARELY in those arms when Deeley's heavy footsteps pounded on the stairs of the beach house.

Olivia whimpered, not even five minutes into her explanation, which required way more.

"Liv!" He tapped on the slider and pushed it open enough to walk in. "Livvie, please, can we talk?"

"I don't want to talk right now, Deeley."

"Please. I did that all wrong and—"

"Yes," she fired back. "Yes, you did."

Bash made a face and scrambled off the sofa, saying something to Teddy, who stood and picked him up. "We're going to find a book to read," she said.

"And I'll take a walk," her mother offered.

"Please, please." Olivia held up her hand. "Don't anyone run off." Bash had already disappeared down the hall, which she thought was better anyway. "Deeley, I need some time, okay? I'm sure you do, too."

"But, Liv, we have to talk."

"I can't right now. Is that okay?"

"No, actually, it isn't. You just told me—"

She held up her hand to silence him. "Please, let me stay here tonight. Take Bash home, get him ready for bed, and let me stay here with my mom. We'll, uh, clean up down at the cabana."

That look of disappointment played over his face again, but the steam had gone out of his fight. "Fine. If that's what you want tonight, Liv, I won't argue. But, you know, you seem to be so worried about what's going to go wrong with us that you can't see what's right."

Olivia just stared at him, trying to process that.

"Let me get Bash," her mother said.

"No, let me." She didn't want to stand here with Deeley and extend the fight. She didn't want to talk about her baby and their future or *anything*. Her head was spinning, and she could actually be sick.

She slipped into the spare room, looking around. "Is Bash in here?" she asked Teddy, who was sitting on the bed.

She pointed under the bed. "He's hiding from your argument."

She heard a muffled sound coming from under the bed.

Her heart shattered. "Bash?" Crouching down, she lifted the bed skirt to find him tucked in a ball, thumb securely in his mouth. "Hey, buddy."

"Wibbie," he whispered as he sucked.

She reached her hand out to him. "Come out from there, little man. No one's fighting, I promise."

He shimmied out from the tight space, climbing right onto her lap into his favorite place in the world. Teddy tipped her head toward the door and slipped out, leaving them alone.

"Listen, Bash," Olivia whispered. "I need you to be a very good boy tonight and go home with Deeley."

He put his thumb back in his mouth, silent.

"He's going to get you dinner and a bubbly fun bath and read to you and put you to bed. I'm going to stay here with 'Liza. Can you do that for me, baby?"

He stayed very, very still and she waited for the typical Bash answer. *No. Don't want to. Want Wibbie.*

But after a moment, he just scrambled off her lap and looked at her, then nodded, and toddled out of the room, sucking his thumb.

With a sigh of defeat and love and confusion and just a little bit of nausea, she slid to the floor and fell back against the bed. Looking down, she spied the words sewn into the pink rug, reading them upside down.

Destiny awaits!

"Destiny." She put her hand on her stomach and for the first time all day, she was overcome with joy. Pure, unadulterated joy. It didn't matter what anyone— including Deeley—had to say. She was having a baby and it was meant to be.

"Destiny," she repeated, grazing the white thread with her fingertip.

Chapter Twenty-one

Eliza

E liza knew that her daughter was never more together or grounded than when she had a plan, a mission, and a goal. And on the day of Camille's surprise wedding, Olivia focused on all of those things, letting go of her worries and tears.

She and Eliza and Teddy had talked late into the night, and Olivia had exchanged a few brief texts with Deeley. He seemed to wisely sense the best thing to do was give Olivia some space and let her concentrate on the event ahead. That response made Eliza more certain than ever that he was the right man for her daughter, but Olivia would have to come to that conclusion on her own.

For most of the day, Olivia stayed zeroed in on the task at hand, issuing directives, taking calls, and, at Eliza's urging, taking a few rests now and then. They brought Camille—so blissfully unaware of what was happening—to the beach house and Eliza, Teddy, Olivia, and Claire all dressed her, and themselves, for "the photo shoot."

Once Claire was ready, she slipped off to the gazebo to host the gathering while they finished dressing. About the time the guests started to arrive, Olivia offered to do

Camille's hair, so Eliza sneaked away to see her sister and check on the progress and guest arrivals on the beach.

She found Claire in the middle of gazebo decorated with lights, flowers, and an "aisle of shells," laughing with DJ, Noah, Buck, and Miles. When she approached, they all made a fuss over how pretty Eliza looked in the blush dress she'd picked. None more than Miles, who beamed at her and held out his hand.

"I hope you're going to dance with me, gorgeous."

"All night long," she promised, nodding toward the oversized dance floor under the tent that had been set up that afternoon.

"How is my bride?" Buck asked.

"In high spirits after her clearance from the doctor, and ready for this, uh, photo shoot."

"So she really doesn't have a clue?" DJ asked.

"Not one. But she will at some point. When do you want us to tell her?" Eliza asked.

"When she sees me," he said. "You're escorting her, right, Claire?"

"Noah and I are going to have her between us," Claire said. "And when she spots you, we'll tell her. And keep her from fainting."

He laughed. "She won't faint," he said, adjusting the boutonnière on his lapel. "But I might."

The women cooed at that, and Miles and DJ laughed at how cheesy he was, but before they could say anything else, a man approached Eliza, tall, with thick dark hair, and sharp features.

"Ms. Whitney?" he asked.

"Yes, hello. I'm Eliza. And you are...?"

"Alec Dornenberg." He reached for her hand, his handsome smile easily reaching blue eyes. "Jeff and Val's son."

"Oh, Alec! I'm so glad you joined us today, although I know you don't know a soul." She shook his hand. "Just one."

"Is she here?" he asked.

Eliza turned and looked toward the boardwalk just as Mia Watson reached the top of it. "She's about to be."

He followed her gaze and Eliza couldn't resist sneaking a peek at the man who unwittingly helped them win *The Last Resort* profile that would get Shellseeker Beach so much business.

But it wasn't the review or even the resort business that made Eliza smile right then. It was the look on this man's face. His whole expression froze in a look of wonder, amazement, surprise, and anticipation. It was like he was the groom today, as excited as Buck.

"Mia," he whispered, certainly having forgotten Eliza was standing there.

Mia fairly floated onto the beach, looking like sunshine in a sweet yellow sundress with her dark blond waves cascading over toned shoulders. She slowed her step as she reached the gazebo entrance, looking from Eliza to Alec, then laughing softly.

Eliza stepped forward to welcome her into the structure. "I guess I don't need to make an introduction to two old friends."

"Not at all," Mia assured her, then gave Eliza a spontaneous hug. "Thank you." When she drew back, she took a tentative step closer to Alec. "Hey, stranger. Been a minute."

"And we're back in the gazebo." He laughed easily and stretched out his arms for a hug that lasted a few lovely seconds.

Beaming, Eliza put her hand on Mia's shoulder. "As you know, you're the cover for our surprise wedding today. Camille thinks she's coming down here for a photo shoot for *The Last Resort*, and we're all wearing clothes from her store, Sanibel Sisters."

"I got you, girl," she said, pulling out a small but expensive-looking camera. "And I'd love to make that a real sidebar in the story. Good for readers to know there's great shopping, too."

"Awesome. Now I better get back to her, but please, enjoy yourselves today."

From the look on their faces when they exchanged a smile, these two would certainly enjoy themselves today.

After a few more quick conversations, Eliza headed back up to the beach house, but halfway there, she spotted Deeley and Bash, dressed sharply and looking heartbreakingly adorable. Both of them.

"'Liza!" Bash let go of Deeley's hand and ran to her, arms out.

"Look at you, handsome guy!" She scooped him up—carefully, since she was wearing a silk dress, but couldn't resist a kiss on his cheek. As she lowered him, she looked up at Deeley, who'd cleaned up beautifully in an open-collar shirt with a sports jacket, his hair combed neatly. "And you."

"Hey, Eliza," he said, maybe a bit sheepishly. "Where's Liv?"

"With Camille at the house." Bash spotted Katie and Harper and ran off to greet them, leaving Eliza with Deeley.

Deeley watched him go, his expression hard to read.

"Have you two talked yet today?" Eliza asked.

"Just texts. I hope I can..." He shifted from one foot to the other. "I blew it, Eliza. Hard, bad, and does it feel like I do that a lot with your daughter?"

She laughed softly. "You two are finding your way with a very unique circumstance." She glanced at Bash. "And it's going to get more complicated."

"Not complicated," he said instantly. "Not...at all."

Eliza searched his face, trying to figure out what he was feeling. "Are you upset about—"

He held out his hand. "Please. Don't think that, not for one minute. I'm over the moon. A baby? I thought..." He huffed out a breath and ran a hand through his hair, mussing it. "I can't stand how happy I am."

Eliza let out a breath of joy and relief. "Me, too."

"But I reacted...and I..." He groaned. "I love your daughter so much, Eliza. I want you to know that. I love her and I really want to spend the rest of our lives together, with *all* our kids, and you and...this place."

"That's what she wants, too, Deeley."

"Do you?" he asked.

She regarded him for a moment, easing back. "Are you, uh, asking for my blessing?"

"I guess I am." He rolled his eyes. "I gotta get this whole 'asking' thing worked out." He cleared his throat and looked at her. "Eliza? May I have your blessing to have your daughter's hand, heart, and soul in marriage?"

She let out a soft whimper. "Don't make me cry and ruin my makeup, Deeley." She reached out, wrapping her arms around his strong shoulders. "Yes, but..."

"But?"

"Promise me you will never hurt her. You will never disappoint her. Olivia Whitney is a diamond, and she deserves to be treated like one."

"Eliza." He put a hand over his chest and closed his eyes. "You have my word I will love her, protect her, and never leave her side. Thank you."

They hugged again but then she felt the phone in her hand vibrate. She'd forgotten she'd even brought it down here.

"They're almost ready up there. Better get this surprise wedding going." She turned and waved to Claire and Noah. "Come on, you two!"

She gave Deeley another quick hug, suddenly heady with excitement for how everything felt right then. With Claire and Noah, she headed back to the house, grateful for the cool February air, the glorious sunset, and all the potential her life had.

For a moment, she had to slow her step, and Claire turned. "You okay?" she asked on a whisper.

"Better than okay. I'm so happy, Claire. So, so

happy." She reached for her sister's hands. "More than I ever dreamed I could be just a year after the darkest days of my life."

Claire squeezed her hands. "I love you so much," she whispered, hugging her.

"All right, you two," Noah teased, putting a hand on both their backs. "Buck wants her to come down just as the sun sets. You stand here and have a love fest for too long, and we'll miss the moment."

Laughing, they darted toward the beach house, and as they came up the stairs, Olivia stepped out, looking beautiful in a pale blue dress that matched her eyes and provided a gorgeous contrast to her dark hair.

"You're stunning," Eliza said, momentarily overcome by the conversation she'd just had.

"Me? Look at..." She took a step to the side and gestured toward the door, and out walked Camille Durant in an off-white lace cocktail dress that literally took Eliza's breath away. "This lovely lady."

"I feel positively..." Camille smiled and smoothed her silky black hair, her signature bob perfectly accentuating her high cheekbones. "Alive."

"You look more than alive," Teddy said, joining them and smoothing her own bright orange frock that floated down to her ankles. "You look radiant, my friend."

Camille laughed and hugged her. "Well, this is a lovely way to have a coming out. A photo shoot! Are the paparazzi here? Because I feel like a star. Oh, Claire and Noah! Look how dressed up you are. Are you in the photo shoot, too?" She put her hands on Noah's jacket, tugging at the lapels. "Do we sell men's clothes at Sanibel Sisters now?"

"No, I…" He managed a self-conscious laugh. "Well, I thought…that…"

"I told him he could be in some of the pictures," Olivia jumped in to say. "So I told him to dress up."

Eliza and Claire shared a secret look, biting back giggles at the lies that would all be revealed in a few moments.

"Then off we go!" Eliza said, gesturing toward the stairs.

As they'd planned, Eliza and Olivia took a few steps ahead, letting Claire and Noah flank the unsuspecting bride.

They wandered past the garden, turning left on the path that led to the cottages, then took the last boardwalk to the gazebo. As they reached the top of that, Eliza and Olivia slowed their step, glancing back.

"What's all this?" Camille asked, seeing the tent and setup for a party.

"Kind of a surprise," Claire whispered.

Just then, Noah took a very formal stance, crooking his arm for Camille. *"Grandmère,"* he said softly. "It would be my honor to escort you."

"Oh!" She looked a little startled but slipped her hand under his arm for stability. "For what?"

They took a few more steps down the boardwalk, and the small crowd gathered in and around the gazebo turned. The first few notes of Beethoven's *Ode to Joy* rang out over the beach, coming through speakers attached to the keyboard Dane had set up, giving Eliza a shiver of happiness. She remembered when her son learned that piece and how frequently he'd played it.

Camille looked stunned, then her gaze landed on Buck, who stood tall and proud in the opening of the gazebo, his blinding smile directed toward his bride.

"To your wedding, *Maman*," Claire whispered, pulling a small bouquet she'd masterfully managed to hide behind her back. "Abner Underwood is waiting for you."

"My..." She paled a little, pressing a hand to her chest. "I'm...oh, *mon Dieu*." She took a deep breath, unable to take her gaze off Buck. "I am so utterly in love with that man. So in love."

They all shared quick and genuine smiles, and Noah patted her hand. "Then let's get you married to him, so that I can have a *grandmère* and a *grandpère*."

She squared her shoulders, lifted her chin, and accepted the small floral arrangement that Claire held out to her. "*Merci*," she whispered.

Eliza and Olivia turned and started walking down the boardwalk, toward the temporary aisle made of seashells laid out over the sand. Eliza went ahead, starting the slow promenade to the gazebo. There, she climbed the two steps and walked down the small aisle, her gaze locked on the handsome man who was offi-ciating.

Miles gave a slow smile with the slightest hint of a question in his eyes. She knew what the question was. She knew. She certainly wasn't ready to hear it, but for the first time in a year, she had a tendril of hope that someday...someday she might.

She reached him and they shared a loving look, then she turned to watch Olivia walk between the sprinkling of seashells along the aisle to come to them and stand next to her.

Dane's music paused for an extended few beats, leaving nothing but the sound of the waves, the seagulls, and the sigh of their guests until he began to play the traditional bridal march.

Very slowly, between her daughter and grandson, Camille Durant entered her own wedding. At seventy-one years old, the French beauty who'd lived a life some could only imagine, who'd loved and married a man who'd never put her on the pedestal she deserved to be on, who'd taken life's blows and sent them off with a shrug and a laugh...this powerful woman finally found her prince.

And there wasn't a dry eye on the beach.

Except for Camille, who didn't even look fazed by her surprise wedding. She owned it, and the man who loved her.

As she reached Buck, he shook Noah's hand, hugged Claire, then took Camille's hand.

"I love you, Cami," he whispered. "And I couldn't wait another minute to make you mine."

"I love you, Abner. And I adore a good surprise."

"Perfect. I intend to give you a lifetime of them."

She sighed and stepped forward as Miles began. "Friends and family, we are gathered here today..."

Chapter Twenty-two

Olivia

"Look at him." Olivia sighed as she leaned into her mother, gazing across the gazebo at Deeley and Bash, currently giving hugs and kisses to the new bride and groom. "Could he be more adorable?"

"The big one or the little one?" Mom teased.

"Yeah, yeah, the long-haired one is cute, too." She gave a wry smile. "But I'm still mad at him."

"You haven't talked?" Her mother seemed surprised. "I thought he was anxious to speak with you."

"Honestly? After the ceremony and Buck's endless toast to his undying love, and then Camille's equally saccharine speech, Deeley made a beeline to talk to them." She jutted her chin. "What is so important that he's that deep in conversation with Camille?"

"I don't know..." But she sounded...like she did. At Olivia's curious look, she just shrugged. "You need to square things with him, Liv."

"If by 'square,' you mean throw my arms around him and forgive him for not jumping for joy at the most important thing in our lives, then sorry. No squaring from me. He owes me a square."

Her mother sighed and nodded, then put an arm

around Olivia. "You're going to be an amazing mother. You already are, you know."

"Well, I've studied under the master."

Her mother laughed. "And you are going to be a stellar, loving, rock-solid, forever wife."

"Except that I forgot to say yes to that not-so-rock-solid, and rather quite lackluster proposal, so—"

The loud dinging of Buck's fork on his champagne glass almost made Olivia groan at the thought of another toast. She couldn't even drink the champagne, for crying out loud.

"Ladies and gentlemen, friends and family. I hope you'll come to our champagne tower, get a glass of bubbly, and join me for a toast."

Seriously? Another one? She turned to say something a tad snarky to her mother, but Eliza had gone off to talk to Miles. The few dozen guests milled about, and it didn't take long for everyone to get a refill of champagne. Olivia thought about getting something non-alcoholic, but then Deeley came over to her with a flute.

"I can't—"

"Sparkling cider," he said, a light in his golden-brown eyes. "Peace offering."

"Oh, Deeley, I don't—"

"Attention, attention!" Buck called out.

"Here we go again," she murmured so just Deeley could hear her. "You love the lady. She's your forever queen. You never thought you could be this happy. *We get it*."

Deeley tsked and tapped her with his elbow. "Such a cynic, Liv. Don't you believe in love?"

She looked up at him, a thousand responses in her head but all she could do was stare at him, because what she believed was that he was the singularly greatest guy she knew, and they were so compatible and perfect.

"I'm on the fence," she whispered with a rueful smile.

"Really? Don't you want to hear a man extol the virtues of his dream woman and announce to the world that he loves her, can't live without her, and never thought he could be this happy?"

Her breath caught in her throat as she studied his expression and tried to imagine what he was thinking. What he meant by that. What he—

"Ladies and gentlemen, friends and family!" Buck boomed. "I have one more important announcement. My bride and I are very happy to share this day with all of you, and even happier to offer the spotlight to another couple."

Deeley looked down at her and murmured, "Because, Liv, if that public display of adoration and emotion is going to embarrass you, well, I apologize in advance."

"What do—"

He stepped away into the center of the gazebo, not far from where her mother and Miles stood, each holding one of Bash's hands. As if choreographed, they inched him forward toward Deeley.

"You ready, Bashman?"

He toddled over to Deeley and met his high-five. "Ready!"

They turned together, holding hands, and walked toward Olivia, who stood utterly speechless. It felt like everyone's eyes were on her, but only two sets mattered right then—the loving gazes of the big man and the little boy she adored.

"Wibbie! We have a question!" Bash yelled in a terribly loud and practiced voice.

Still holding his hand, Deeley came right in front of her. "Olivia Elizabeth Whitney."

She slowly pressed her hand to her lips as she realized what was happening. And the next breath caught in her throat as Deeley bent down on one knee. Everyone hooted and cheered, loud enough to startle Bash.

But Deeley reached for him and guided him into the very same position, down on one knee.

After noisy *awws* from the crowd, Deeley cleared his throat. Maybe. She couldn't hear much thanks to how hard her heart slammed against her ribs.

"Liv, I have loved you from the moment I laid eyes on you." Her heart may have been pounding, but she most certainly could hear the ache and truth in his voice when he said those words. "From that day to this, you've made me a better, happier man. You challenge me and thrill me and make me laugh every day. You love with your entire being, like you do everything, and being on the receiving end of that is probably the greatest thing that ever happened to me." He put his hand on Bash's shoulder, who gazed up with a face so serious and angelic, she nearly melted. "The greatest thing for both of us."

She managed a breath...barely.

"I can't imagine life without you, Livvie, and I don't want to," Deeley continued. "I want to be by your side until we're seventy-five and come out here to this gazebo to renew our vows, with our kids—*all* our kids—and grandkids and family right here with us." Deeley looked down at Bash with a meaningful nod, and he popped up and reached into his pocket, struggling to find something for a second.

"I got it, Deeley," he muttered, frowning until his little fingers produced a small black box that nearly caused another loud "awww" from the crowd and a whimper from Olivia.

Bash handed the box to Deeley, who held Olivia's gaze as he opened it to reveal a breathtaking solitaire.

"I love you with all my heart and soul, Livvie. Please make me the happiest man in the world and say you'll marry me."

A tear dribbled down her cheek as she stood speechless, doing nothing but letting the moment wash over her. Then Bash jumped up and down, and exclaimed, "Wibbie! Be my mommy!"

She just collapsed to her knees, coming face to face with both of them, throwing her arms around the two men she loved most in the world.

"Yes, yes, yes," she whispered through a cascade of kisses and tears and the echo of a resounding cheer around them.

"I love you," Deeley whispered into her ear. "I can't wait for us to have a baby together. Another baby. And more. I can do anything with you, Liv."

She kissed him and tasted the salt of both their tears, then leaned back to let him slide that gorgeous rock on her finger.

"Bash and I picked it out today," he said proudly. "I got some advice from Camille, who had no idea she'd be sharing the spotlight with you, but she's cool with it. That's what I had to clear with them."

"I bought the ring, Wibbie!" Bash announced. "I picked it!"

"You did great, little man." She kissed his head. "You and Daddy did...." As the word slipped out, she lifted her head. "I mean Deeley."

"I kinda like Daddy," Deeley said, inching close to kiss her.

As they came to their feet, they were almost immediately circled by all the people she loved pouring congratulations all over them.

"Camille!" Olivia squeezed her. "This was supposed to be your day."

"It's *ours*, my Sanibel sister." She kissed Olivia's cheek and hugged her. "Congratulations, *cherie*."

"And you, partner."

Finally, she got to hug her mom, who'd hung back and watched with tears in her eyes.

"Did you know?" Olivia asked.

"He asked for my blessing right before the ceremony."

"Oh." She covered her mouth again, tears welling.

"And you know what, Liv?" She took Deeley's hand

and drew him closer to the two of them. "Dad would have loved this guy."

"Thanks, Eliza," Deeley said with a tight smile. "That means...everything."

Just then the Turners came closer, and Asia gave her a hearty squeeze.

"Told ya he'd be happy about it."

For a millisecond, Olivia was confused. Happy about...oh! Yes! The baby! She'd totally forgotten! She'd been so caught up in the moment, she actually forgot the reason for all this. Except...one look at Deeley and she knew the baby wasn't the reason. This was inevitable. They were inevitable.

And that proposal rocked her world.

Floating on air, she finally accepted the sparkling cider Deeley had offered, laughing as he toasted her with his and managed to scoop up Bash in the other hand. Just as he did, her gaze drifted over Deeley's shoulder, catching sight of her mother walking with purpose toward the boardwalk. Running, almost. Did they forget something? Was she...

Then she saw what Mom was rushing toward...disaster.

Five people—two adults, three kids, and one pack of problems.

"What are *they* doing here?" she whispered, and Deeley whipped around to follow her gaze, grunting when he saw the Brennans.

"I'm going to get rid of them once and for all." He lowered Bash to the floor.

"How?"

He huffed out a breath. "I'm going to tell them to get lost or get legal and if they do, they will fail miserably. I'm going to tell them we're not giving up. Ever."

"I'm going with you." She put her hand in his, and Bash reached up to take hers.

"I come with you, Wibbie."

She exchanged a look with Deeley, who nodded his approval.

"Forever, my darling, Bash," she whispered, squeezing the hands of both her men. "Forever."

It took a lot to rile Connor Deeley. For a former warrior, he was a surprisingly peaceful guy, who preferred a long paddleboard ride to a confrontation. But as they marched across the sand, Olivia could practically feel the steam coming off him.

"This is not a good time," he announced, his fiery gaze locked on Jenny.

"I'm afraid this is the *only* time," the woman said, putting a hand on her oldest son's shoulder. "Riley, can you kids take Sebastian to—"

"No, you will not take Sebastian," Deeley ground out. "Anywhere, anytime. You will no longer discuss taking Sebastian. Is that clear?"

Next to her, Bash pulled on Olivia's hand, looking up at her with confusion in his eyes. She scooped him up and put his head on her shoulder, stroking his hair as she stood next to Deeley in family solidarity.

The bearded pastor looked pained as he sighed. "Listen, Connor, this isn't going to be easy, but we've done our due diligence and met with the county court, and now we have a legal order that states that as Sebastian's blood kin, we are entitled to challenge your guardianship."

"What?" Olivia whispered the word, clinging to Bash.

"You're out of your mind," Deeley said, his voice low and taut. "And I will literally fight you to the death if you think you're going to touch this kid."

Jenny nudged her husband. "Show him the paper. We have the law on our side, Mr. Deeley."

"I don't care if you have *God* on your side—"

Olivia spun and looked at her mother, who stood a few feet away, taking it in.

"Honey, you go with 'Liza now," she whispered, passing Bash to her. "Mom, get Claire over here."

Her mother took him and cooed sweet things in his ear, hustling back to the gazebo as Olivia turned to hear Deeley say, "You want to know what's best for Bash? What's best is that you leave this beach right now before I say or do something everyone will regret."

"Please don't threaten us," Will said. "We do have to—"

"Get out!"

At the edge in his voice, Jenny returned her hand to her oldest son's shoulder. "Take Caleb and Bella down by the water, dear. Find some shells. Give us some adult time."

No surprise, he obeyed, leaving them alone when Jenny stepped closer, raw determination in her eyes.

"Show him the court order, Will," she insisted.

With another put-upon sigh, he opened a folder Olivia just noticed him carrying and produced a legal-sized packet of papers. Just seeing it made Olivia sway on the sand.

They were going to take Bash? Now? *Right now?*

"We can do this very simply," Will said, handing the paper to Deeley. "We have a suitcase full of clothes and toys for Sebastian, a car seat, and everything he needs."

Olivia almost sputtered. "And you're just going to drive off with him?"

"Or we can come back with local law enforcement," Jenny said. "Who will honor the order of the court."

"What is wrong with you?" Olivia demanded of the woman while Deeley skimmed the legal paper. "Why are you hellbent on taking someone's child? Who died and left you in charge of this kid? Not his mother!"

"Olivia, I know this is difficult, but my grandmother died and made a request that we fix a broken family," she shot back.

"By breaking ours?" Olivia demanded.

"But you're *not* a family," she said, the words spoken so softly, Olivia had to lean closer to hear. "Bash is our family, our kin, our blood. Please see this from our point of view. We want to be sure he's somewhere secure and balanced."

"He is!" Olivia exclaimed.

"And you based this whole guardianship on texts that might not have even been real," Jenny continued as if she hadn't even heard. "No one has challenged you, and we believe that's not right."

"What's right is my own court order that states I'm his legal guardian until he's eighteen." Deeley growled the words without looking up.

"Please read carefully, Mr. Deeley," Jenny said, pointing to the paper. "We've established without a shadow of a doubt that you and Olivia have only known each other for a matter of months. Olivia has no legal or legitimate connection to Bash, and who's to say you'll stay together? This living situation is simply far too unstable for our comfort and..." She bit her lip and gave Olivia a sad, sorry expression. "The Honorable Richard M. Foster in the Lee County Family Court agrees."

Just then, Claire swept over, putting a hand on Olivia's back. "Can I help here?"

Olivia stood speechless, unable to make the introduction as Jenny's announcement landed on her heart.

Claire took over, her whole body straight with authority and confidence. "I'm Claire Durant, Olivia's aunt, and this family's attorney," she said with a direct and unrelenting look to Jenny.

At that moment, Olivia never loved this woman more. She was smart enough to know this was a legal issue and risky enough to claim to be their attorney, even though that was truly pushing the boundaries of the law and her license.

"Can you look at this?" Deeley asked, handing the court order to Claire.

Olivia watched her expression as she read, aching for a clue to how real this nightmare could be, but Claire had a completely serene poker face. The opposite of the man next to Olivia.

She put a hand on Deeley's arm, adding a squeeze. "It's going to be okay."

"When these people leave, it will be."

Will huffed out a breath. "Honestly, we didn't want to do it this way, but—"

"But you are," Deeley said. "And, frankly, that tells me everything I need to know about you and what kind of priority you place on Bash's health and stability."

"This is a temporary change of guardianship," Claire interjected, flipping to the second page.

"Is it legit?" Olivia asked.

Claire's sigh told her everything she needed to know, sad enough to make Olivia's whole body want to fold in the sand and cry.

"There is legal precedent for this," she said quietly. "And it is cited here. In the case when both parents are deceased and neither left a legal will—"

"Just text messages," Jenny interjected. "And, let's be honest, anyone could have written them. They weren't vetted, no investigation was done, and we've been able to establish that Bash's mother was known by acquaintances and previous employers to have addiction issues. You can't decide a child's entire life based on text messages found in a phone owned by a woman like that."

Deeley bristled, unable to deny anything she'd said. Good heavens, this family had done their homework.

"But can they just take him?" Olivia asked Claire.

"The closest kin can make the argument that the child belongs with family," Claire finished.

"We are family," Deeley insisted.

"Not by blood," Jenny said. "His DNA test tracked right back to the Royce side of my family."

Olivia let out a soft mew of disbelief and Claire took her arm. "Come here and talk to me privately," she whispered. "You, too, Deeley."

Olivia followed her and glanced at Deeley, expecting him to come closer. But he was leaning over, staring daggers at the pastor. "If you so much as touch that kid..."

"We would never hurt him," Will said.

"You *are* hurting him," Deeley shot back.

"Come on." Olivia took his arm. "Let's hear what Claire has to say."

Still glaring at the guy, then throwing another dark look at Jenny, he stepped away, joining them.

"Please tell me they can't do this, Claire," he said.

"I'm afraid they can," she said.

"Then we're taking Bash. Let's go, Liv. We can—"

Claire held up her hand. "And get charged with kidnapping? Not the solution."

"Then what is?" Olivia pleaded. "Can we call the police?"

"Law enforcement will most likely honor this order and put Bash in a car with them."

Deeley muttered a curse, dropping his head back like he wanted to howl.

"How is this possible?" Olivia said. "There has to be some way to delay this until we can get to court and fight them. They can't take him to Minnesota!"

Panic crawled up her chest as a wholly different kind of nausea rolled over Olivia.

"Can't we buy time?" Deeley insisted.

Claire looked at the paper again. "I might be able to argue some of this if we could get in front of a judge, but it's Saturday night."

"What about that Macgregor guy who did probate on my grandfather's will?" Olivia asked. "He's Miles's good friend."

"Jonathan Macgregor!" Claire's eyes widened as she nodded. "Let me ask Miles if he could get him here."

Deeley didn't wait, but spun around and whistled, silencing the whole wedding, although things had grown quiet as this drama played out. "Miles! We need you! ASAP!"

As Miles jogged over, Claire flipped the page of the document, frowning again.

"What is it?" Olivia asked, hearing the desperation in her own voice. "Do you see something, Claire?"

"Maybe..."

Olivia clung to that as Miles headed over and, behind him, her mother with Bash on her hip, followed.

"Maybe what?" Deeley pressed.

"Well, their main 'stability' argument is predicated on the fact that..." Claire shook her head and looked a little confused. "You're living together and... Livvie, are you pregnant?"

Olivia glanced at her mother, who was a few feet away, holding Bash and listening. "As a matter of fact..."

Claire's face lit up but then Miles joined them. "Hold that thought," she whispered, handing the paper to Miles. "Any chance you could get Jonathan MacGregor here very, very quickly? He might be able to issue some kind of counter order based on personal knowledge of Deeley and Liv. It's a stretch, but worth a try."

Miles took the paper and walked away. "Let me call him."

When he left, Claire turned back to them, taking each of their hands. "Listen to me," she said. "Their entire argument to the judge was predicated on the fact that your relationship is temporary and short-term. They argue the fact that you're pregnant—"

"How does she *know* that?" Eliza asked.

"She saw me buying pregnancy tests in Bailey's."

"Then I'm sure that's what sealed the deal," Claire said. "Not that there's anything wrong with an unwed pregnancy, but in the eyes of a family court, considering that there is no legal will from either parent, this judge saw that as a measure of—"

"We don't have to be unwed!" Deeley said.

Everyone just stared at him, including Olivia, who wasn't sure she heard right.

"I'm serious! Let's get married right this minute, Liv. Right now, in front of everyone we know and love.

There's an aisle, a crowd, a cake, and…and…Miles and whatever else we need."

"Would that work?" Olivia asked, breathless.

Claire tipped her head. "If you're actually married by an official and he happens to have an extra marriage certificate, then it would make a powerful argument to Judge MacGregor. You can snag a license on Monday, but I think he'd kill this order with one of his own."

Deeley put both hands on Olivia's shoulders and held her with a grip of steel. "Liv, I know this isn't the big white wedding you wanted, but—"

"Are you kidding? To save Bash from those people? Yes! Everyone's here and—"

"He's on his way!" Miles called, returning at a fast clip.

"Did you happen to bring a spare blank marriage certificate?" Eliza asked Miles. "Please tell me you're that prepared and amazing."

Miles just grinned. "Why, yes, Eliza Whitney, I am all that and more."

"Then we're getting married!" Deeley announced, snagging Olivia's hand and managing to slide Bash out of Eliza's arms. "Be my best man, Basho!"

Olivia grabbed her mother. "Maid of honor, follow me!"

Claire gave a squeal and Deeley let out another ear-shattering whistle. "Ladies and gentlemen," he called out. "Clear the aisle! Because here comes another bride! And she's all mine!"

There was suddenly commotion and movement and

noise and laughter and the whole world felt like it was spinning out of control in Olivia's head.

Deeley, five steps ahead of her, suddenly stopped, hoisted Bash a little higher and turned to her. "You're sure, right, Liv?"

She stared at him for a minute, loving his fire and determination, the way he held that boy, and the pure love in his whiskey-gold eyes.

"Never been more sure of anything in my life, Connor Deeley."

He hooted and shoved a victorious fist in the air.

"Woohoo!" Bash echoed, throwing his fist up, too.

"We're gonna marry Wibbie, Bash!"

"Yaaay!"

With that, they zipped into the gazebo, with Deeley shaking hands and slapping backs and practically dancing to stand in the same place Buck had. He stopped to talk to Camille, bending over to whisper something in her ear, then throwing his head back in a laugh at whatever she said in response.

"Liv." Mom put her arm around one side. "You ready for this? I mean, I know you live for control, no doubt longing for a good plan and to-do list."

"Eh." She shrugged, channeling her inner Camille. "All that control is overrated."

Her mother laughed. "Good thing you think so, because with a baby and a toddler and a brand-new husband, you can kiss control goodbye."

Olivia smiled. "And kiss my new life hello."

"That's my girl."

She slowly turned and looked over her shoulder, catching sight of the Brennans, who had gone halfway up the boardwalk, but still watched with far too much interest.

"Ignore them," her mother said. "Focus on your moment."

Nodding, she took a deep breath and centered herself, not sure what she was waiting for, but then Teddy came down the gazebo steps side by side with Camille, who had a wide smile on her face and the bouquet still in her hand.

"I'm so sorry," Olivia said breathlessly. "This is so unfair to you, Camille!"

"Hush." She handed the flowers to Olivia. "Carry these. No bride should walk down the aisle without flowers. I gave Deeley my brand-new ring to borrow, but I want it back."

"Oh, thank you! It's something borrowed."

"And your dress is blue," Claire said with a laugh. "Now all we need is old and new."

"This is new." Olivia touched her belly. "Baby's less than six weeks old."

A few of them laughed, a few gasped, but then Teddy stepped closer. "And this is as old as the Earth." She handed Olivia a smooth pink crystal. "For good energy to carry you through your whole marriage."

Olivia felt her eyes well as she hugged a woman who'd truly become her grandmother.

"Now, off you go, Livvie Bug." Mom gave her a nudge. "Surprise Bride Number Two."

"Oh, Mom." Olivia hugged her the hardest. "I love you so much."

"I love you, too," she replied. "Do you want to walk alone or would you like Dane to give you away?"

She thought about that. "Let him play the music. You go first, Claire, then Mom. I'll make this walk alone." She bit her lip and put her hand on her stomach again. "Not entirely alone, though."

Mom gave her a quick squeeze while Claire headed back to the side of the gazebo, talked to Dane, then returned.

In a few seconds, the next rendition of *Ode to Joy* started, and they all three gave a nervous laugh. Then Claire walked, and Mom walked, and Olivia waited for Dane to switch to the song every little girl sings when she dreams of this moment.

No, this wasn't quite what she imagined growing up, but that didn't matter. This was her path, lined with seashells and high hopes, and it was taking her exactly where she wanted to go.

She took her time, even though this was the most rushed ceremony in history, walking slowly toward Deeley and Bash, who stood next to him with his precious face set in a solemn expression. These were her men. Her family. Her future.

Once again, Miles cleared his throat and began to speak. "Friends and family, we are gathered here today to witness the matrimony of...."

Olivia just closed her eyes and let the joy wash over her.

Chapter Twenty-three

Dane

Little Blue's was hopping for open mic night. To make tonight extra special, Jimmy Thanos stepped back in time and played the blues and jazz songs that made him famous, surprising people who had no idea he was anyone other than the long-haired guy who served the beer.

While he played and wowed the crowd, Dane served the drinks.

When Jimmy finished, he invited anyone who wanted to sing to sign up at the bar, then he came back, his eyes bright with the rush that came from playing to any size of crowd.

They tapped knuckles and just as Dane was about to congratulate him on a set well played, Jimmy looked over his shoulder at the door.

"*Aja...*" Jimmy sang, hitting the high note of the well-known Steely Dan song. "I run to you..."

Dane smiled and waited a beat before turning, knowing that the moment he laid eyes on her, his heart would kick a little. It did, of course.

He was still getting used to the fact that she...liked him. And not as a roommate or a friend. Ever since the wedding—weddings, if he counted his sister's sponta-neous marriage that day—he and Asia had just *clicked*.

Behind Asia, Liv and Deeley came in laughing, as they had been since that same day. The plan had worked masterfully, sending the offending family out of town when a second judge issued an overruling court order and allowed them to file adoption paperwork right then and there on the beach at sunset. Deeley and Liv would legally adopt Bash very soon, well before child number two arrived.

And right behind Deeley and Liv, his mother joined the party with Miles.

"And there she is," Jimmy said under his breath. "Dang, son. Mama didn't age at all."

Dane's eyes flashed at the remark, but he had to smile at another kick he felt—this one of pride that his mother was such an attractive woman, confident and glowing. Also a little bittersweet sadness that Dad wasn't here to appreciate that. And some real admiration at how strong Eliza Whitney proved to be.

But most of all, he just loved the heck out of her.

Putting down his rag, he came around the bar and headed to the door to greet them.

"Welcome to my humble place of employment," he joked, putting an easy arm around Asia and grinning at his sister as she looked around, taking in the bar vibe and the woman on stage currently singing the blues.

"At least it's not...what did you call your last job?" Liv asked. "Soulless?"

"Soul we got plenty of at Little Blue's." He extended his hand to Deeley. "Good to see you, man."

Deeley shook his hand in greeting, the connection easy now between the two of them.

"Hey, Mama," Dane said lightly, knowing the name would make his mother smile, even if she had no idea it was an echo of what Jimmy had called her.

"Honey, this is nice," she cooed, looking around. "A local place, for sure."

"Local *dive*," he joked. "But I saved you a great table by the stage. Hey, Miles."

"Dane." The other man gave him a warm smile but did not remove his hand from Mom's back. That was odd —he was usually so deferential and rarely touched her when Dane was around.

But out of the corner of his eye, he saw Jimmy approaching and realized why. Couldn't blame the man for claiming what was...his.

Dane turned to bring Jimmy into the circle and make the introductions. But before he got the first one out, his boss made a beeline for the woman in the center.

"As I live and breathe, Eliza Vanderveen. You are off the charts, woman. I can't believe you're here."

"Jimmy." Her greeting was muffled by his shoulder as the much bigger man folded her into a tight embrace that lasted one beat, maybe two, too long. Certainly too long for Miles, who just cocked a brow as he rubbed his short, silver goatee.

"Jimmy," she repeated, inching away. But he put two possessive hands on her shoulders and held her still.

"Eliza V. I cannot believe the gods have put us together again. It's fate, don't you think? Kismet? Serendipity?" He gave a hearty laugh. "One more and I'll have written a song about you."

She smiled, flushed enough to show the compliments were hitting the mark, then managed to slip out of his touch.

"Jimmy, let me introduce you to Miles Anderson."

"Oh, I know Miles. He's been drunk in here before." He put a hand on Miles's shoulder, who just snorted.

"Jimmy. How are ya?"

Dane felt himself bristle, somehow just knowing that if Miles had ever been drunk, which he sincerely doubted, it wouldn't have been here. And Miles was even too classy to rise to his own defense.

Dane stepped in before Jimmy said another word. "This is my sister, Olivia, and her...husband." He chuckled. "Still getting used to that."

"I'm not," Deeley said. "Feels too good. Jimmy, it's a pleasure." They shook hands, and Jimmy greeted Liv, but went right back to Mom before a moment passed.

"Please tell me we can sing together, Eliza. I can whip up a song from that play we did together. What was it? *Jukebox Nights*? I know I can remember your solo. *Step In My Direction,* right?"

Her jaw loosened a little. "You might remember it, Jimmy, but I sure don't. And this isn't my night to perform." She easily backed up, a little closer to Miles, her message subtle but clear.

Jimmy grunted and rolled his eyes, looking from one

to the other. "Is this serious? Like I do not have a snow-ball's chance?"

"Not one," Miles deadpanned. "Not a single chance."

They all looked at him with a little surprise—including the woman in question—but no one was more surprised than Dane. Miles really cared about her. Like, truly.

Maybe he'd underestimated this man.

Next to him, Asia curled her fingers into his hand, secretly sending her support and, he suspected, knowing what he was thinking. He glanced down at her, silently communicating how very grateful he was for her. She'd opened his eyes, somehow, made him see his mother, this island, and the whole world differently.

Everyone deserved someone like that in their lives, even a woman who'd only been widowed for a year. *Especially* her.

"Understood," Jimmy said, drawing them deeper into the bar. "Then let me get you all a round while you get comfortable at the VIP table." He gave a soft hoot. "Which is not too different from the *not* VIP tables, only it's closer to the stage. Easier to throw stuff at the lousy acts."

"Which you will not be," his mother said, pointing to Dane.

"He better not. Paul Margolis just texted that he'll be here any minute, and Slick here is our evening's spot-lighted act."

He hustled off to the bar.

"Slick, huh?" Livvie elbowed him. "You nervous?"

"Weirdly, no." He glanced down at Asia, who'd done nothing but build him up, help him practice, and sing their song with him. He hadn't told Mom or Liv about *Guts and Glory* and had decided to surprise them with the tribute to his father. "Come on. Your table is a really good one."

They crossed the bar and he nodded to some regulars, keeping his hand on Asia's back as they settled in. He took a drink order and walked back to the bar to fill it, getting a strange look from Jimmy.

"What?" he asked.

"What do you think? I'm kinda crushed." He winked at him. "Your mom's a dime, dude."

He gave a fully disgusted face, making the other man laugh.

"Miles is gonna wife her right up and I missed my shot. Again." He jutted his chin. "What are they drinking over there? It's on the house."

Wife her up?

He turned to look at the table just as Miles stood up, leaning over to say something to Eliza, making her laugh. And share a peck on the lips.

He waited for the resentment to rise, but once again, it wasn't there. But if he did "wife" her up? How would Dane feel about that? It was one thing if they dated, but...

Miles strode across the bar, threading a few tables, and stopping at one to give a high-five and hello to some locals. He reached the bar just as Jimmy put drinks on a tray for their table.

"I thought you might need a hand," Miles said. "But I see you got this."

"I'm good," Dane assured him, then reached for the bottle of Heineken that Miles had ordered and handed it to him. "This one's for you. Jimmy says it's on the house."

He lifted the bottle toward Jimmy and nodded. "Much obliged, sir."

Jimmy froze in the act of pouring a shot and leaned forward. "Just know this, my man. If you slip up, one little, tiny centimeter, I will move in on that woman so fast, you will not know what hit you. So, if I were you, I'd start building that pedestal and keep her on it or you will find yourself alone."

Miles's green eyes flickered as if he wasn't sure if that was a joke...or a genuine threat. "The pedestal is built," he said coolly. "And no one is going to slip."

Jimmy just nodded and finished his pour, turning away to leave Miles and Dane alone.

"Kind of expected that warning from you, not him," Miles said.

Dane gave a tight smile. "Yeah, I guess you would. Look, Miles, I don't..." He huffed out a breath. "I don't want my mother to be unhappy or lonely or grieving. I hope you know that."

"I do know that."

"But I don't want her to rush into anything, either. If I've seemed like I've been less than enthusiastic about your relationship, that's why. And I'm sorry."

Miles put a hand on his shoulder and looked him right in the eye. "No one is rushing her," he said. "But I will be honest with you, as I have been with her. I'm not in this for a casual thing. I'm hoping this goes all the way, and I'm going to do everything in my power to make that happen."

For a moment, Dane just stared at him, the echo of Jimmy's expression still in his head.

Wife her up.

"She'll never marry again," Dane said softly, weirdly confident of that.

Miles lifted a brow. "Never say never." Then he gave a mock toast with the beer he hadn't tasted yet. "If you're going to stick around Sanibel, I propose that we become friends. Fish, hang out, hit a bar now and again. I would like that, and so would Eliza."

Once more, he waited for the resentment, the desire to scoff at the invitation that he'd hang with the man who kissed his mother. But suddenly, that felt incredibly small and immature and dumb.

And deep inside, he knew his father would hate anything but the right response to the invitation. So he held out his hand to Miles. "I'd like that."

Miles shook it, and returned the smile. "Great. And if I'm not mistaken, the guy walking up behind you is that record label executive. Let me take this tray of drinks to the table for you, while you make his acquaintance."

Dane froze and let go of Miles's hand. "Thank you."

Grateful for the assist, he waited a beat before turning to meet the steely-eyed gaze of the man who might hold his future in his hands.

"Paulie!" Jimmy jogged over. "I want you to meet

your next songwriting gold mine. Dane Whitney, this is
Paul Margolis of Palm Valley Records. Paul, prepare to
have your socks knocked off."

After the introduction of a lifetime, Dane was well
and truly nervous when Jimmy literally turned on the
spotlight and announced his name. Paul Margolis could
change his life with the purchase of one song or, if he was
thinking huge, a contract to write for various Palm Valley
artists.

Basically, the next three minutes of his life were the
most important in the last twenty-eight years.

As he walked up to the stage, he put his hand on
Asia's shoulder and lifted a brow with a silent question.

"I'm here for you, Music Man," she whispered,
pushing up. "No guts, no glory."

He heard his mother gasp softly and give a questioning look to Livvie, but he didn't stick around to
answer any questions. He would, in a second.

While he sat at the piano, Asia stepped up to the mic
that the last singer-songwriter had used and turned to
him, holding his gaze with one so beautiful and real, he
couldn't even believe it.

"Okay," Dane said into the instrument mic, getting
used to the sound of it. "Thanks, Jimmy, for that introduction. I'm going to play a song I wrote these past few
weeks, and this gorgeous songbird is going to belt it out
way better than I ever could. This is Asia Turner, and
she's a poet who helped me...in every way."

A smattering of applause gave him a second to get his
thoughts together as he realized he'd never practiced this

speaking part. But he knew it was important to let this audience—and Paul Margolis—know that the song was from his heart and not just some notes thrown on a page.

"This one's called *Guts and Glory*, and it's a tribute to a man who had both. And a lot of heart, and a lot of soul." He glanced at the table closest to the stage, catching his mother's sweet smile.

He put his hands on the keyboard and played the simple, melodic opening notes. On the second bar, Asia started to sing.

Living on an island of fear and uncertainty,
Looking for the answer to where I gotta be.

She eased in with the low notes, a beautiful treble in her voice as she sang about a man she'd never met. She sang of Dad's easy laugh, his giant heart, and the words of wisdom that he'd impart. And then she belted out the chorus, with a hooky downbeat and sticky melody and words that hit him so hard.

You taught me then, you teach me now,
You show the way, you tell the story.
You make me know that when I'm down,
I gotta have the guts to find the glory.

He closed his eyes and let his head sing the words as his fingers flew up and down the keyboard, channeling every swirling emotion in his heart into the notes, rising, falling, slowing, speeding, and finally reaching the crescendo that Asia delivered flawlessly.

The hairs on the back of his neck stood up and there was a lump in his throat as he finished, holding the closing chord long enough to let the room erupt in applause. When he finally looked up, the first face he saw was his mother's, with tears rolling down both cheeks.

"I loved it," she mouthed, wiping her face.

Next to her, Livvie beamed through the same teary eyes.

But it was Miles's expression that caught him by surprise. A look of...defeat? Fear? Maybe he just realized the memory he was up against.

Dane didn't have time to think about it, because the crowd wanted an encore, so he and Asia slid right into *Change of Pace*, the other song they'd been writing these past few weeks.

When they finished, he stood and gave Asia a hug, then hopped off the stage, where Paul Margolis leaned against a speaker, nursing a beer.

"Can we talk?" he asked.

"Sure."

"Bring your co-writer. I want you both."

He and Asia exchanged a look and right at that moment, Dane knew his whole life just shifted. And for the first time in his life, he didn't hate the change. He welcomed it.

GIDDY. Dane and Asia were downright giddy for the rest of the night. After the preliminary negotiations were done and they'd made plans for Dane and Asia to visit the record label in Miami, Paul took off. They shared the news that together they would sign a contract with Palm

Valley Records to sell those two songs, and four more. If any of them were recorded by one of the label's singers, the payoff would be juicy.

They toasted with champagne, since Roz had Zee for the night, and spent the evening in a state of shock and ecstasy.

They laughed, they drank, they kissed a few times, and the rest of the people around the table joined in the fun that lasted until Livvie—designated pregnant driver —dropped them off at the Tortoise Way complex.

"Music Man!" Asia exclaimed as they climbed out in the parking lot and slid their arms around each other to walk to their unit. "Do you realize what has happened?"

"Um, the songwriting deal of my dreams?"

"No. You made magic on a piano that wasn't, you know, the *Precious*." She dragged out the word, Gollum-style, making him laugh.

"I guess I can play on other instruments."

"But you might not have to," she said. "Because if this contract works out, I say we move into a bigger place that can hold the Precious."

Did she say *we* move? *Yes*, he thought with a smile. Yes, she did.

As they neared their unit, he pulled her into his side. "I don't think it was the piano that won the night. It was you."

"No!" She turned, letting him wrap his arms around her and clasping his neck. "It was you!"

"You're my muse, Aje."

She dropped her head back and let out one of her

arpeggio laughs, exposing the sweet skin of her throat and tempting him to take a taste.

"What?" She straightened her head and looked at him. "What are you thinking?"

"What do you think I'm thinking?" he asked.

"I *think*..." she giggled. "That we should *think* of better words if we're going to be the next songwriting duo that takes the music industry by storm."

He laughed, easing her closer. "I didn't know you were in the market for a new career."

"It's a side hustle," she said. "And I didn't know, either. I also didn't know I was in the market for..." She bit her lip and melted into him. "A new man."

He could barely breathe. "Then maybe we need to negotiate a new, uh, roommate contract. Since we're in the contract negotiating mood tonight."

"Yeah?" Her brows shot up. "Let me hear all the weighted pros and cons, please."

He laughed at that. "Weighted pro...you and me, together in every way."

"Mmm." She smiled up at him. "Very pro."

"Weighted con?" He slowly shook his head. "There isn't one."

"No con, huh? Well, then...let's renegotiate." She sighed and lifted her face to kiss him, no words necessary. They deepened the kiss just long enough for a car to drive by, the lights illuminating them uncomfortably.

"Come on," he said, tugging her toward the town-house. "Let's take this inside."

They walked arm-in-arm as Dane pulled out his

keychain. When they came around the corner and approached the door, his gaze dropped to something on the welcome mat, a black...stick?

"What is that?" he asked, frowning at it, then at Asia, who suddenly froze, gasping with wide eyes.

"Don't worry," he said on a laugh, bending over. "It's not a snake or a bug, it's—"

"Don't!" she exclaimed. "Don't touch it!"

"Asia." He scooped up the small item, which was plastic and paper and light. "It's a toy that someone dropped." Realizing what it was, he snapped it open, revealing a black folding fan with a red dragon spread across the ribbed center. "See?"

Her chest rose and fell with strained breaths, and she looked like she might faint right then and there as she stared at the open fan in abject horror.

"Asia? What's wrong?"

She closed her eyes and fought a sob. "It's all over, Dane," she whispered. "It's all over. Everything. Everything is over."

"What?"

"Quick." She looked left and right then pushed his arm holding the keys. "Inside. Inside!"

He stuck the key in the lock and twisted the deadbolt, and she practically pushed him in, then yanked the door closed, flipping the lock into place.

"What the heck is going on?" he demanded.

"I have to pack. I have to leave. I'm sorry, but I have to."

It felt like all the blood drained from his face. "What are you talking about?"

"He found me."

"What? How do you—"

"And that means he'll find Zee. That can't happen. That can *never* happen. I'm sorry, Dane. But I'm leaving. Tonight." With that, she ran off and all he heard was a sob and her feet as she bolted up the stairs.

He fell against the door and sank to the floor, staring at the cheap toy fan that had somehow changed his life once again.

A change he hated. A change he...refused to let beat him. No. No. Not this time. He would not let change beat him ever again.

Pushing up, he followed Asia, marching up the stairs to find her like a human whirlwind shoving clothes into a bag.

"Asia!"

"Not now, Dane. I have to think. I have to move. I have to *run*."

He got right in front of her. "You have to stop."

She froze, looking up at him, her eyes frantic and panicked. "You don't know—"

"Yes, I do." He put his hands on her shoulders to still her. "I know this, anyway. That whatever—*whoever*—has reared an ugly head, he will have to go through me to get to you. And no one, absolutely no one on this Earth, will get near you, or Zee. Trust me."

"I do, Dane," she sobbed his name, some of the fight gone. "I trust you."

It was all he needed to hear. "We'll get through this together, Asia. But you will not run, hide, or cower in fear. We will get through this together. Whatever happens, we can handle it."

On a sigh, she fell deeper into his arms. "I hope you're right." She looked up at him, blinking back tears. "Because this isn't going to be easy."

"No guts, no glory, right, Aje?"

She smiled through her tears. "No guts, no glory, Dane."

*Don't miss the exciting conclusion of the Shellseeker Beach series. **Sanibel Moonlight** finishes the stories of this found family that stays together through every crisis, supports each other through every moment, and always has the humor and heart to face what life throws at them!*

The Coconut Key Series

If you're enjoying Shellseeker Beach, you'll love Coconut Key, Hope Holloway's first, now completed, series set on the sun-kissed sands of the Florida Keys!

The Shellseeker Beach Series

Come to Shellseeker Beach and fall in love with a cast of unforgettable characters who face life's challenges with humor, heart, and hope. For lovers of riveting and inspirational sagas about sisters, secrets, romance, mothers, and daughters...and the moments that make life worth living.

About the Author

Hope Holloway is the author of charming, heartwarming women's fiction featuring unforgettable families and friends, and the emotional challenges they conquer. After more than twenty years in marketing, she launched a new career as an author of beach reads and feel-good fiction. A mother of two adult children, Hope and her husband of thirty years live in Florida. When not writing, she can be found walking the beach with her two rescue dogs, who beg her to include animals in every book. Visit her site at www.hopeholloway.com.

Made in the USA
Columbia, SC
15 April 2025